My Steps
Are Ordered

My Steps
Are Ordered

Michelle Lindo-Rice

www.urbanchristianonline.com

Urban Books, LLC
97 N18th Street
Wyandanch, NY 11798

ISBN 13: 978-1-60162-667-7
ISBN 10: 1-60162-667-3

First Trade Paperback Printing August 2014
Printed in the United States of America

10 9 8 7 6 5 4 3 2 1

This is a work of fiction. Any references or similarities to actual events, real people, living or dead, or to real locales are intended to give the novel a sense of reality. Any similarity in other names, characters, places, and incidents is entirely coincidental.

Distributed by Kensington Corp.
Submit Wholesale Orders to:
Kensington Publishing Corp.
C/O Penguin Group (USA) Inc.
Attention: Order Processing
405 Murray Hill Parkway
East Rutherford, NJ 07073-2316
Phone: 1-800-526-0275
Fax: 1-800-227-9604

My Steps
Are Ordered

by

Michelle Lindo-Rice

*What happens when her husband finds out
she's in love with his brother?*

The Second Installment in the On the Right Path series

Praise for *Sing a New Song*

"*Ms. Lindo-Rice writes with heart, humor, and honesty . . .*" –**Shana Burton,** author of *Flaw Less* and *Flaws and All*

"*Michelle Lindo-Rice has written a sweet story of the power of love despite the main character's (Tiffany's) sordid past . . .*" –**Michelle Stimpson,** best selling author of *Falling into Grace*

"*The author's writing is crisp and her characters' emotions are authentic . . .*" –**Pat Simmons,** award-winning and bestselling author of The Guilty series.

"*The author did a phenomenal job in drawing the reader's heart and spirit into the characters . . . Ms. Lindo-Rice developed an endearing, engaging, multilayered story with realism and redemption . . .*" –**Norma Jarrett,** *Essence* bestselling author of *Sunday Brunch*

Praise for *Walk a Straight Line*

"*I could feel the breeze and smell the scent of the flower garden the wind was carrying with it; that's how fresh this story is . . . I loved how the story flowed.*" –**E.N. Joy,** BLESSEDselling author of the New Day Divas series

"*The message of resilience in Colleen's story is powerful and important . . . as is the message of commitment, love, and friendship that comes through . . .*" –**Rhonda McKnight,** bestselling author of *An Inconvenient Friend* and *What Kind of Fool*

Acknowledgments

I acknowledge my Lord and Savior, Jesus Christ. My heartfelt gratitude goes to my sons, Eric and Jordan, or my "two eyeballs," for their encouragement and understanding.

To my parents, family, loved ones and friends at Agape Church of God and the Charlotte County public schools, I thank you for being in my corner. Special mention goes to Glenda Clark and Colette Alexander, who support me every step of the way. And I owe a very special mention to my unpaid "editors" and feedback crew, Zara Anderson, Sobi-Dee Ophelia, and Jane Adams.

I want to extend a special thank-you to Rhonda McKnight. Her skill and craft are helping me become a better writer. I still have much to learn.

I would also like to thank Felicia Murrell for her editing skills. She's fast, thorough and has an eye for details.

And I wish to thank Victoria Christopher Murray, a best-selling author, who encourages me. Her willingness to advise and share speaks about her character.

And Joylynn Ross, the acquisitions editor, literary genius, and author at Urban Books, deserves my thanks for taking a leap of faith in me and for believing in my work.

Finally, I must express my deep appreciation to all the new readers who reach out to me on various social media and who make it all worthwhile. To all the book clubs and bloggers who feature me and read my work: Thank you.

A Note to My Readers

*"The steps of a good man are ordered by
the Lord: and he delighteth in his way."*
—Psalm 37:23

For many of us, the road to salvation has been paved
with many mistakes and failures. Sometimes, we know
better but choose to go our own way and to satisfy our
wants. But we can delight in knowing that we serve a
perfect God, who loves us and who forgives us all our
sins. When we accept Christ, He throws our past in the
sea of forgetfulness and remembers it no more. However,
we do have consequences that we might have to face, but
He will be with us every step of the way.

As Christians, we are flawed and human, but we have
an advocate in Christ Jesus, who pleads for us and sends
us His Holy Spirit to comfort us. We also have a secret
ingredient for abundant life—hope. Though we face the
same battles and trials as everyone else, we hope for a
brighter day, when God will wipe away all tears and our
sorrows will be turned into joy.

Thank you for choosing to read my work. It wasn't by
accident, but by divine ordination. Be entertained. Be
blessed.

Sincerely,
Michelle Lindo-Rice

Dedicated to

Glenda Momrelle-Clarke,
A sister, a friend, woman of God, and one of my biggest
cheerleaders.

We Agree

We came into this world alone
But we were not destined to end it that way
We yearned for someone with whom we could share
The myriad paths in life just waiting for us to choose
Our lives were full but without true meaning
We developed our talents but were still dreaming
Then we awakened and discovered that our souls
connected
And we acknowledged finding that missing link
The person with whom everything clicks
The one who invigorates, rejuvenates, entrances,
The mind, body and soul
At first, admission was a struggle
But eventually we accepted defeat
For love had conquered
Our wandering, seeking hearts
And captured the essence of who we are
Now we are tightly woven
Where does she begin?
Where does he end?
That is a mystery
Only God holds the key
For what He has joined together

Dedication

No man can put asunder
So from this day onward
We walk together
For the two of us,
We agree

.

Written by
Michelle Lindo-Rice
For Glenda and Andrew Clarke Jan. 22, 2006

Prologue

The present day . . .

It can't be.
No. It's impossible.
Immobilized, Pastor Keith Ward felt suspended in time. His breath caught. His yellow tie, sprinkled with tiny red polka dots, threatened to choke the life out of him.

The voices of the choir faded in the distant echo. All around him people praised and rejoiced while Keith felt the scales around his heart chip away.

Time stood still.

Leaning forward, Keith squinted to focus into the distance. That's her all right. She was here. His psyche must have known something. No wonder she'd been on his mind.

Gina Ward.

His brother's wife.

And, the mother of Keith's child. Yes, he was a father.

Keith's heart slammed into his chest. Its beating sounded like thunder booming to his ears. Gripping the handles, Keith eased his body out of the chair, intending to pursue the woman who had twisted his insides and stolen his heart.

He had to go to her.

As he soon as he stood, Keith felt a moment of disorientation; belatedly realizing the crowd was standing and cheering. It seemed as if they were giving him a standing ovation. Flabbergasted, Keith watched Gina leave. All of his thoughts about his sermon left the forefront of his mind.

He turned his head to see his assistant, Natalie Henderson, or as he called her, "The Hawk," gesturing towards the podium. She mouthed the words, "Go. Go," with frantic hands.

Keith gritted his teeth, clenched his fists and closed his eyes. *Lord, help me. Help me.* He repeated scriptures to temper the need that filled his being.

The crowd shouted praises, presuming he was hearing something from God. Summoning every ounce of self-control he possessed, Keith stepped up to the stage. He opened his Bible, worn from use. He'd refused to get a new one. This one had sentimental value.

Then, with authority and anointing, he addressed his parishioners waiting on a word from God.

Chapter One

Three years earlier . . .

"Say you'll be here for Gina's party. Colleen and Terence can't make it, so I'm counting on you to show your ugly face. Trey's been asking for his favorite uncle Keith." Michael Ward, Keith's brother, threw in that last tidbit for emotional blackmail.

Keith Ward grinned, picturing the rambunctious little boy giving the pint-sized Gina a run for her money. "I'm his only uncle Keith. Is he still running like his pants are on fire?"

"Yup, and you should see Gina try to pick him up. He's already half her size."

Sitting in a leather chair in his office located on Queens Boulevard in New York City, Keith propped his foot on another chair and looked up at the ceiling. Going to Atlanta would mean that he would be seeing *her* again. Gina. His blessing and his curse. Who was he fooling? Of course he'd be there.

"Okay, I'll come. Let me know if you need me to take care of anything on my end," Keith offered. As soon as he ended the call, he grabbed his briefcase. He needed to head to the courthouse, located two blocks away.

While he'd been on the phone, his secretary had handed him a message that the judge was ready to make a ruling on the Harper Wills case. After two grueling months, he was glad a decision had been made.

As he walked, Keith took a stroll down memory lane. Michael had been love struck when he'd met Gina Price, her name at the time, at his business partner, Terence Hayworth's wedding. His brother tended to attract psychopaths, so Keith had been prepared to dislike and dismiss this new woman who had his brother spellbound. But the moment he'd seen Gina Price, Keith had gotten the shock of his life.

Before Gina, Keith hadn't known there was such a thing as instant love at first sight or even real animal attraction, but that was how it had been. Before her, he'd only been in love once, with Vanessa Arnold. Sadly, she'd been killed by a drunk driver. However, Keith's feelings for Vanessa paled in comparison to what he felt for Gina.

Gina was like a fire that consumed him.

Keith stopped. He stood at the foot of the ten steps leading up to the entrance of the courthouse. He dragged his hands down his face, pulling on his cheeks, as the memories flooded him.

Twice. On two sweet occasions, he'd been with Gina.

The first time was right before his brother's near fatal car accident. When Gina and Michael were dating, she found out Michael had cheated with his crazy ex, Karen Newton, and had broken things off with him.

To Keith, this had been fate giving him his chance. He had rushed to Gina's house and he hadn't had any reservations about professing his love. It sounded like the plot of a cheap romance novel, but he'd been convinced that Gina was his destiny. This was his time—his moment, he'd told himself. His heart rang with joy when Gina confessed she'd felt the same way.

And he'd had her, for one sweet night that he'd hoped would last forever. However, for Gina and Keith there had been no happy-ever-after. They shared one of the most mind-boggling, emotionally charged intimate experiences uniting their soul . . . Remembering, Keith felt the old guilt begin to eat at him again . . . and, then the call came.

Michael, feeling guilty about cheating on Gina, had lost control of the vehicle while speeding to her house and crashed, almost killing himself.

Keith remembered how his body had shaken with fear when he'd learned that Michael was in a coma. The wait had been agonizing. By some divine intervention, Michael had awakened with no residual brain damage and Gina patched things up with him. At her urging, Keith and Gina agreed never to talk about what transpired between them.

Plagued with guilt, Gina pressed, "It never happened."

After his near death experience, Michael had wasted no time in putting a rock on Gina's finger and wedding plans commenced with so much speed that Keith felt like he was in a time warp.

Keith trudged up the stairs as her words pounded in his head. *It never happened.* He made a fist. But, it had once.

And again.

There had been a second time. Keith shrugged. He'd better leave that as a secret of the past.

Entering the designated courtroom, Keith put his briefcase on the table, pulled out the battered leather chair, sat, and waited for his client, Harper Wills, to arrive. Keith drummed his fingers on the table, his mind on Gina.

He couldn't control the quivers of anticipation that rocked through his spine. He ached to see her. Soon . . . soon he would. He felt like a kid who was about to be given an all-you-can-eat day in a candy store. However, lucky for him, while he sat there musing, none of his thoughts showed on his face.

When he left the courthouse, he was going to go gift shopping. It would be late, but he lived in the city that never slept, so he wasn't concerned. After the guilty verdict, as soon as the gavel hit the desk, Keith went through the motions, entered an appeal and shot out of there. He knew just the perfect gift.

The days flew by, and before he knew it, Keith found himself scurrying to catch the flight from JFK Airport to Atlanta. Since he carried only a small carry-on, he made it to the plane right before the final boarding call. With a dismissive glance at the other passengers, he settled into his seat. There was enough legroom for him to stretch out.

As he watched the clouds during the plane's ascent, Keith sighed. He was grateful Michael had planned the trip. He relished leaving the hustle and bustle of New York, and its crazy, demanding work hours, for five days. Taking a deep breath, he settled deeper into the comfy seat. He could feel the muscles in his neck and back relaxing already.

His plane made good time and landed without incident. With his height of six-three, Keith had no trouble spotting Michael, who was awaiting his arrival just outside the security checkpoint.

"Hey, big bro!" Michael gave him a hearty hug.

"It's been a while," Keith replied, feeling good about seeing his brother. It had been almost six months since his last visit.

"I've missed you," Michael declared, a little misty-eyed.

"Same here, bro," Keith said.

"What about me?"

Keith knew whom the small voice belonged to. "Hi, Trey," he said. Two little fists clutched his trousers. Keith bent to peel Trey's hands off his pants. His chubby fingers were sticky. Not caring, Keith held out his arms.

"Yippee!" Trey squealed and jumped into his arms.

Keith's heart expanded with indescribable joy. "You've gotten so big, Little Man."

Trey nodded and opened his mouth to show off his new tooth. Keith noted that the boy's honey-colored complexion, curly hair, and hazel-green eyes were a gift from his grandma Gerry. At four, Trey was already so tall that Keith was convinced that he would overtake him.

"You guys are going to have to watch the women." Keith looked at Michael. "He's probably breaking hearts in preschool."

Michael chuckled. "Don't I know it? I predict he's going to be like you, a magnet for the ladies."

"What did you bring me?" Trey asked his uncle.

"Trey." Michael was annoyed at his son's blunt request, but Keith laughed.

He waved off Michael's rebuke. "It's okay. I like the direct, up-front approach." Keith's biceps expanded as he adjusted Trey in his strong arms.

Michael poked Keith in the ribs and whispered, "Still affecting the females, I see."

Keith harrumphed. He looked around, noticing a group of women eyeing him, then ignored them. He was here for his family, nothing else. "Don't start," he warned and walked off.

Michael grabbed Keith's carry-on and said, "What? You can't blame them for being entranced by a movie star in their midst."

"Spare me the humor, Michael."

"Well, when you've got it, you've got it. I'm just saying you missed your calling." Michael listed Keith's physical attributes all the way to his car. "Accept it. You're too pretty for words."

"Michael." Keith gritted his teeth as Michael clicked the locks to open the car doors. Once Trey was buckled into his car seat and both brothers were seated, Keith closed his eyes and prayed for strength. Sometimes his brother took a joke too far. "Enough. I think you have way too much fun jabbing at me."

Michael surrendered and started the drive to his home. They moved on to safer topics, mostly business, which Michael was much more serious about. He had expanded his ventures from architecture to acquiring real estate properties, fixing them, and flipping them for a profit. Keith was so proud of his brother's success and told him so.

"I'm looking to get into investing next," Michael said.

"You're going to be the next Donald Trump," Keith declared. "Next, I'm going to be watching you on TV, saying, 'You're fired.'"

His brother grinned. "And you know it! I'm just grateful to Tyler Simmonds for giving me my first break in the big leagues. He and his wife, Camille, should be at Gina's party."

Keith nodded. Michael had referenced the owner of Simmonds Synthetics. Though he didn't respond, as Michael was pulling into the driveway of his and Gina's palatial house in Suwanee, Georgia.

The front door opened, Gina stepped through it, and Keith's heart stopped. He didn't have eyes for the well-manicured lawn or the lilies. He didn't mention the beautiful landscaping, which he knew Michael had spent a fortune on to create and then maintain.

No, Keith had eyes only for Gina. She had her medium-length hair in big, bouncy curls, and she looked a little rounder than the last time he'd seen her. Her extra weight only added to her appeal. In short, Gina was beautiful to him. Her size was insignificant. Keith was in love with the woman . . . her essence.

"Mommy!" Trey squealed, holding out his arms.

Gina came over to hug her son. "Mommy missed you," she said, helping him out of the car seat.

Keith saw her check him out from under her lashes and patted his stomach. He was in top physical shape from working out.

"Hi, Gina. It's been a long time." Keith offered the perfunctory salutation in a low, calm tone. On the inside, he was a veritable mess. He didn't know how he was able to stand there, so poised, when the woman of his dreams stood mere inches in front of him. He commanded himself to refrain from snatching her into his arms.

"Keith," Gina breathed as she walked into his arms and gave him a warm hug.

It was like she'd read his mind. Keith tightened the embrace. He inhaled her scent. She smelled like a sun-ripened peach, and he determined never to let her go. If only . . .

"Hey, get your big paws off and quit mauling my wife," Michael joked. "You need to give some of that loving to the ladies ogling you at the airport."

Here we go again, Keith groaned silently. The two parted with a small, awkward chuckle at Michael's wittiness. This was one moment when Keith was thankful that though his brother was a shark in the business world, he was clueless when it came to matters of the heart.

A blind man could see the combustion, the sizzling electricity between he and Gina. It crackled and swirled around them like a tornado. A dormant animalistic urge that surfaced every time they were within feet of each other. That's why he'd nixed his plans tot move to Georgia once Michael and Gina did. He needed to keep his distance.

Michael, however, remained blissfully unaware, which made their guilt enormous. How could he be so naïve?

"It's a good thing I know I can trust you, big brother, or it'd be on," Michael jested, reaching inside his car for Keith's carry-on.

Keith and Gina locked eyes but didn't respond.

"I'll help you, Daddy," Keith heard Trey say, but he was still looking at Gina, who now had a slight blush grazing her face.

She was rubbing at her arms, and he knew she felt the loss like he did. When she placed her finger over her lips, he knew exactly what she was thinking.

"Stop reading my mind," she mouthed at him.

Michael preceded them into the house, with Trey in tow. Gina gave Keith a thoughtful look as she took his hand to lead him inside.

"No, I haven't found anyone," Keith volunteered.

"How do you do that?" Gina whispered.

"It's always been like that with us," Keith returned for her ears only. He gave her hand a small squeeze. "Why should this instance be any different?"

Gina nodded but didn't comment. Her silence meant she knew he told the truth. It was how it had always been between them. They were able to know instinctively what the other was thinking, connecting on a mental level that defied words. They didn't need small talk. They didn't need anything . . . just each other.

Chapter Two

June 18 . . .

"Whoo-hoo! This is how you bring in thirty-four!" Gina exclaimed, swinging her arms in beat to the tune of "Turn the Beat Around." The deejay was on a seventies kick, and she was loving it.

Her actual birthday had been the day before. Michael had taken her out to a special dinner. This party was a complete surprise. Wearing an Anne Klein coral-colored halter dress that was a gift from Michael, Gina had danced with everyone at the party except for Keith. She was too afraid of what might show on her face and what her body language would give away. It was diabolical that the one she yearned to dance with was the one she had to avoid. She wanted Keith, and she was afraid she wouldn't be able to hide it.

Keith's arms were folded across his chest as he leaned against the wall. Their eyes met. She knew Keith had been checking her out all night from under hooded eyes. It was disconcerting. Not knowing what else to do, she reached up and twirled her hair with her fingers. Willing herself to look away and maintain discretion, Gina sought Michael. She watched as her husband left a group of friends and walked over to his brother.

Since Keith's arrival, the two brothers had been joined at the hip. They had taken Trey all over town. It did her heart good to see them both so relaxed. They worked hard and deserved the playtime. She had stayed in, not wanting to intrude on their time together.

Besides, she treasured her solitude.

Once Trey was born, Gina epitomized the ultimate stay-at-home mom. But it did not give her much time to herself. She could afford at least ten nannies but wanted the hands-on experience of raising a child. She did not want to miss any part of motherhood. In fact, she and Michael were talking about more children. Growing up an only child, Gina wished she'd had siblings, so she didn't want Trey to be alone.

Caught up in her musings, it took a minute to register that someone was calling her name, frantic to get her attention. "Gina! Come quick. It's Trey. He's fallen!"

What? Gina's maternal instincts went into overdrive. Her feet catapulted her in the direction of all the commotion. Since Michael and Gina had friends with young children, like themselves, his invite had encouraged parents to bring their children to Gina's party. He had hired sitters and set up entertainment for the children in their basement. Trey must have left the children to seek out his parents, as he was upstairs.

A small crowd had gathered around him, but they parted like the Red Sea when Gina dashed over to her son. She told herself not to panic, but that did not stop her quick intake of breath and her sheer terror when she saw Trey lying lifeless on the floor.

"Trey!" She looked around. "What happened to him?"

Michael was right by her side. "Did he fall?"

"He passed out," someone said.

"Don't move him," another cautioned.

Gina wanted to do nothing more than pick him up in her arms, but she knew it was best not to lift him. Her hands grazed her son's face. She ran her fingers through his hair, willing her shaky hands to calm down. She heard the distinct wail of an ambulance rushing in the distance. Her heart hammered. She covered her ears, willing herself to calm down. Gina remained rooted to the spot until the fire truck and the ambulance arrived. Her legs felt like rubber as she jumped in the ambulance, which would transport Trey to the Children's Healthcare of Atlanta in Duluth, a six-minute ride from their home in Suwanee. Keith and Michael followed behind.

Hours rolled by. The emergency room physician called for a pediatric critical-care specialist, Dr. Newman, who ordered test after test. Trey was assigned a private room. Gina's head spun from the number of people who entered the room to do this or that. Her mouth felt dry from having to repeat the same medical history whenever a new face popped in.

"Yes, Trey had been eating less. I don't know if he felt faint."

"No, I wasn't concerned."

"His father and uncle had been running him all over town."

"No, I don't know if Trey had a fever."

She resisted the urge to scream, "Don't you guys read the chart? Isn't it all on the computer?" What she wanted was answers, but all they had for her were questions. She felt herself caving. She was going to lose it. She dropped her head against her husband's chest, and he wrapped his arms around her.

"He's going to be okay," Michael whispered. "We have to wait for the test results to come back, but we must remain positive."

Gina raised her head and nodded. Of course, Michael was right. Michael was always right. She looked over his shoulder. Keith was leaning against the wall, with one foot propped and his arms crossed. She'd been avoiding his eyes since he'd come to her house, but now he was staring at her with deep intensity. She allowed herself to get lost in those eyes, to find comfort in them.

"He was with you guys," she said. She hardly recognized her own weak and pitiful voice. "Did you notice anything different?"

Michael released her. "He was . . . I don't know . . . maybe tired, but I thought that was from all the running around."

Gina marched to Trey's bedside. She gripped the bed railing with both hands, closed her eyelids tight, and tried to remember what he'd been like when she was dressing him for the party, when she'd dressed him earlier that day, at breakfast, at bedtime the night before. She shook her head. She'd missed something. She had to have missed something. Kids didn't pass out without some kind of warning.

"I'm going to step out and return Mom's call," Michael said. "I left a message earlier to let her know what was going on."

Gina nodded. Calling her mother-in-law hadn't crossed her mind. The door squeaked as Michael made his exit. Fatigue was setting in. She used a hand to massage her neck. That was when Keith put his hands on her shoulders and squeezed for her. She let her head drop back against his chest. She knew it was wrong. She knew Michael could walk in at any time, but she needed to draw from Keith's strength.

"He's going to be okay," he whispered, kissing the top of her head.

"You promise?" She clung to his words.

He squeezed her shoulders again. "I promise."

Gina turned into him and began to cry.

Keith stretched his arms behind her. He pulled tissues from the box on the table and swiped under her eyes. "Baby, you don't want to upset Trey. You don't know what he can hear," he shushed.

She sniffed, "You're right. I know it. I just . . ." *Get it together, girl.* She blotted her nose and lifted grateful eyes to him. "I'm glad you're here."

"I couldn't be anywhere else. I love my nephew, and God help me, I love you."

Not knowing what else to do, she decided to take her best friend, Colleen Hayworth's advice and pray for her son. She'd called her hours ago, and Colleen and her husband, Terence, were storming heaven with their prayers. As she whispered to God, the sobs welled up within her. Gina put her hands over her mouth to keep from wailing. Her eyes remained peeled on the door as she willed the doctors to come and tell her it was some kind of weird bug that could be treated at home with medication and rest. The wait was nerve wracking.

"Do you want me to go see what is taking so long?" Keith asked.

"Yes, but maybe Michael's talking to someone. He's been gone awhile."

Keith covered her hand with his briefly. "Maybe," he said. On cue, the door swung open, and Michael reentered the room.

"Where have you been?" Keith sounded annoyed.

"I . . . I was sick. My nerves . . ." Michael replied.

"Come here," Gina beckoned to him. She had a slight whisper of a smile for her penitent spouse. She had not eaten much of anything, or she also would have been throwing up. So she could relate.

Michael complied, and she found herself sandwiched between the two men. She shifted and leaned into her husband. She'd hoped he would hold her the way Keith had, but true to who he was, Michael was caught up in his own grief. He wouldn't be able to comfort her. Not really.

Keith shook his legs and stretched.

She knew Keith wanted to be the one holding her. But Michael was her husband and the father of her son. He was the one with whom she shared that bond of parenthood. Keith could empathize, but she doubted that he would understand until he had his own child.

After an interminable time, Dr. Newman entered the room. Sensing their eagerness, he didn't belabor the point. "We're still running some tests, but the preliminary scans have me a little concerned. I don't want to worry you, but I have to be sure before diagnosing. I have ordered a complete blood cell count."

Trey squinted from the doctor's touch, but otherwise he remained still.

"What are you looking for?" Gina asked, with a tremor in her voice.

"I know it's hard, Mrs. Ward, but hold on a little longer," the doctor soothed, ending his investigation.

By this time, both Keith and Michael had moved into his space. Dr. Newman was of medium build and average height with blond, curly hair, so the Ward men towered over him. The doctor didn't appear the least bit intimidated. He was the best in his field and one of the leading pediatric specialists in the nation.

"Was it something he ate?" Keith asked. "Could he have ingested something by mistake?"

"No, we've already ruled out food poisoning. We didn't find any foreign objects in his body and we've also ruled out appendicitis," Dr. Newman replied, already anticipating the next question. "His liver and spleen are swollen, so I ordered a spinal tap, as well. I'm waiting for the result of the test. I should know more in the next few hours. I will be back once all the labs are in and I have taken a look at them."

Dr. Newman gave them a curt, but sympathetic smile and left the room.

"That told us nothing." Michael clenched his fists. "I need to know what is wrong with my son. Like, yesterday." He expelled a loud breath and then tried to inject humor into the situation. "Well, this is one party no one is going to forget anytime soon."

No one smiled.

No one responded.

Feeling awkward, Michael declared, "I'm going to call Mom again," before leaving the room.

Chapter Three

As soon as the door swung shut, Keith stalked over to Gina, pulled her into his arms, and kissed her. The kiss was short but fiery and said everything he could not say with words.

"You shouldn't have done that." Gina wiped her hand across her mouth. "How dare you make this about you and me when my son is . . ."

"You're right. I'm sorry," Keith said to appease her, though deep inside he wasn't the least bit apologetic. He needed to have some sort of physical contact.

"A hug would've sufficed," she said, reading his mind. Gina looked into his eyes and raised her hand to graze his cheek, and he knew he was forgiven.

Without breaking eye contact, she moved her hand down to his shirt. Keith had been dressed in a light brown suit, but he had discarded the jacket sometime during all the commotion. Her hand came across a small box in his pocket. Curious, Gina looked at him.

"Your birthday present," Keith offered. He pulled it out and handed it to her.

Gina looked at the box and bit her bottom lip. "I feel tacky taking a gift from you while my son is fighting for his life."

"Open it," Keith commanded. "Trust me. It's okay."

Gina complied and with jittery hands opened the package. "It's a locket." She lifted it with care and tried to pry open the small clasp. She was all thumbs.

Some things never change. With a rueful smile, Keith undid the clasp for her. He remembered another time when he had to help her with her buttons. Gina was so graceful in many ways, but when it came to fine motor tasks, she could become klutzy.

She peered inside the tiny locket. "There's a picture of Trey." A fresh load of grateful tears fell. "I love it, Keith."

Keith felt pleased that his gift had brought Gina some measure of comfort. He put the chain around her neck. Gina held on to the locket while Keith held her.

A few minutes later Michael returned with news of their mother's impending arrival. "I had my driver go get her." He juggled three cups of coffee. Keith saw that he had also raided the snack machine, buying a plethora of candy and chips, though no one felt like eating.

It was a little after dawn when Geraldine Ward rushed into the room. By then, Michael had nodded off in a corner chair, and Gina had drifted into a light sleep, resting her head on Keith's shoulder. Keith smiled at the sight of his mother and placed his finger over his lips before pointing to Gina and Michael.

He saw her nod with understanding. Her silver-gray hair was styled in a sophisticated bob. Dressed in black pants and a beautiful metallic gray top, with silver earrings dangling from her ears and a matching necklace around her long, graceful neck, Gerry looked years younger than her fifty-eight years and at times was mistaken for Keith and Michael's older sister instead of their mom.

Keith eased Gina off his arm, and her eyes popped open. He walked over to his mother. He gave her such a tight hug that her feet lifted in the air.

Michael stirred and awoke. "You made it!" he exclaimed and welcomed Gerry with visible relief.

Gina squirmed under Gerry's knowing glance. She experienced a moment of déjà vu as she thought about another hospital and another time. When Michael was in a coma at Long Island Jewish Hospital, Gerry had walked in on her and Keith in a similar cozy position. She envied Keith's nonchalance then and now. He wasn't the least bit bothered by what his mother thought, but she was. Gerry knew how she felt about Keith. The older woman had even advised her not to marry Michael out of a sense of obligation. However, Gina had been adamant that she loved Michael. And that was the truth. Breaking eye contact with Gerry, Gina looked over at Michael and smiled. She did love Michael, in a way.

She was just a somersaulting, crazy fool in love with Keith. Gina shot to her feet and greeted her mother-in-law with a hug. Gerry offered all the right sentiments, and in the face of this maternal warmth, Gina felt tears threaten again.

It was times like these that Gina missed her own mother, Lucille Price, who had died from a sudden stroke. She was nineteen when her mother passed, and the pain hadn't receded with time. Lucille hadn't lived long enough to see Gina marry or to meet her grandson. Gina also yearned for a father to call, but while growing up, she hadn't known little more than his name. Feeling overwhelmed, Gina excused herself and stepped outside the room to be alone with her thoughts.

"Are you all right?"

Gina turned toward the voice. Michael had concern written all over his face. "Yeah," she said.

"What's wrong? Well, besides the obvious." Michael bent over, then tilted her chin upward, looking directly into her eyes.

Gina knew how perceptive he could be, but she wasn't sure if she was up to talking about it. She shrugged and released a small sigh. "It's nothing."

"It's never nothing."

Gina saw the question reflected in his eyes and decided to explain. "Well, I know my mother is gone, but I wish I knew my father. Because then I would have someone to call, like you did."

"Oh, baby." Michael cradled his wife in his arms and they re-entered the room. "I know you're terrified. I've made several trips to the nurses' station to find out if there is any news. I know that they're doing their job, but those nurses know what's wrong. However, they wouldn't cave, no matter how much I ranted."

The door swung open and Dr. Newman entered the room.

Everyone gathered around the doctor with fear and dread.

When they heard the news, Keith had to hold on to his mother to keep her from falling. Gina fell into Michael's arms.

Chapter Four

Trey had leukemia.

Acute lymphocytic leukemia, a common form of cancer in children Trey's age. His bone marrow had produced a large number of abnormal white blood cells. These defective white blood cells were unable to protect his body against disease. However, since his white blood count was below fifty thousand, he had a good chance of beating the disease. Gina clung to those words like she would a lifeline.

Trey would be transported later that day to the Aflac Cancer and Blood Disorders Center at Children's Health-care of Atlanta at Scottish Rite. It was about twenty miles from where Gina and Michael lived. Trey would be in his own private room. Dr. Newman had referred Trey to Dr. Milliner, a renowned oncologist.

In a daze, Keith drove Gina home to throw some clothes in a small suitcase and to grab some of Trey's toys. There was space in the hospital room for one parent to stay overnight. She intended to take advantage of the twenty-four-hour access. Michael and Keith were given twenty-four-hour ID badges, so they could visit at any time. Michael and his mother remained behind with Trey. He received his first dose of chemotherapy before his transfer.

While Keith showered, Gina sat at the dinette table and tried to eat breakfast, which Keith had ordered her to do. She dropped the turkey bacon, fighting the feeling that she was about to empty her stomach of all its contents. She knew her son was at a great facility, but she didn't know those nurses and she didn't trust them. She had to be with Trey.

Gina's single consolation was that Trey had been conscious and alert when she left him. He'd been playing just before she left—unaware of the disease that was attacking his body. She hadn't been able to hold back her tears when Trey started crying as she walked out the door because he wanted to go home. He was too young to understand the full implications of what was happening and he was scared.

Gina stopped eating. It felt like she was eating cardboard. Her stomach felt like it had rocks in it.

Gina couldn't fathom how Trey could have been playing happily one week ago and be in this condition today. There had been no real warning signs. She racked her brain, trying to figure it out. It was so weird, because Trey had always been a picture of good health. She could not even recall the last time he had been sick. Again, Gina tried to remember any telltale signs of his illness, but there had been none. He had not seemed pale or breathless.

Or had she been too focused on Keith lately to pay really close attention to her son? She mulled over that question until he entered the kitchen. She caught a whiff of Axe body wash—she loved that scent called Phoenix. Michael used it at times.

Eyeing Keith's stealth-like movements as he approached the dinette, she wanted to resent him for causing her to take her eyes off of Trey. But the longer she looked at him, the less angry she felt, even with herself. He needed a shave. He was as tired as Michael and she were. He loved her family. It wasn't his fault that she found him so sinfully distracting. She closed her eyes and shook her head. Right before her party, she'd wished Keith wouldn't get on the plane and go back to New York. Well, she had her wish. *Be careful what you wish for*. She hung her head and began to cry.

She felt Keith's arms circle her.

"I don't get this. How could cancer rear its head like this? He was fine, and now, all of a sudden, he might be dying." Gina said.

Keith sat down across from her, taking her hand. "I don't know, Gina. I'm at a loss myself. But Trey's a fighter. He'll pull through this."

She couldn't ask for anything more. Except for a miracle from God. A God she didn't know, and one who didn't seem to still be giving those out. He hadn't done anything to save her mother from dying of a stroke, and He hadn't kept cancer cells from invading her child's body.

A week of seeing her son squirm with discomfort and battle nausea from the chemotherapy tore Gina to her core. All she could do was wash the sores in his mouth and wipe his pale, drawn face. She fought to hold herself together, but she felt she just wasn't doing enough.

After one such episode, Gina felt a dam explode. She charged out of the room and ran smack-dab into another woman.

"Ouch!"

"I'm sorry! I didn't see you," Gina said, apologizing. She rubbed her elbow.

"It's okay. I wasn't watching where I was going," came the cheerful reply, though the woman hugged her chest.

Gina looked into the greenest eyes she'd ever seen and let out a small gasp when she realized the woman was rocking a small bundle in her arms.

"This is Kendall, my boy. It's hard to tell, but he had a head full of curly hair and the fattest cheeks you've ever seen. Then at five months . . . we got the news. He had his first birthday yesterday." She held him out for Gina to see. He looked gaunt, pale. He had no hair at all—no eyelashes, no eyebrows, nothing. Gina placed her hand over her mouth. He didn't look like a one-year-old. In fact, Kendall looked more like a three-month-old baby.

"Is he . . .? Is he . . .?" Gina gulped. She couldn't say the words.

The woman tilted her head, requesting that Gina follow her down the hallway. Why was this woman so upbeat when her child looked so frail and sick?

Gina looked at her watch. Trey had fallen asleep five minutes ago. She knew from experience that he would be out for a while. She followed the woman to the end of the hall. They entered the last room on the right. It took her a moment to realize this was Kendall's room. It was smaller than Trey's. Seeing the sparse surroundings, Gina's heart overflowed.

"I'm Kelly, by the way. Kelly Olson. My husband, Herman, left me when he saw how sick Kendall was. He blames me for it since cancer runs in my family." With a hum, she placed her child in the bassinet provided and swaddled him in the baby blue blanket. "There, there, my son. Close your eyes and rest your head."

Gina couldn't help it. She had to ask. "How are you humming and smiling after what you told me? If it were me, I'd be crying my eyes out, angry at the world."

"I learned early on to accept what I can't change," Kelly replied. "I know it sounds crazy, but instead of being mad and depressed, I choose to remember the gift God gave me for the short time I've had him." Gina saw her reach out to pat Kendall's little bottom. Her heart melted.

"Why are you talking about him in past tense?"

"He's dying," Kelly said. "That's why Herman left. He refused to watch his son die. I stayed because I refuse to leave him while he still lives. Every day, after I get off from my shift at the restaurant, I come here. No matter the time, I come. It's tough doing it on my own, though. I never had to worry about providing for Kendall's basic essentials before, but he keeps me going."

Her optimism was remarkable. Gina shook her head. "I can't even begin to understand your drive, but I'm glad I ran into you."

"What about you?"

For the first time in a while, Gina smiled. "I have a son. His name is Trey. He's getting sick from the chemotherapy, but he's fighting."

Kelly nodded. With a pained voice, she whispered, "Good for him. Good for him." She turned toward her child and with a singsong voice said, "If only you could fight, little one, but I know you'll soon find rest."

Overcome, Gina rushed out of the room. She didn't stop moving until she stood outside Trey's room. She couldn't believe what she'd encountered. She wondered if Kelly was cuckoo. No one in their right mind would be so accepting of their child dying.

Her compassion stirred, though, as she thought of Kendall.

Gina cracked the door open and retrieved her iPad. She logged on and went to Macy's website. After a great number of clicks, she reviewed her loaded cart, inputted the hospital's address, chose the next-day delivery option, and hit the PAYMENT button. She logged off, anticipating her delivery.

The next day Kelly sought her out. Her face was puffy from crying. "I know it was you. You're my angel. After you left, I kicked myself for not even getting your name. Never did I imagine that I would see all those clothes and toys in Kendall's room. For a moment, I wondered if I'd read the room number wrong." She hugged Gina. "That you would be so generous when your son is fighting for his life means so much to me. Thank you."

Gina's chest expanded. "I was glad to help. I've also asked Dr. Milliner to consult on your case. I know I took some liberties, but I'm covering the costs if you agree. I've already spoken to my husband about it, and he's on board."

Kelly's mouth popped open. She wrung her hands. "I can't accept it. It's too much. I'm a stranger."

Gina held on to both her arms. "When I bumped into you, I was aggravated and at a loss. You did something for me. Watching you with your son empowered me to keep going. It's you whom I have to thank."

"Five minutes," Kelly replied. "That's all it was."

"Those five minutes were enough to teach me about gratitude."

"Do you think Dr. Milliner can help Kendall?" Her voice sounded hopeful.

"I don't know, but he's the best," Gina said. "If you'd like, when Trey's asleep, I can sit with Kendall." She didn't even know why she was offering, but it pained her to see the baby in there by himself. She had walked past his room a few times and heard his little whimper. Gina knew she had Trey, and she'd put him first, but in her heart, she knew Kendall needed help.

Such was her pattern for the next few weeks. She'd read with Trey, care for him, and then sit with Kendall. Finally, with Kelly's permission, the staff brought Kendall into Trey's room for most of the day, until his mother returned. Keith, Michael, and Gerry fell in love with him. Gina also volunteered to start a story hour with some of the other children in the ward. Sometimes, while Trey was asleep, she'd take Kendall with her when she read to them.

Then, on August 5, Dr. Milliner informed them that he recommended a bone marrow transplant for Trey as the chemo treatments hadn't been successful. So Gina and the entire family had to be tested to see if they were potential bone marrow donors. They gave blood and had their cheeks swabbed. They would know soon.

Please, let there be a match, Gina thought at least one hundred times that day. She looked at Kendall. He was getting better. To everyone's surprise, his little cheeks were fuller than before. She felt good that she was able to help someone else.

She looked at her son. If only she could help her own child. He'd lost most of his beautiful curls. Even his eyelashes and eyebrows were gone. She gulped. All she could do was hope.

Then the results came. None of them were a match.

"No, no, no," she wailed, clutching her stomach.

"What are our next steps? What can we do?" she heard Michael demand.

"Our next step is to get him on the national donor list," Dr. Milliner said.

"Consider it done," Keith stated and grabbed his cell phone. "I'm on it."

To Gina, everything was happening too fast. She was experiencing such a whirlwind of emotions that she felt like she was in a bubble. A daze. Michael and Keith were a blessing, because all she could think of was Trey. Everything else for the next couple weeks was a blur.

Keith had made himself at home at their house as they had more than enough space in their home to accommodate him. Since Gerry lived forty minutes away, it was more convenient for her to spend the night, as well. She went home only to check on things and switch out clothes.

It was late July. A month had passed since Trey was hospitalized, and Gina was again expressing her gratitude to Keith.

"I know you've been a godsend. I don't know what you did to get him to the top of the donor list, but I'd be lying if I said I didn't appreciate it," Gina said, bouncing Kendall on her lap as she sat in Trey's hospital room, "And I felt a little hopeful when Michael told me that childhood leukemia has a remission rate of ninety percent."

Michael was a man on a mission. For months he'd been on the Internet with his laptop searching out information on leukemia. Now he sounded like a textbook, talking doctor lingo with the best of them. Gina applauded Michael for his efforts, because she knew that he would look out for their son. She also knew this was his way of escaping and not having to sit in the hospital and deal with the minute-by-minute agony.

Gina bunched her fists. "Trey has the spunk to beat this disease, and I'm going to hold on to that. He's got to because—" Kendall reached up to tug on her hair. Despite her worries, she couldn't help but smile at the cherub on her lap.

"I've been going to the chapel and praying for him every day. I believe God will come through," Keith said, continuing their conversation. He held his hands out to take Kendall from Gina.

Gina nodded, but inside she couldn't help but blame God. Why would He allow a little child to suffer? Still, she welcomed all the prayers on her son's behalf. She continued, "I'm so glad Trey has Althea to provide round-the-clock individualized care."

A petite and stately immigrant from Russia, Althea Watson was no-nonsense and reserved all her charm for her young patient. She had been with Trey for two days. Even a blind man could see that he was in good hands.

"I think you and Michael could convince Dr. Milliner to send Trey home if Althea's willing to go home with you. I know he's been wanting to go home."

Gina jumped at his idea. She felt there was no place like home, sometimes. She'd miss Kendall and the other children, but Trey was her first concern. Besides, she and Kelly had forged a bond. Kendall was in remission and would be discharged the following week but they would remain in touch.

Gina remembered Kelly's reaction to the good news. "God has heard my prayers," Kelly had said.

Looking at the cherub, Gina had rejoiced with her. However, she couldn't stem her bitter feeling about her own situation. *God doesn't hear my prayers.* She couldn't see God coming through twice, but she had kept that to herself.

By the end of the week, Trey was home and in his own bed under Althea's watchful eye. For the first time in weeks, Gina slept through the night. She didn't even know that she had fallen asleep. When she opened her eyes at 3:58 p.m., Michael was standing over her with a pensive look on his face.

Gina shot up, with alert, wide eyes. She clutched her chest. "What? Is it Trey?" Her heart was in her throat. Gina jumped out of bed and grabbed her pants. She slinked into them before Michael took her in his arms.

"Calm down." He kissed her forehead. "Trey's fine. I wanted to talk to you about something."

But before he could continue speaking, their door opened and Trey bounced into the room. Thrilled to see him, Gina embraced him, forgetting that Michael had something on his mind. She didn't even notice when Michael left the house.

"I want to play, Mommy."

Trey took her hand, and they ventured into the living room area. He ran to his toy chest and started playing with his Legos. He loved creating all kinds of things with the little connecting pieces. Even at a tender age, he showed signs of ingenuity and giftedness. His artwork and reading comprehension skills were beyond his years. He was the product of good genes. Gina was so proud of him.

Keith must have heard them, for he came out of his room.

Since Gerry had retreated to her guest room, Keith and Gina had a moment alone. They walked out of Trey's earshot, but Gina kept her son in her line of vision.

"I can't believe this is all happening. I'm having a hard time processing everything. It's sort of surreal to me," Gina said before shifting gears. "How are things with your job?"

Keith waved his hands in a dismissive gesture. "My job is secondary to everything going on here. There was no way I could've gone back to work with Trey sick. I would have been too busy worrying about both of you to be of any real use to anyone." He touched her cheek. "Gina, I can't leave, knowing you are facing one of the most traumatic experiences of your life. Unless I'm a complication and you want me to go."

"No. I do want you here, and it is selfish. I know I shouldn't, but I depend on you."

"I love you without any strings attached. You're not only family, you're also the love of my life. I wouldn't be anywhere else right now."

Gina's heart expanded. How could she respond to that? She put her index finger across his lips to stop him from saying anything further.

"Gina," Keith said with a fierce whisper. "I've never minced words, and I'm not about to start pretending. You're the love of my life, and I have to live with that. I have to live with seeing you in my brother's arms." He pointed over to Trey. "I had to see you carry Michael's child. I had to be happy for you, all the while wishing he was mine. And now that he's sick, I want to be here for you, but not as a brother-in-law."

Keith pulled her into his arms. She pushed against his chest. His muscles bulged beneath her palms. Keith refused to release her. She stole a glance in Trey's direction. He must've lost interest in his Legos, because he was watching television in the family room.

"Keith, your mother could come in here," Gina reminded him in low tones.

"Right now," Keith informed her, "I don't care. I just . . ." Keith stopped as his voice broke. With regret, he released all but her hands. "Anything I say will only sound distasteful, considering the circumstances."

Still holding both her hands, Keith nudged Gina until they were hidden in the shadows in the hallway. He had a good vantage point and could see anyone approaching. Leaning over, Keith pressed his mouth against hers. *You should stop this,* Gina told herself, though she yearned for more.

Lucky for her, Keith took a deep breath and ended the kiss. With a tender smile, he touched the tendrils of her hair. Since he'd moved his hands, Gina took the opportunity to move out of his arms.

"You taste as sweet as I remember," he moaned.

"I have to put distance between us," she said in a shaky voice. "I can't be responsible for my actions when I'm close to you." She released three huge breaths to regain control of her emotions. Against her will, Gina honed in on his lips. They looked inviting. She touched her own lips, remembering the brief kiss he had planted there moments ago. "I can't think. I need to focus on Trey. You're making me question the kind of mother I am. And I am your brother's wife."

Her barb hit its mark. "And whose fault is that?" Keith snarled.

Gina took two steps back. She knew he was lashing out at her because his man juices were flowing and she had put a brake on his groove, but his comment was undeserved.

"I'm sorry," Keith said, apologizing, and groaned. He ran his hands over his head. "That was uncalled for. I'm the one who was at fault. I caused this." He motioned between them, moving his hands back and forth.

Gina reached out and touched his arm before saying, "You fell in love, Keith. I did too. It was poor judgment on both our parts."

Bitterness gave his voice a distinct edge. "*Poor judgment* is not the term I would use to describe a man who pursued his brother's woman with dogged persistence. *Traitor* is more like it." He turned and headed to the family room to check on Trey.

Keith bent down in front of Trey and gave him a smile. The boy's color looked good. He slapped his knees and stood. At that moment Keith called himself every kind of a fool. How had he morphed from a decent and honest guy into someone who would feel up his brother's wife in his brother's home?

On the job, his discretion and integrity were applauded. He didn't use cutthroat methods and he never relied on charm and manipulation. He used his brains and wits to get ahead. But when it came to Gina, all his morals and scruples flew out the door. Keith detested himself, but he could not control himself around her. Anytime he came within five feet of Gina . . .

Keith shoved his hands in his pockets. Tomorrow. Tomorrow he'd get out of this house. He'd get a rental and find somewhere else to stay, because being under the same roof as Gina was unbearable. He would lose his mind or do something stupid if he stayed. And his brother, Michael, didn't deserve this. He rubbed his hands on his forehead and squeezed his eyes closed. He groaned. He could still see Gina.

With an imperceptible nod, he retreated to his room. He stayed there until Michael returned. Then Keith borrowed a car and searched for a short-term rental in the neighborhood. The nearest hotel was too far, and he needed to be in the vicinity.

Chapter Five

"We have six bedrooms, for crying out loud! So I don't understand why Keith felt the need to get his own place when there's more than enough room here," Michael said, fuming. "He has found a place and is flying home to lock his house down and get more clothes."

Gina watched her husband pace like a caged bull in their bedroom, nearly wearing a hole in the carpet. Perched on the tiny stool by her night table, she paused from brushing her hair as the news impacted her body. Her stomach constricted.

Keith was leaving.

Gina's insides trembled. She didn't want Keith to go; however, considering their encounter the evening before, Gina knew his moving out was the honorable thing to do. It was signature Keith to do the right thing. Well . . . er . . . to try to, anyway.

"Maybe he wants his privacy," Gina said, though she knew the truth.

Michael stopped and gave his wife a piercing look, weighing her every word. Gina maintained eye contact, but her heart rate increased. She knew it might be her guilt working on her, but Gina could swear Michael suspected something. Her knees buckled, even though she was sitting.

"Oh, I see . . ." Michael replied, with a knowing grin. He wagged his eyebrows at her. He had arrived at a different interpretation of Gina's words.

Gina turned and continued brushing her hair, not wanting Michael to see her natural reaction to his insinuation. She attacked her hair with vicious strokes, acknowledging to herself that she felt a pang of jealousy.

Then she became upset at her irrational response. She didn't have any dibs on Keith. He was a normal, healthy male, and she couldn't expect him to remain celibate, waiting for any scraps she could give him. She continued brushing her hair, caught up in her thoughts. Correcting herself, Gina accepted that a part of her was hoping Keith would wait for her, which was selfish, because she had no intention of leaving her husband. Trey needed his father. Michael had given her no grounds to doubt his fidelity.

Unaware of Gina's turmoil, Michael threw a quick kiss Gina's way. She watched desire fill his eyes, knowing he would seek physical release. It was a good outlet for coping with their son's ordeal. Gina felt herself respond knowing she also needed the human contact. She opened her arms.

Their interlude was cut short when Trey called out.

Upon hearing Trey call his name, Michael grabbed a storybook and left the room. It was their bedtime ritual. Michael would somehow contort his huge frame and snuggle with Trey in his twin-size bed. He read everything from fairy tales to stories from Greek mythology with such exuberance that Gina could hear their peals of laughter from her bedroom.

She never intruded, knowing how much their bonding time meant to each of them. She would peer in to see Trey's little head crooked under Michael's arm, and her heart would melt at the sight.

Feeling faint, Gina grasped her chest. She grappled with the fact that her son was now on borrowed time. She could not even begin to think about how many of these moments would be lost to her if Trey died. Thoughts of also losing Keith magnified her uncontrolled emotions.

Tossing her hairbrush down in frustration, Gina walked into her bathroom and shut the door. Leaning against it, Gina felt tears come to her eyes. She wiped her tears away, feeling stupid for even crying over Keith.

What was she even crying about? Keith? He was not her husband. Losing him to another woman was in no way comparable to losing her son. But she still felt acute pain. Gina commanded herself to feel happy for Keith if he ever found someone. She knew that day was inevitable.

She knew she would never be ready for it, but in all fairness, Keith needed to get married and have children of his own. He was going to be a devoted husband to one lucky woman and a wonderful father to a lucky child. Gina shrugged her gloom away, feeling ridiculous and selfish. She lifted her hands, physically trying to swat away the twinge of jealousy. If Keith found someone, it would serve to help put their relationship in proper perspective. He wouldn't be honing in on her anymore. She pursed her lips, conceding she wouldn't like it. She could relate to how Keith must feel and agreed his moving out was the best thing for both of them.

The next day, Gina and Michael took Trey to the hospital to get a CAT scan and blood work done. Since they had no choice, Gina and Michael headed to the waiting room after handing off their son to the nurses.

Gina's eyes widened when she saw a couple seated in two of the chairs in the waiting room. Squealing, Gina ran into the room. "Colleen!" Her emotions bubbled to the surface, and she started crying. She needed to see her best friend more than she'd realized.

The two women hugged and cried. They stood apart and laughed and cried some more, happy to see each other.

"I can't believe you're here!" Gina said. She had called Colleen to break the news about Trey and insisted her friend stay in New York. But now, seeing her lifelong confidante in person, Gina was glad Colleen hadn't heeded her instructions. Colleen and Gina had met in middle school. The two had been inseparable from their first meeting.

"We had to come and check on our god-son," Colleen insisted.

"Where are the girls?" Colleen and Terence were the proud parents of twins. Their daughters, Kimberly and Kaye were two years old.

"They're at the hotel with Francine and Lionel," Colleen answered, referring to Terence's mom and step-dad. "We didn't want to bring them here to the hospital with us."

Gina nodded with understanding. "I can't wait to see them."

Terence tapped her on the shoulder to give her a hug. He'd already greeted Michael while she and Colleen had been chatting. The four sat down.

Terence pulled out his Bible and flipped through the pages. "Colleen and I have been praying nonstop. We have our prayer warriors on the job, as well. I wanted to share a verse with you, which has encouraged me time and time again. It's Psalm 91:2." He held out the Bible, pointed the verse out to Gina, and asked her to read it.

"I will say of the Lord, He is my refuge and my fortress: my God; in him will I trust."

"I know you're going through a difficult time, but God is with you. You can trust Him. He can get you through anything. He's a miracle worker, and I believe Trey will receive his healing," Terence told them.

"Amen," Michael said.

Gina nodded at his words. For Trey's sake, she hoped against hope he was right. There was a time not too long ago when Gina could not stomach being in the same room with Terence Hayworth. She had been staunchly against Colleen marrying Terence and had not been shy about airing her opinions, but Terrance had proved himself to be worthy not only of her friend, but also of her admiration.

Dr. Milliner entered the waiting room. He gestured that he needed to speak with Gina and Michael. They followed him out of the room.

In a serene tone, the doctor addressed Gina. "Your husband called me and said you two were considering having another child."

Gina's mouth hung open. She was a private person, and right now it felt like her personal life was on blast. Of course, she wanted more children, but she wanted it to happen naturally in a year or two, when Trey was in school. This all seemed so . . . contrived. She looked back and forth between both men, not wanting to have this conversation with the doctor standing right there. Right now she felt more like a receptacle than a human with feelings.

"A sibling is often a viable candidate," Michael noted.

"I don't feel comfortable with the idea of having one child for the sole purpose of saving another," Gina confessed.

"I'm surprised you feel that way. It's not as if we haven't spoken about having another child," Michael replied. "We would just be doing it a little faster. I am thinking about Trey here. I want my son to live, and if this is the only way—"

"Are you saying that I'm not thinking about my son?" Gina snapped.

Dr. Milliner must have sensed her volatile emotions. He cut in the conversation and addressed both of them. "Mr. and Mrs. Ward, I know this is a lot to take in. Please take all the time you need to think about it. In the meantime, we will keep searching for a donor."

"Thanks, Doctor," Michael stated.

Gina and Michael joined Colleen and Terence in the waiting room. About an hour later, Keith arrived at the hospital and found the four friends in the waiting room. After greeting Keith, Colleen and Terence reluctantly announced that they had to head back to their hotel to get their daughters tucked into bed. Before leaving, both Colleen and Terence volunteered to see if they were potential donors for Trey. Gina appreciated the gesture and told them so.

Once they left, she couldn't get the conversation with Dr. Milliner out of her mind. She felt stifled. She wanted another child, but she did not want it that way. It seemed kind of cold to have a child for the purpose of saving another. Gina left the waiting room. She needed air. She wandered to the gift shop. It was a little after six thirty, and the gift shop didn't close until eight o'clock.

Michael watched Gina's departure, and his mental radar beeped. He strolled over to Keith. "Gina is ticked off at me."

"What's going on, Mike?" Keith asked.

"I called the doctor to speak about us having another child. A brother or sister is often a better match than parents or even grandparents."

"Well, I can understand that." Keith arched an eyebrow, indicating that Michael should continue.

"I didn't speak to Gina first, though, and Dr. Milliner mentioned it before I had a chance to speak with her." Michael scrunched his lips, knowing he'd made a grave error.

"Not cool." Keith shook his head. "I can understand Gina's agitation. You should have spoken to her in private, instead of airing your personal business in front of everyone. You know better."

"I know." Michael exhaled. "Unfortunately, hindsight is twenty-twenty." He paused, as if he was trying to figure out what to do. "Can you talk to her for me?"

Keith shook his head. "Michael, you're pushing it. Gina is your wife. You have to be the one to fix this."

"I know, but I know you two have a special relationship. I know I should be jealous, but it's times like now that it comes in handy." Michael chuckled.

Keith lifted both eyebrows. "A special relationship?"

"Yeah," Michael replied. "I'm not blind, you know. She respects you. I can tell. So go talk to her."

Keith put his hand on his chin and contemplated Michael's request. Then, without another word, he rose and strolled out of the room to search for Gina. He shook his head again. Without knowing it, his brother had given him an opportunity to do the one thing he wanted to do . . . spend time with his wife.

"There you are," Keith called out, beckoning Gina to him with a slight nod of his head. He'd checked a couple of rooms before venturing into the gift shop. He'd seen the top of her little head as she roamed the aisles.

She'd bought a small pack of honey-roasted peanuts and a pack of gum. She offered him a handful of peanuts, but he declined. Gina unwrapped a stick of gum and stuck it in her mouth. They walked out to the benches near the entrance.

"Michael sent me," Keith said, sitting next to her.

"I had a feeling. It's not the first time he's sent you in to do his dirty work." There was an edge in her voice.

Keith knew Gina was referring to one particular time. His memory took him back to the night when Gina found out that for the entire time she and Michael were dating, he'd had Karen Newton living in his penthouse. Gina's anger had known no bounds, and Michael had sent him to mend fences. But that was the night they made love, their emotions too raw to ignore. It had been unforgettable.

"So I guess Michael told you," Gina said, unaware of Keith's darkening pupils and his shallow, quickening breaths. Gina continued her tirade. "I can't believe he went behind my back to talk to Dr. Milliner without talking to me first."

Gina turned to Keith, unaware that she was entering a lion's den. A hungry, dangerous lion. She raised her hands in a gesture meant to curtail his response. "Now, don't get me wrong. I'm going to do whatever is necessary to save my son. You'd best believe that. But I don't like the way in which Michael went about it."

"Michael is only acting on Trey's behalf," Keith said, defending his brother. He willed himself to ignore her heaving chest and the heat rising within.

"I know," Gina said. She bent her head to study her shoes.

"You're exhausted. Your feelings are getting the best of you," Keith explained. He was fighting a serious distraction, because she looked real good in the V-necked shirt she was wearing.

"I guess so." Gina picked her head up and gave Keith a rueful grin.

"Come back with me. Michael is out of his mind with worry, and Trey must be asking about you." Keith wiped his sweaty palms on his legs and held out his hand.

Gina and Keith rode the elevator to the third floor. In the close confines of the elevator, he reached over and his hand brushed against her chest by accident. That was his undoing.

Keith pressed the STOP button. The elevator jerked to a halt. By then he was already having second thoughts. He could've kicked himself for giving in to the impulse. It would take backtracking, but he figured he could still do the right thing without Gina catching on to his original intentions. She locked eyes with him and arched an eyebrow. He knew she must be wondering what was wrong with him.

"I wanted to apologize for kissing you," he said quietly. *Great.* Why did he mention kissing? Now he *really* wanted to kiss her.

"I had no right letting you," Gina said, letting him off the hook. She licked her lips.

"So you understand why I moved out?"

"I do," Gina said. She grabbed Keith's arm. "Keith, it's time for you to move on. Find love. You deserve it," she said beseechingly.

Chapter Six

Count to ten . . . Count to ten . . .

Michael struggled to catch his breath. He took deep breaths to calm himself. He could not believe Gina was being adamant about something that was a no-brainer. They needed to have another child. None of his family members were a match, and she had none. Colleen and Terence had given blood samples, but the odds were slim to none. They needed more relatives. Gina had no one.

Except her dad.

He put his hand on his chin and mulled that over for a moment. What if he found her dad? Gina had mentioned him the other day. He knew there was a huge gap in her heart for the man who had contributed to her existence. She had never expressed an interest in locating him, but he figured this constituted as good a time as any.

He snapped his fingers. This would be the ultimate way to kill two birds with one stone. Reunite Gina with her long-lost father and find a prospective donor. He figured Gina's father owed her that much. He had not been a help to her thus far, so this would be one way he could make it up to her.

Michael paced as he pictured Gina's reaction, and smiled. It was a win-win situation. He would do it. Why hadn't he thought of this much sooner? *Better late than never,* he told himself. Gina would meet her father, and he would be the one to do that for her.

He keyed in a speed-dial number on his cell phone. His lawyer knew the right people to handle this delicate matter. Frank Armadillo answered on the second ring.

Michael sketched out what he needed done. Frank promised he would find Gina's father and stated that he had the right individual in mind for the job. This person could find anybody, with professionalism and discretion.

Michael made another call. Within minutes, he'd lined up Keith to babysit Trey that night. He needed some alone time with Gina to talk her into getting pregnant. He then called Althea and gave her Keith's address so she'd be there in case any emergency arose. He did a quick mental check in his head. "That's right. I almost forgot." He placed a call to his personal doctor. He needed to have a physical to make sure all his "swimmers" were ready and raring to go.

The last call he made was the one he dreaded the most. Michael felt like he had a mouth full of sand. He had to lay on the charm to persuade Gina to let Trey out of her sight and stay with Keith. She argued, but after much debate, Michael won. Gina caved once he told her a private nurse would be on duty at Keith's to look after Trey.

As soon as he entered the house, Michael noticed that Gina had dressed with care. She wore flats and a form-fitting navy blue sheath dress. There had been tension between them at home, and he knew it was not good for them or for Trey. The little boy did not need his parents in conflict right now. Children could pick up on when their parents were at odds. Trey was fighting for his life. He needed to know his parents were united and were fighting with him, not because of him.

Michael walked over to the dining-room table, where Gina was lighting the last candle, and saw that she had prepared grilled chicken breast with Alfredo noodles for dinner. The lit candles sparkled, and the chandelier tinkled from the light breeze the open window provided. His mouth watered.

"This looks delicious." He almost forgot the flowers he held. With a wide smile, he said with a husky voice, "These are for you." He handed her the two dozen white roses he'd ordered.

Gina put her hair behind her ear—a sure sign she was moved. "Thanks," she said under fluttering lashes. Then she arranged the huge bouquet in a vase on the sideboard before placing the arrangement on the table as a centerpiece.

They sat and ate in silence. As they were finishing their meal, Gina began to speak. She splayed her hand across the table before moving it between them. "Michael, I know what this is all about, and I want to say that my answer is yes."

"Yes!" Michael clapped his hands and gave a whoop. "Gina, I love you." He stood and reached for her. Gina placed her smaller hand in his. With a slight tug, Michael led her into their bedroom and undressed her with care.

"I'm so relieved, Gina. You've no idea," Michael murmured in her ear.

Their union was beautiful and bittersweet. He treasured their lovemaking and spooned her body next to his, not wanting to let her go. He wasn't one to be so emotional, but he wasn't ashamed of his feelings, either. Soon he drifted off to sleep.

It was around three o'clock in the morning when Michael jolted awake. *Trey.* He left the bed, careful not to awaken Gina, and wandered into Trey's room. He lowered himself and sat on the edge of the small bed. The sheets were cool to his touch. *Trey should be here, bundled under the covers.*

With a sad smile, he patted the pillow where his son would lay his head. Then he eyed the room. Seeing that Trey's toys were strewn over the floor, Michael rose and put them in his toy chest. He could purchase the best toys and gadgets the world had to offer, but he couldn't do anything to save his son.

He saw the picture of Trey smiling as he stood next to a clown, and picked it up. Michael remembered that day like it was yesterday. He had taken the day off from work and pulled Trey out of school to go to the circus. They had had front row seats, and Michael had basked in the wonder written all over Trey's face when he watched the different acts perform.

He then stood in line with the other parents so that Trey could get his picture taken with the clown. Other kids his age had been scared, but Trey had shown no anxiety. Michael remembered how he puffed out his chest with pride at his son's bravery. Michael cradled the photo in his hands. He ran his thumb over Trey's smiling face.

Unable to control himself, Michael choked up.

His precious son was now in a battle for his life. He didn't know what he would do without Trey. He couldn't even picture what his life had been like before Trey. "Empty," was the easy, immediate answer.

Michael comforted himself with the knowledge that he was doing all he could for his son. He would move mountains and crawl under rocks if it meant Trey had a fighting chance.

He left Trey's bedroom, walked to his office, and turned on the computer. His research was now a part of his daily ritual. If there was a new treatment, he was going to find it and get it. If there was a new doctor, he was going to reach out.

That was why he was on a mission to find Gina's father. Michael could not ignore or neglect a potential donor. He hoped Frank would come through. All he needed was a name and a location. He would do the rest.

Chapter Seven

Gina woke up around eight o'clock the next morning and noticed that Michael's side of the bed was empty. He must've fallen asleep in the computer room again. She'd better go wake him, she thought, or he'd have a crick in his neck and a monumental backache. She swung her legs to the side and pushed her feet into a pair of plush red slippers. If she knew him, he'd be stretched out on the sofa. It was a sofa bed, but Michael never pulled the bed out.

Gina heard the doorbell as she headed down the hallway and made a quick U-turn. "That's probably Keith and Trey." She peered through the window in the foyer and smiled at her guests. They entered the house, and Trey made a beeline for the television screen. Keith and Gina shared a smile as they watched him channel surf.

"He doesn't have a care in the world," Gina mused.

"He knows he has parents and a family who dote on him," Keith replied. "So he does not have to worry about a thing."

"Michael is asleep in his office," Gina offered, anticipating his question. Then, without taking a breath, she asked, "Where's your mom?"

"I drove her home this morning. She needed to check on a few things. I told her I would pick her up later."

"Or Michael can send a car for her."

"I don't mind the drive. I welcome it, even, because I get a chance to think."

"That's a dangerous pastime," said a male voice.

Keith and Gina turned toward the voice. Michael sauntered into the kitchen and grabbed a peach from the bowl on the island.

The kitchen was the reason why they had bought this house. It was huge, roomy, and equipped with state-of-the-art appliances that were every woman's dream. The stove heated water in thirty seconds, and the cleanup was easy. Michael and Gina had enjoyed good times in this kitchen with Trey. And if Michael's plans succeeded, they would enjoy even more good times.

Michael's cell phone rang, and he excused himself with a harried "I'll be back. Business."

Gina didn't spare her husband a glance. She was too busy watching Keith play with Trey to give her husband a second thought.

Within five minutes of Michael's departure, Terence and Colleen arrived at Gina's house with their two-year-old twin girls. Kim and Kaye were dressed in identical blue plaid summer dresses.

"They're so adorable," Gina cooed.

As soon as the girls spotted Keith, they made a beeline in his direction. Gina didn't know what it was, but he was a magnet for kids. Within minutes, all three children were jumping all over him. She could hear his laughter at their antics as he swung the girls high in his arms and on his legs. She figured a good fifteen minutes passed before he put out toys for the children and turned *Caillou* on.

Gina tapped the spot next to her on the love seat and Keith took a seat next to her.

By this time, Colleen and Terence had decided to offer up a word of prayer. At the end of the prayer, Colleen sang a verse from "What a Friend We Have in Jesus." Her sweet voice resounded off the walls.

When she was finished, Terence opened his mouth. "I wanted to talk about Jesus's healing power. There is nothing too big for Him. He's a miracle worker, and He left His Holy Spirit, a Comforter, Teacher, and Friend. The Holy Spirit is here to help us through every situation."

Gina listened to Terence's words. While he was talking, she thought about how far he had come. He had been transformed from a weasel into a witness for God. Gina no longer found him repulsive. Instead, she felt a keen sense of respect and admiration for him. Never in her life would she have imagined that she would be sitting here while Terence admonished her with the Word of God. He was a living testimony of how God could do the impossible. Terence encouraged her to look to God.

Gina nodded her head in agreement. She did need God at this time. She needed to believe God could do anything. She had never been a churchgoer. She viewed most pastors and deacons as hypocrites. She believed most of them were lechers preying on the single sisters in their congregation. Countless pastors had made headlines for their outrageous behavior.

But Colleen had pointed out the fallacy of this to her. In fact, there were many more pastors and men of God whose motives were pure. They had a genuine love and passion for God and did not provide fodder for the media, which thrived on sensationalizing mistakes. They were not considered newsworthy, but their names were written in the Book of Life, which, Colleen declared, was what mattered in the end.

Gina responded appropriately to her friends' sincere belief in God. But deep in her heart, she acknowledged she was not ready. She was a literal thinker. The kind of faith that Terence and Colleen spoke about just didn't make logical sense to her. Gina couldn't understand trusting in a God she could not feel. She believed God ex-

isted, but she couldn't conceive of how to make Him real
to her. He seemed unattainable. She was used to Terence
and Colleen by now and tolerated the drill because she
wanted them to pray for her son. But she herself didn't
buy into what they were saying. Gina believed God was
for those who were helpless and poor. She was neither.
She did believe in the power of prayer, but she saw God
as a resource to call on when she needed help. She did not
yet see Him as a Friend or Comforter.

"I want to know God," she heard Keith say.

Gina's eyes were like saucers when she heard Keith's
request. "What's going on?" she asked, but no one was
paying her any attention. She shook her head. Keith was
a highly respected attorney at his law firm. He dealt with
logic and sound reasoning. What was he doing? Was he
serious?

Truth be told, she wondered why God would appeal
to someone like Keith. Gina could see him moving up in
political circles to become a national figure. He had no
real need for God, no illness that he needed God to fix.
She eyed him. He was fine in every sense of the word.
Nope. She didn't get it.

She studied Keith some more. In all the years she'd
known him, Gina had never seen him look so young and
vulnerable. She couldn't discern what was going on with
him. Nevertheless, she showed respect and remained
quiet.

Keith listened with keen intensity to Terence's words.
He felt something strike his heart when Terence uttered,
"One day every person will have to acknowledge Jesus
as the living God." He thought about the Holy Spirit and
wondered if He could really see all his actions and hear
every single thought.

Squirming in his seat, Keith felt like a little whip was
hitting his heart. He knew he had done terrible things,

and the idea that there was an all-seeing God made him wary. He gripped the love seat to keep from looking over his shoulder to see if anybody was watching him. He then glanced at Gina and wondered if she was as affected by Terence's words as he was. Keith felt like crying, and he did not know why. Terence's words were reaching him.

Colleen must have seen the myriad emotions crossing Keith's face, for she stood and came over to him with an understanding smile. She held out her hands. Keith grabbed Colleen's hands as if they were a lifeline and stood to his feet.

"Hallelujah," Colleen said, rejoicing, interpreting Keith's surprising actions.

Keith bowed his head in supplication. He did not know what this feeling was, but he reveled in it. It felt like God was beginning to set him on a path, and it felt scary good. One minute he felt like his heart was being pierced, and another he felt like singing. "Pray for me," he said beseechingly. "I want to know God the way you're talking about Him. I want to know more about His Holy Spirit."

Terence and Colleen began lifting up words of praise and praying in earnest.

"Yes, Keith. Allow God to order your steps. He will never steer you wrong," Terence told him.

Keith welcomed the prayers. This was the second time he had experienced this calm. The first was at the hospital, when Gina was praying. He wasn't sure he could express his emotions, but it was not an eerie feeling. Instead, it was reassuring. There was something about the name of Jesus that impressed upon him that all hope was not lost.

Then Terence and Colleen prayed for Trey and anointed his little forehead with olive oil.

Before he and Colleen left, Terence addressed Keith in private. "Find a church. Let God finish the work He started."

Keith nodded. "Okay. I will."

After Colleen, Terence, and the twins departed, doubt reared its head, attacking Keith's conscience, though it felt like physical lashes across his spine. *Do you think God would want you? You're in love with your brother's wife. You've betrayed your own flesh and blood. What use would God have for a traitor?*

Chapter Eight

"Where's Terence?" Gina asked when she noticed Colleen was alone. "I actually thought you were Diamond. She is a college student and my part-time babysitter. I help her with her papers. She lives right down the block." Gina strolled down her driveway and pointed a couple houses down. "It's been a while since I've seen her, as I've been caught up with Trey."

Colleen smiled. "Well, you'll have to settle for plain old me. Terence is at the hotel with the girls as Francine and Lionel flew back to New York last night. They send their love by the way. I'm here to drag you out of the house, and I'm not taking no for an answer. I made reservations for us at Good Hair by Shelley's." Gina had been going to this salon on Butner Road for years. "We're going to get our hair and nails done. It's my treat."

Gina hesitated. "Trey's my main focus right now. Not my appearance." She touched her hair, knowing she did look like a hot mess.

"Well, I took the liberty of calling Michael and he assured me that he and Keith will watch Trey. He promised to call if anything changes." Colleen put her hands on her hips and waited.

Gina caved. "Okay, let me get a quick shower."

Once she'd showered, Gina decided to wear a sundress. It was a nice blend of browns and pinks. She matched it with a pair of brown, strappy sandals.

Several hours later, Gina and Colleen's hair had been relaxed and styled. Colleen's tresses had been straightened out and hung by her waist.

"Your hair's gorgeous," Gina declared.

Colleen pooh-poohed the compliment. "Please. It won't last. Terence will have it frizzy by midnight. He loves when I get my hair blown out. But then his hands will be all in it, and that will be the beginning of the end."

Gina saw her secret smile and giggled. "I can imagine. Well, Michael knows better than to touch mine." Her shoulder-length hair was so full of body that it moved with every turn of her head. It looked like a wig or a weave, but Gina could claim every strand as her own.

They prolonged their excursion by going to a diner for an early dinner. Both women ordered frozen strawberry lemonade and garden salad with chicken. Ever the persnickety eater, Gina ordered her salad with French dressing and declined the onions and Roma tomatoes. The two women chatted about any and everything, with Colleen doing most of the talking, and Gina a lot of laughing.

Near the end of the meal, Colleen wiped her mouth with a napkin and asked, "How is Keith?"

"Keith?" Gina was stymied. "I would never have expected you to ask about him." A thought occurred to her. "Are you asking because of the other night?"

"Yes," Colleen admitted. "He seemed touched by the Word. I sense Keith is on the brink of making a decision."

A vision of Keith becoming a Bible-thumper floated through Gina's mind. Her heart rate escalated from fear and denial. "A decision about what?" Gina hated asking questions she already knew the answers to, but she could not help this one.

"Accepting Jesus as his Savior and allowing God to take control of his life."

"I don't know," Gina said with caution. She didn't want to have this conversation. It was making her feel uncomfortable. She loved gospel music and singing inspirational songs, but she was no fanatic. Gina felt like she was under a spotlight. Soon Colleen would turn the questions in her direction. She liked having money and being able to do what she wanted. To her, serving God was all about sacrifice, and there were some sacrifices she was not ready to make.

Be honest with yourself, she thought, her conscience prodding her. *This is all about Keith. You don't want to stop thinking about him and the way he makes you feel. You want him all to yourself. If he decides to serve God, it means you cannot continue this emotional affair. You would have to let him go. Gina, you cannot be jealous of God. That's plain ridiculous.* She scolded herself and prayed that Colleen would talk about something else. Not knowing what else to do, Gina toyed with her straw and then picked up the dessert menu.

Colleen leaned forward. "I told Terence to give him a call."

Gina lifted her head and closed her eyes. Colleen was not going to let the matter rest. "What Keith does is none of my business." This time she busied herself with her napkin.

Colleen smirked. "Tell that to someone who does not know you well. I have seen you come close to giving your heart to the Lord, but every time you come close, something pulls you back. Or, rather, someone."

Her tone grated on Gina's nerves, but she played innocent. "I have no idea what you are talking about," she declared with a resolute shake of her head, denying the truth. Her hair whipped her in the face. Gina sputtered when a strand of hair hit her tongue. She hated when this happened. She used her thumb and forefinger to snag the pesky strand.

"I think you do," Colleen replied, pressing. "You want to hold on to this dead-end road with Keith."

"Colleen, what are you talking about?" This time she wasn't playing dumb. She needed clarification.

"You revel in your feelings for Keith. You love the fact that such a gorgeous man is all about you. You don't want to let him go. You'd rather let God go."

Gina was put out by Colleen's frank observations. She remained silent, opened her pocketbook, and dug through its contents for her hand sanitizer. Her fingers felt yucky after sticking them in her mouth to retrieve that errant strand of hair. When Colleen rose from the table, Gina did the same and trailed behind the taller woman. They took care of the check at the cash register and departed the restaurant.

While they walked, their sundresses swayed in the wind. Colleen's long legs were briefly exposed, and Gina laughed at her efforts to keep her dress down. Gina took a deep breath. She could smell bread as they walked by a bakery. It called to her, but she fought the craving. Carbs were not her friend.

It was such a beautiful afternoon that Gina did not want to continue with the topic at hand, but she was no chicken. She fought to speak with a semblance of calm and addressed her dearest friend. "You think I would put a man before God? Colleen, I'm married to someone else. His brother, I might add."

"Admit it, Gina," Colleen said, prodding her. "I'm not going to let you cop out. You've got to face the ugly truth. Keith is your stronghold, and you will not let this thing between you two go."

"Then why won't God let me have him?" Gina demanded, though she already knew the answer.

"Because you are married, Gina, and you cannot commit adultery and expect God to condone that. And every moment you spend pining after Keith, that's what you are doing—committing adultery. You have a good man and a son, Gina. It has been five years. Let it go. You chose Michael over Keith. That is the end of it. Accept what you cannot change."

"I . . ." Gina paused. She came to a complete halt, heedless of the other pedestrians, who now had to circle around her. Colleen's supplication had hit the bull's-eye. Her love for Keith had her twisted and turned upside down. What was wrong seemed right. Gina knew her morals and values were now in question. "Maybe you're right. But if I cannot be honest with God, to whom can I tell the truth?"

"Talk to God, Gina. Tell every sordid detail to Him," Colleen urged. "But at some point or another you're going to have to let that man go and grab on to God. He will give you everything your heart desires."

Gina thought a lot about Colleen's words as they walked. The two stopped into a gospel gift store and looked at the Bibles. It had been an eternity since she had read the Bible. Gina bought two of the Bibles, one for herself and one for Keith. She paid extra to get his Bible engraved with his name and a dove on the front. Gina also bought DVDs for Trey to watch and one of the Noah's ark play sets.

Miraculously, Colleen didn't comment on her purchase, and for that Gina was grateful. Gina didn't think she could have tolerated Colleen putting her two cents in.

At home that night, Gina practiced what she would write on the dedication page. She didn't want to make any errors or have the ink blur. Then she penned, with careful precision, the following note.

Dearest Keith,
May God grant you all your heart's desire. Hold on to Him. He will see you through.
Love always,
Gina

Chapter Nine

He couldn't believe it. This couldn't be true.

Michael walked out of his physician's office, deflated. The envelope he held slipped out of his fingers. He bent over and picked up the envelope, the contents of which had left him dumbfounded. He crumpled the envelope and clutched it tight within his fist.

Robotic, he used every ounce of resolve he possessed to locate his truck and jumped into the driver's seat. He slipped the key in the ignition. But instead of starting up the engine, Michael sat there, frozen in time, like a zombie.

He opened his fist and hurled the envelope onto the passenger seat.

The only part of his body that moved was his eyes. Their rapid blinking indicated a valiant attempt on his part to come to terms with what he had seen.

The August heat penetrated his senses. He turned the ignition to blast the AC. Michael grabbed his chest. He felt as if his heart had been crushed into a million pieces. Overcome, he rested his head on the steering column and stayed in that position for several minutes before he lifted his head off the wheel and reached over to retrieve the envelope. He extracted the crumpled letter within, smoothing it out with his hands.

Michael hoped his eyes had deceived him. He could have misread or misinterpreted the letter's contents. He looked again at the printed information, even while knowing the words in black and white would be the same.

He sobbed as tears flooded his eyes. He swiped his face with the sleeve of the shirt, not caring that it had cost the equivalent of someone's weekly earnings.

Michael knew he was on the verge of a breakdown. Never in his life had he felt this kind of despair and dis-illusionment. He felt as if someone had taken a hammer and smashed his heart into shards. He used the back of his hand to wipe his forehead.

Michael looked out his window and saw he was attract-ing the attention of a passerby. After starting up his truck and putting it in gear, Michael backed out of the parking spot with such force, his tires squealed. Heads turned in his direction. Someone even shouted that he needed to slow down.

Michael was past the point of caring. He needed to get to the bottom of this. He needed answers. If everything on that paper was true, then his life as he knew it was a farce.

On the other side of town, Keith called Gina on her cell as he pulled next to her SUV at her home. "We're in your driveway," he said and waited for her to come outside. He and his mother had decided to tag along with Gina when she took Trey to the medical center for his checkup and blood work. He'd headed to her house where they agreed to meet up once he had picked up Gerry. They all piled into her car and were in good spirits until the results came in.

The findings weren't good. Dr. Milliner decided to admit Trey, as he had a fever.

Gina and Trey joined Keith and Gerry in the waiting room. She was frantic as she relayed the bad news. "Let me try to get ahold of his father."

Keith looked at Trey. No matter how good he looked, his nephew was terminally ill. He couldn't fathom life without the little boy. Keith shook away the bad thoughts.

"I don't understand why he's not picking up," Gina wailed. She looked at Keith. "I've tried calling Michael several times on the telephone, but I keep getting his voice mail. And he's not even answering my text messages."

This was atypical behavior for Michael. He had not even called to inquire about Trey, and that was out of character. No one cherished fatherhood the way Michael did. Seeing her distress, Keith decided to give Michael a call and ended up leaving a message. Keith furrowed his brow in concern. He recalled Michael's suspicious behavior the other day and wondered what was going on. Keith knew it had to be something major for Michael to be missing in action.

Gerry told them that she would try her luck. She called her younger son and left a stern message. Once she rang off, Gerry touched her chest, worry evident on her face. "I hope he's okay. I know I shouldn't do this, but I can't help thinking he may have gotten into an accident."

"Mom, don't drive yourself crazy with possible scenarios. If something were wrong, we would have heard," Keith said, jumping in to reassure her.

Gina nodded her agreement and folded her hands in a protective gesture. But a moment later her own fears got the worst of her. "I wish Michael were here. Where is he? I'm trying not to imagine the worst, but what if Gerry's right? How do we know Michael's body isn't slumped over somewhere or his car isn't wrecked beyond recognition?" She sobbed. "And Trey will soon be connected to all sorts of gadgets and devices and beeping . . . I don't know if I can do this." Gina cried some more. Then she wiped her face and walked over to the windows to look out at the visitors' parking.

Seeing Gina suffer in silence, Keith called his brother every evil name in the book. Whenever his brother decided to show his face, Keith was going to knock some sense back into him. Michael's absence was inexcusable.

Heedless to his mother's presence, he walked over and stood behind Gina. He leaned forward and hugged her. Cradling Gina against his large frame, Keith whispered reassurances in her ear. The botanical scent of Gina's hair filled his nostrils, and Keith inhaled, taking a sharp, quick breath. He tightened his grip and snuggled closer to the petite woman. She felt so fragile in his arms. He wanted to protect her from monsters and dragons, but he was powerless against this disease.

A loud cough brought Keith to his senses. He dropped his arms and turned to face his mother's prying eyes. She rolled her eyes at him with disapproval. Keith raised a single eyebrow and dared his mother to voice her thoughts. Gerry remained silent. Keith excused himself to use the restroom. When he exited the restroom, however, his mother was waiting by the door. He stopped short.

She tapped her feet. Her face contorted into a frown. "Keith, do you know what you are doing?"

"Yes. I was using the restroom," Keith quipped, knowing full well what his mother meant.

"Don't play dumb with me, Keith Ward. Those dimples and that smart wit do not affect me. Gina is vulnerable now, and she needs her *husband,* your brother," Gerry said emphatically. "I make it a rule not to pry into your private affairs, but this time I'm not going to sit back. I see trouble brewing a mile away, and I'm not going to be embroiled in any mess."

Keith fought his resentment. "I know whose wife Gina is, Mom. You don't have to tell me."

"Yes, I do. She married Michael. *Michael.* Not you. Son, I know you've been hurt and you're in love with this woman, but you have to let it go," Gerry begged.

Keith turned his head away from his mother, which was a sure sign that he was not going to heed her advice.

Nevertheless, Gerry persisted. She was more stubborn than both he and Michael combined, and she was going to say her piece. "Find someone else, Keith. Your love is going to lead to hurt and pain. Consider your brother."

"I have," Keith spat out. "I have, Mom. If I didn't put Michael's feelings first, then I'd be with Gina right now."

"But you're not."

Keith felt bitterness rise up within him. He felt his throat tighten. Keith was disgusted with his feelings but was helpless to quell the remorse that suffocated him every day.

"Envy and jealousy are terrible diseases," Gerry said in a gentler tone. "You've never been this way before about anything in your life. Please give your actions serious thought." She sighed. "I love Gina, but that girl is going to give me more gray hairs. She's turned my two intelligent sons into two unrecognizable bumbling idiots." Though Gerry's words were harsh, she reached up and gave her son a tender kiss on the cheek.

Keith embraced his mom, conceding that she was right. He had to get some perspective and set his life in order. Keith thought about how he had felt when he was praying. He promised himself he was going to pray about this situation.

He didn't know why he could not shake his feelings for Gina. He didn't want to hurt his brother. He knew he was playing a dangerous game.

Keith felt grimy.

God still wants you. The thought hit his mind. *Could that be possible, for real?* He wondered.

When Keith and his mother entered the waiting room, Gina was sitting with Trey. She was holding his tiny hand and whispering words of comfort. Gina turned with an expectant gaze at their entrance. Keith could see her looking around his shoulder for Michael. He watched as her shoulders slumped with disappointment.

Before long they were escorted to Trey's hospital room. When Trey fell asleep, Gina announced that she was going to get water, but Keith knew better. He could see the tears threatening to fall. Following his instincts and his heart, Keith grabbed a box of tissues and followed her out the room.

Chapter Ten

The box of tissues in hand, Keith followed Gina as she ambled outside the hospital. Gina had taken the elevator and he had taken the stairs. With his long legs, he caught up to her in no time. He held the box of tissues out to her. She pulled a couple out. He knew Gina needed a good cry. They walked over to Gina's SUV. She disengaged the alarm, and the two of them sat in the front seat.

"I don't get where Michael could be," Gina cried. "This isn't like him, and I don't know if something happened. I am already worried about Trey. God, where is he?" Her chin quivered, and the tears fell.

Keith waited for Gina's tears to subside. He had left another message for Michael and did not have a clue. He did not want to exacerbate the situation by announcing that he'd noticed Michael's furtive actions of late.

Gina took a deep breath and composed herself. Then she perked up. "I almost forgot something." She reached behind her to get something from the backseat. Grabbing a box, she held it out to him.

It took a moment for Keith to register that the box was intended for him. After a brief hesitation, Keith took the gift and tore off the wrapping paper. He opened the box, but in the SUV dim interior he could not see what was inside. He turned on the interior light and was surprised to see a Bible.

He outlined the insignia bearing his name with his fingertip. The leather-bound Bible was exquisite. He opened it to the dedication page and read Gina's profound words. "This is beautiful, Gina," Keith said. "I love it."

Gina reached up and held her locket. Then, looking at Keith, she smiled. "We both seem to know the kinds of gifts to give each other. We have always been so in sync."

"So why are you constantly looking over my shoulder for my brother?" he asked. "He should be here, but he's been occupied with something else of late. I'm here for you. I don't want to be a substitute."

"That's kind of selfish of you. Michael's been a substitute for years." She threw her head back against the seat rest. Silence filled the car until she spoke again. "He's Trey's father. I can't ignore that."

"You could have avoided all this," was his curt reply. He looked at the gift in his hand, then back at her large, sad eyes. "I'm sorry, honey. I didn't mean to say that."

Gina nodded. "It's okay. At least it's coming from the right place. It's coming from love. I need that."

Keith shifted. Her comments warmed his heart, but his mother's warnings still rang in his ears. He couldn't dismiss his mother's concerns. If he didn't watch it, he and Gina would be wading into dangerous waters. He decided to resist that tempting conversation and asked a question about Trey.

Gina followed his cue and changed the subject. She asked him if he had gotten any word from Michael. Keith responded no.

Okay, that was a dead-end conversation, he thought. Keith felt her eyes on him as he looked out the window. "Let's go back in," he suggested.

Gina agreed. He decided to leave his gift in her car for safekeeping, and the two climbed out of the vehicle.

Gina walked to the rear of the SUV and popped open the trunk. She reached in to snag one of the bottled waters she kept there. "I'd better hit the restroom before going back into Trey's room. I don't want him to know I've been crying."

Keith turned his eyes when the shifting of Gina's gray pencil skirt exposed a lot of her legs. She had on a button-down, red silk shirt and wore matching pumps. When they stepped into the elevator, Keith heaved a sigh of relief. He had pretended not to notice Gina's eyes on him in the close proximity of her car. He felt good. He had resisted and defeated the urge to make physical contact.

Gina turned to Keith and apologized.

"What are you sorry for?" Keith queried.

"This." Gina pressed the STOP button. The elevator squeaked to a stop. She backed him into a corner and grabbed his shirt for balance.

No, Gina, Keith thought. *Don't do it, Gina.*

Though she wore heels, Gina still had to get on her tiptoes. She moved her hands up to hold Keith's head. The silky material felt good against his skin.

No, Keith begged with his eyes.

Gina closed her eyes and pressed her lips against Keith's. "I need this right now. I need your strength." Somehow, the top two buttons of her shirt had come undone, and Keith saw the flimsy undergarment she wore. He growled and deepened the kiss with all the passion he had repressed.

God help him. He wanted this woman. He loved this woman. He would take whatever he could get. Keith ran his hands through her hair.

"Oh, yes," Gina breathed.

You know this is wrong. Keith heard his conscience. Michael's face appeared before him. Adamant, Keith closed his eyes tighter and focused on the wonderful sensations flowing through his body. But he was no match for divine intervention.

Keith's cell phone vibrated. The two sprung apart. Reason returned. Guilt prevailed. He looked at his phone. "It's Michael."

Gina pressed the button to put the elevator in motion. As she buttoned her shirt, he saw her visible relief at his brother's call.

When the elevator stopped on their floor, Keith signaled to Gina to go ahead without him. As soon as she stepped out of the elevator car, he pressed the DOWN button and headed back to the lobby.

Keith walked out of the hospital and climbed into his brother's Escalade. He didn't care about the smooth leather interior or the smooth bass playing in the background, because the minute he entered the car, the stench of alcohol hit him full force. Michael peeled out the parking lot before Keith could buckle himself in.

"Have you been drinking?" Keith asked, enraged. Without waiting for a reply, he demanded, "Michael, pull over."

No more words were exchanged as the two men switched seats.

Keith gripped the wheel hard. He was so angry with his brother he could strangle him. What would possess Michael to even touch alcohol? And, worse yet, get behind the wheel while intoxicated? The last time he'd been reckless, Michael had almost lost his life.

"How could you?" Keith bellowed. "Your wife is upstairs, half sick out of her mind with worry, and you are busy getting sloshed. She thinks something happened to you."

"Don't talk to me about my wife," Michael snarled and twisted his body to look out the window.

Keith was taken aback by the bitterness in his brother's voice. He had no idea where such venom was coming from, and he wasn't sure he wanted to know. "What about

Trey, your son? Remember him?" The music blasted in the background. With gritted teeth, Keith punched the buttons to turn off the device.

"Ha!" Michael shouted. Then he stewed, saying nothing more.

Keith could see that Michael was battling with something, but he needed answers. Not sure of where he was going, Keith finally decided to go to his place. It was obvious there was something amiss, and he knew they needed to hash it out without fear of interruption.

Michael was out of the car and storming up the entry to the house before Keith had even put the gear in park. Sighing, Keith jogged to the other side of the car to close the door Michael had left open in his haste.

As soon as Keith unlocked the front door, Michael rushed inside. Keith stood on the steps and pondered his brother's odd behavior. Michael was in a sad condition. Keith activated the car alarm then went inside.

Inside, he found Michael in the kitchen. By the looks of things, his brother was searching for something to drink. "I have only water," Keith stated through clenched teeth. He placed the house keys on the table and watched his brother in silence. He didn't have a drop of alcohol in the house, so he didn't have to be concerned about Michael finding any.

Disgusted, Michael curled his lips with disdain. On surprisingly steady feet, he stomped into the living room and dumped his huge frame on the chaise lounge. His long legs hung over. If it weren't for the dire circumstances, Keith would have ribbed him about it.

Seated on the couch across from him, Keith observed his brother with controlled patience. Michael appeared to be stone cold sober, despite the huge amount of alcohol he must have consumed. That was a minor consolation, Keith thought. "Look, Michael just spit it out. It does not take a rocket scientist to figure out that something is wrong."

"Gina." Michael said her name like it was something he picked off the bottom of his shoe. "Gina is not who I thought she was." Michael stopped and shook his head. Then he placed his hand over his head and moaned. His dramatic antics tore away the last shreds of Keith's patience.

"Where is all this coming from?" Keith shouted. In two strides, he marched over to his brother and snatched him to his feet. "You'd better start explaining yourself fast, or I won't be responsible for my actions." Keith realized he was overacting to the situation, but he could not stomach hearing the disgust in his brother's tone.

Even with Keith's nostrils flaring in his face, Michael remained unaffected. He shrugged out of Keith's grip and dug his hand into his pocket. Without saying a word, Michael extracted a crushed piece of paper and handed it to him.

"What is this?" Keith asked while he undid the creases in the paper. He had a strange feeling he was not going to like what was on the paper. Keith read its contents. His brows furrowed with confusion, but within seconds, his eyes bulged with incredulity. Flabbergasted, Keith read and reread the paper to make sure he was seeing right. It was the results of a DNA test. Trey was not his brother's son.

"Do you know what this means?" Michael screamed. "Trey is not my son. He is not mine. Gina lied to me! She is a—"

"Michael!" Keith had to shout to stop his brother from screaming obscenities.

Michael leaned against the wall before sinking to his knees. With his head in his hands, he rocked and rocked until the tears came. Michael cried and cried.

He was overwhelmed by pain, but Keith felt powerless to help him. Keith was too dazed to offer any words of consolation.

Keith's cell phone rang in the huge space. He dropped the paper and moved toward the sound. He had placed his phone next to the house keys on the table. He noticed Gina's face and name pop up on his phone. Keith swiped the REJECT button to let the call go to voice mail. He sent Gina a covert text message saying he'd call her later.

Fresh out of tears, Michael sat hunkered down with his head in his hands. Defeat was evident all over his body. Keith decided to take charge of the situation.

"Michael, how conclusive are these results? How can you be certain this is not some crazy mistake? It happens all the time."

"Don't you think I would have demanded another test?" Michael asked with a resigned sigh.

Keith strode over and picked up the paper. Yes, he'd read it right the first time. He folded it before putting it in his pocket. This was becoming one crazy, unforgettable night. "But what made you decide to even do a DNA test in the first place?"

"Well, Gina and I have been trying to conceive for the past few months. So to cover my bases, I decided to get checked out. I'm getting older, and I don't know . . . I decided to see a urologist. My plan was to find out the quickest way to get Gina pregnant, even if it meant freezing my sperm . . . artificial insemination . . . whatever did the job." Michael released a heavy sigh. "So I did a semen analysis. I have a low semen count and a semen motility grade of one. You know what that means?"

Keith could only shake his head. "But you exercise, and you're healthy . . . I don't get it."

"Yeah, well, that's the other thing. All that exercise, football, cycling—I don't even know where to put the blame—may have caused a blockage. But what it boils down to is my chances of having a child are slim to none. I'm useless," Michael moaned out of self-pity. "I feel like I am not a man."

"Nonsense," Keith said with vehemence. "You're not the only man in the world that's . . ." He paused, realizing the subject matter required sensitivity on his part.

"Go ahead and say it, Keith," Michael demanded. In one urgent motion, Michael bounced to his feet. "Say it. Infertile. Infertile. I have lazy sperm, and I can't have children, so Gina has been passing off a bastard kid as mine."

"Michael!" Keith yelled. "Don't you ever call Trey such a degrading name again. Ever. In every way that counts, he is your son. No DNA can change that."

"Get off your high horse, Keith," Michael retorted. "If it were you this happened to, I guarantee you wouldn't be responding so rationally."

"That's a preposterous remark," Keith responded. "If Trey were mine, I'd . . . I'd . . ." Keith's voice trailed off as a thought occurred to him. Keith felt his mouth go dry. He turned his back to his brother. The truth hit his entire being like a ton of bricks. He staggered under its impact. He would have fallen flat on his face if it weren't for the fact that his brother was a few feet away from him.

Was Trey his?

Keith performed quick calculations in his head. There was that second time, two days before her wedding. His mind rejected that thought. But it had been rushed . . . a frantic good-bye. He couldn't have gotten her pregnant in . . . What was it? Like, five minutes? Could he?

Of course, he could have.

He glanced over at Michael, but his brother was too caught up in his own pain to pay him any attention.

Trey could be his son. *No*. If he wasn't Michael's, then Trey *was* his son.

Keith conjured up a mental image of Trey. Now that he knew the truth, he could see so much of himself in Trey. Keith could see himself mirrored in Trey's attitude, intelligence, and his natural curiosity. It was remarkable how alike they were in terms of personality. His chest filled with pride.

Keith wanted to blurt out the truth then and there, but he knew he had to speak to Gina first to get confirmation. He considered the ramifications of his claiming his son but dismissed them. He did not care what anybody thought or felt. He was going to claim his son. The problem was, would Trey understand that his uncle was his daddy and that his daddy was his uncle? That gave him pause. Talk about confusing. Keith realized he needed time to think without Michael around.

"You would what?" Michael asked. "See? You cannot even say anything, because you know you would find a way to make her pay for her deceit. Keith, I love Gina enough to accept her son if she had told me the truth. Why didn't she come clean?"

Thinking on the fly, Keith gave a suitable response. "Maybe she doesn't know, Michael," he stated with a calm that belied the agony churning on the inside. "Maybe Gina genuinely believes that Trey is your son."

"But she knew that she'd been with someone else, and it's obvious she didn't use any protection," Michael said. "She flipped about me and Karen, but all along she was laid up with some other guy."

"Even if that was true—"

"What do you mean, even if that was true? Bro, the proof is on the paper. Trey didn't come from the stork!"

"Okay, so it's true, but you guys don't live in New York anymore, so she made a clean break."

Michael shook his head. "You know what? I don't know if that's true. I love Gina, but she isn't always *there* with me, you know. It's weird. Hard to describe. I wouldn't be surprised if she had some other guy in her head."

Recognizing the dire need for a change of subject, Keith said, "Michael, forget about this other guy. The focus is on Trey. He's your son in every way that counts. Are you going to turn your back on him now, when he could be on his deathbed?"

Hearing his own remarks ring in his ears, Keith knew that this would not be the right time for Trey to learn the truth. Keith's mind was in turmoil. He could be jumping the gun. For all intents and purposes, Trey could be someone else's child.

And that would be tenable if Trey did not have an uncanny resemblance . . . to him.

Keith looked at his brother. He knew it would not be long before Michael put two and two together, and when he did, the repercussions would be . . . He didn't want to think about it.

It was only a matter of time. Keith's days were numbered. If he were a man of a different constitution, Keith would be worried. But he was man enough to step forward and shoulder the blame. It was Gina who he was worried about. There was no way she would be able to cope with this now. Her emotions were too fragile.

No matter how hurt he was, Michael would not inflict any of his anger on his . . . on Trey. He was innocent.

"Take me to see him," Michael commanded. "I need to see Trey."

"I'm not taking you anywhere. You're drunk, and you need to sleep it off. You're of no use to anybody in this state. Tomorrow, when you're sober, I'll take you."

"You don't have your car," his brother pointed out.

It was a wonder Michael had noticed that, drunk as he was. Keith helped to get him situated in the guest room. "It's at your house. We'll stop by your house first, so I can get my car. Then I'll drive behind you to the hospital. For now, get some rest. You're going to have a vicious hangover in the morning."

Chapter Eleven

Gina threw herself into Michael's arms when he appeared in the doorway of Trey's hospital room the next day. "Thank God, you're here," she cried.

Michael hated Gina's tears. They served to remind him of those he'd shed the night before.

He rubbed his temples, having awakened with a vicious headache, which he'd treated by popping two painkillers.

Michael was still furious at her deceit, but he would not be insensitive and voice his true feelings aloud. Seeing Gina's deceptively innocent face made it worse. He wanted to hurl insults at her, but Trey was in the room, so he curled his fists and kept his lips closed. Trey was ill. Trey was the one who mattered now. His heart could wait.

With every ounce of resilience he possessed, Michael patted Gina on the arm. He closed his eyes, trying not to visualize the letter and its contents. This was not the time or place. But he couldn't be the bigger person. She'd played him for a fool. He slid out of her arms and headed over to his sleeping son.

I can't pretend. I can't move on as if nothing has happened. His life had been turned upside down by that DNA test result.

He reached over and patted the top of Trey's head. He recalled all the fun times they had together and all the firsts that Trey had already experienced.

Shock ran through his system like a thunderbolt.

Michael realized that deep down he didn't care about who was responsible for Trey's existence. He was here. He was his son. His son. His name was on the papers. He had a legal right to Trey. He had been there from his birth, had cut the umbilical cord, patched up his skinned knees . . . He was Trey's dad. Nothing would change that.

Unbeknownst to Gina, Michael studied her. He watched her every move with Trey and her display of genuine love and devotion. Michael was so glad that he had heeded Keith's advice. He would have regretted storming in here and shouting expletives, which would've unsettled Trey and gotten him kicked out.

If he were being reasonable, Michael could not fault her for finding solace in someone else's arms after the way in which he hurt her. He had cheated on her with Karen. He acknowledged taking advantage of Gina's goodness and naïveté, which had led to him almost losing her.

Michael recognized that a part of him had held Gina to a standard of perfection, which wasn't realistic or possible. He had to reconcile in his mind the fact that she was human and thus predisposed to err.

Who was he kidding?

It pained him to think of Gina with someone else. He tried not to picture her finding ecstasy with . . . Ugh. The image was too difficult to conjure.

Michael redirected his thoughts back to his son. Trey needed him. Michael did not know that it could be possible, considering the new revelation, but he loved Trey even more.

It was like God had given him something he could not have had on his own. He could not abandon Trey. He was, for all intents and purposes, a gift from God.

From his chair across the room, Keith watched the conflicting emotions cross Michael's face. He saw the pain caused by Gina's indiscretion mingled with the devotion to Trey. Michael didn't know it, but Keith knew love would win. Gina was a prize, a good woman. His brother wouldn't let her go. In time, Michael would jump over this hurdle.

He wasn't too sure about his own recovery. He was the "other" man and the true biological father. He couldn't help but stare at the solitary figure lying in the bed. His son.

Keith was also drawn even more to Gina now, and he had never fathomed that could be even remotely possible. They shared a bond. Their love had brought to fruition a little boy who lay sick and helpless on a bed not even three feet away from him.

A boy who needed his mom and dad. For Keith, it was torture to remain silent. He did not know how he was able to withhold the truth. He felt his heart tighten. Keith wanted to shout the news from the rooftops. He wanted to claim his son. But this was a terrible, twisted situation in which he had become entangled.

In vain, Keith tried to remain stoic, but his heart felt both sorrow and joy. Everything he wanted, everything that was so precious, was within his reach, and he could not declare it. He had to remain a silent observer.

This went against his nature. Keith did not know how to resolve this dilemma without someone important in his life getting hurt.

The truth shall set you free.

Keith knew he had to come clean if he was going to stay sane. He couldn't keep this lie to himself for the rest of his life. He couldn't pretend that he was not a father. However, Trey was young and impressionable. He would find it hard to understand how his uncle was now his dad, and his father was now his uncle.

But on the other hand, Trey was young enough to adapt. Keith couldn't imagine waiting until Trey was a teenager to break the news—news that could cause irrevocable damage.

How could he not step up and claim him? Every child deserved to know where he or she came from. Yet how could he destroy his brother's life? Keith looked at his brother and his son. The truth would hurt both of them in some way. How could he choose?

Torn apart, Keith traipsed out of the room. He found the chapel and headed to the front pew. His conscience battled him. Keith remembered the Bible that Gina had given to him. He considered getting it but waved the thought aside. He felt too sullied and too unworthy to even open the good book. However, he could talk to God. Terence and Colleen had assured him that he could, and Keith clung to that hope with every fiber of his being.

Releasing his tears, Keith could not even find the words to say to God. Thoughts rushed at him, but his quicksilver tongue was silenced by the harsh reality of his actions. He had slept with his brother's wife. A couple days before Gina had pledged her eternity to Michael, she'd given herself to him. They had created a child, who was now ill, without a donor.

The guilt weighed him down. His conscience attacked him, granting him no reprieve.

Keith felt as if God was punishing Trey because of his misdeeds. He was a terrible, ruthless reprobate, but Trey shouldn't pay for that. "Please, God. Hurt me instead. Take your wrath out on me, but spare my son." Keith was too overcome to say anything else.

God loves you.

Keith turned his head and looked around the room. He was so distraught that he hadn't heard anyone enter. Feeling embarrassed, Keith looked around the vestibule.

There was no one there. But he heard the persistent sound again.

God loves you.

The powerful sentiment was a ubiquitous presence, resonating through his heart and echoing in his ears. It felt like a loud crescendo lifting him out of the mire of sorrow he had spun. Then it became a smooth, calming thought that soothed his entire being.

Keith felt comforted. He felt awed. God's Holy Spirit had spoken to him. At that moment, though he did not know how, Keith knew everything would work itself out.

Chapter Twelve

If Michael responded with "Just have a lot on my mind," one more time, Gina was going to scream!

Something was wrong. She sensed it. But each time she'd asked him, he'd assured her that he was fine. Gina didn't know how to interpret Michael's sudden, aloof demeanor of the past two days.

At the breakfast table that morning, she'd voiced her concerns. "Michael, I can't pinpoint it, but your concern seems somewhat . . . forced. Our conversations—when you do talk to me—are stilted, and I can't help but feel as if you're keeping something from me. You're usually up-front with me, and it's not like you to keep anything from me."

He looked like he'd been about to say something but he must have changed his mind. Instead, he'd said, "I'm going to the hospital. Are you coming?"

"I have a quick errand to run, but I'll meet you there." Gina felt guilty for lying, but going alone to the hospital was ten times better than sitting in a car with Michael and enduring his silence.

As soon as she heard Michael's car pull out of the driveway, Gina dialed Colleen's cell phone.

Colleen answered mid-ring. "You're going to live a long time, because I was just thinking about you. I just picked up the phone to call you to find out if there was any update on Trey's condition."

"No," Gina sighed. "However, no news is good news."

"So what's up?" Colleen inquired. "I can tell from your tone that something is bothering you. Talk to me."

"It's Michael." She needed to express her sentiments aloud to make sure that she was not being paranoid or supersensitive. This was an emotional time for everyone. Gina wanted to make sure that she was not overreacting.

"Okay," Colleen replied. "Give me more, or this is going to be a long, drawn-out conversation. I'm looking at the clock, and we have about an hour before the twins wake up, so get to talking, girl."

"I think something is bothering him, and I am not sure what." Gina twisted in her chair. Her position was as awkward as the conversation.

"Well, his son is in a hospital with a deadly disease. I think that's a valid reason for him to be bothered."

"Colleen, I know all that. I can't put my finger on it, but it is more than that. It's the feeling I get when he is around. He pulled a disappearing act the day before yesterday. At first I attributed it to all this stress, but he has been acting odd around me. He looks at me in a way that makes me uncomfortable, and it's freaking me out."

"Have you asked him about it?" Colleen said.

Gina nodded, though Colleen could not see her, and replied in a dejected tone, "Yes and his reply is that he's got a lot on his mind. Then he changes the subject. I'm walking on eggshells. I can't sleep because I don't know what is going on. He's like a brick wall." She leaned into the phone to hear Colleen's words.

"You should confront him. It could very well be nothing. You sometimes get too tuned in to people's moods. He feels helpless because there's nothing he can do for Trey. Men take that much harder than we do."

"Colleen . . ." Gina lowered her voice, even though there was no one around to hear her conversation. "Do you think he's found out about Keith and me? That's the only thing I can think of."

"I don't think so. Michael strikes me as the kind of man who would go ahead and have it out with you about it. It's your own guilt causing you to see things that aren't there."

Gina couldn't let it go. "I think it's possible that he knows, but he's trying to play it cool for Trey." Her stomach was in knots. She did not want to consider the magnitude of Michael's hurt and wrath toward her and his brother if he found out.

"I think you're paranoid and worried about nothing."

"I just have this feeling. Call it instinct," Gina insisted.

"What does Keith say?" Colleen asked.

"I haven't spoken to him. I did call him, but he has not returned my calls. He's pulled a disappearing act."

"Now, *that* I find unusual. When it comes to you, Keith drops everything."

Gina didn't even bother denying Colleen's words, because her friend spoke the truth. "That's another reason why I'm beside myself right now." Gina fought to keep a sob out of her voice. "Neither one of them is acting right, and that has me rattled."

"Stop worrying about those men." Colleen's voice held an edge of frustration. "Focus on your child."

"I've tried, but they're my family, Colleen. Other than you, they're all I have."

Colleen tried to reassure her some more, but once they hung up the phone, Gina realized the conversation with Colleen had done nothing to pacify her doubts. Gina felt like kicking herself. She would not be going through this turmoil if she didn't have a guilty conscience.

Some would say that it was fair play, but she had to be honest with herself. Michael had cheated on her, but that was no validation for her sleeping with Michael's brother. Being with Keith had not been about getting even. Michael was the last person on her mind when she made love to

Keith. It had been about Gina and Keith expressing their love for each other. Gina sat at her kitchen table and eyed the fruit bowl. She picked up a banana and peeled back its skin. She took a bite. Maybe Keith had been right. He'd pushed for them to tell Michael the truth. If they had done so back then, maybe Michael would have been able to get past it and move on in time. She and Keith would have married, and they would not be in their own private hell, sneaking kisses and touches like high school kids.

Her stomach turned. She couldn't finish the banana. She tossed the remaining portion into the garbage can, washed her hands, and wiped them on her jeans. Her mind wandered back to the elevator kiss. Gina was still ashamed at her brazenness that night, but a part of her was glad that she had done what she did. She craved Keith's touch and his lips. Even though five years had passed, her body had never forgotten him, because Gina was still in love with Keith.

She was at it again. Thinking about Keith. Gina cautioned herself to stop. There was no use pining for something that she could not have. There were times when she felt like blurting it all out and hightailing it back to New York and into Keith's arms. But there was Trey to consider. She could not do that to her son. He needed both his parents, and Gina was not going to mess with his childhood to satisfy her selfish desires. When Trey started school, Gina wanted to be able to check the box that said he lived at home with both parents. Her selfish desires no longer took center stage once she became a parent.

Trey was worth every sacrifice—even the pining of her heart.

Chapter Thirteen

Keith forced his eyes open. His alarm clock was blasting, telling him to get up. Lethargic, he reached over and put the clock out of its misery. He had slept only about four hours.

With an angry grunt, he made himself sit up. He needed to get over to the hospital. He wanted to see Trey. His progeny. He also needed to be present to deflect Michael's cantankerous disposition as his brother wavered between feelings of love and hate.

The news that he was infertile had to be driving Michael up the wall, and the natural reaction was for Michael to transfer all those emotions right to Gina. But Keith would not allow that. It was not Gina's fault that Michael was infertile. But it was her fault—well, both their faults—that Trey wasn't his.

On the other hand, Keith admired Michael's restraint and deference in the face of what were delicate circumstances. Finding out that you were infertile and that the child you thought of as your son was not your own was no easy dish to be served. Keith could attest that Trey was the sole reason why Michael was trying to be a better man. It was a tough pill to swallow, and Michael had told him as much.

After a quick shower and a small breakfast, Keith drove over to the hospital, arriving just after eight o'clock. On impulse, he decided to enter the chapel on the ground floor. He opened the door to the small vestibule and then sauntered up the aisle to his usual spot in the front pew. There was a Bible on the bench. Its worn pages testified to the many people who'd sought comfort by reading the words.

A bookmark protruded from the book. Keith slid it out to take a look at what was written on it. It was "Footprints in the Sand." He knew this poem, and at the moment he really appreciated it. Though he was strong and capable, he needed someone. He closed his eyes.

Right at this moment, he felt alone. He wished he had his own woman to talk to right now and give him a little solace. He had dated—and hadn't been a monk—but he was in love with Gina. He wouldn't do that to another woman. Keith sighed. He needed to unburden himself, because he was conflicted. He knew that Trey was his son. He didn't know if he could remain quiet about that for long. He wasn't the sort of man who would deny his own child.

Keith did not know how he had ended up in this situation.

How? His conscience jeered him.

Okay, he thought. He knew how.

Keith slumped over and clasped his hands. He stayed in that position but couldn't summon up the words. However, somehow, he felt surrounded by a comforting presence. It was like God was giving him a hug.

Keith stayed in the chapel until Michael texted him.

Where R U?

Downstairs, in the chapel, he texted back.

On my way. With Gina.

Keith met up with Michael and Gina by the elevator. The three of them got on the elevator and went up to the lobby. When they walked out into the lobby, Michael grabbed Keith's arm, indicating he wanted to talk in private. The two men lingered, allowing Gina to walk ahead so they could talk.

"I'm not going to do it," Michael confessed. "I'm not going to confront her. Not now. Maybe not ever."

Keith nodded his assent. "I'm impressed with your decision. Right now Trey is who is important, and I applaud you for being the bigger man."

After spending the entire day and evening at the hospital playing with Trey, Keith bid farewell to Michael and Gina but not before he grabbed his Bible from the backseat. He felt a strong pull to read God's Word. He wanted to experience again that closeness that he had felt in the chapel.

When he arrived home, he took care of his nightly ablutions before settling in bed. Keith opened the Bible and scanned the crisp pages. He turned the pages back and forth, unsure of where to begin reading. Finally, he decided to look for a passage that sounded interesting, figuring that since the whole book was from God, it shouldn't matter what he read. His eyes caught a phrase. "What time I am afraid, I will trust in thee." It was from Psalm 56. Curious, Keith decided to read the entire chapter. He read another part that said, "In God I will praise His word, in God I have put my trust; I will not fear what flesh can do unto me."

He was hooked. He noticed that there were little italicized letters on the page and, being a quick study, realized that it must be a reference. The reference note read, "Ps. 118:6 and Heb. 13:6." Keith wondered what on earth Ps. and Heb. were.

Then he chuckled, realizing that they must be books in the Bible. He brought the Bible closer to his eyes, and sure enough that "Ps." and the "Heb." had periods at the end, signifying they were abbreviations. Keith thought for a moment. Then a light bulb lit up. He looked at what he called the table of contents at the beginning of the Bible.

Aha! He found it.

"Ps." stood for "Psalm," and "Heb." was Hebrews. There were also page numbers listed, so Keith could find the books. He read the introduction, which revealed that the Bible was divided into two sections: the Old Testament and the New Testament. It was then divided into books, and then into chapters and verses, so that locating scripture would be easier.

Keith laughed at his own ignorance. He appreciated that little introduction, which made navigating the Bible much easier and less daunting. It was obvious that his law degree was of no use here. He was going to need divine assistance.

Keith checked out the rest of the Bible and found a concordance and even topical studies in the back. It was interesting to note that there was a Bible verse for almost everything. He learned that the little numbers by some of the verses meant that there was commentary on those verses below. He knew that he would be absorbed in this book for hours. When he read Psalm 118:6 and Hebrews 13:6, the references there led him on another escapade.

Getting on his knees, Keith prayed a short but earnest prayer. "God, I'm not an expert at praying, but I know you can hear me. I thank you for this Bible. Please open my mind so that I will be able to understand what I'm reading." Then Keith ended his prayer with, "And, please bless Gina and Michael and Trey. Amen."

He grabbed a pencil and wrote little notes and questions while he was reading. He was not sure if people wrote on the pages of their Bible, but that was what he had done with his college texts. He was going to purchase a highlighter, as well, so he could mark those verses.

Keith read and studied for hours. He was so engrossed in the Word that it was 4:00 a.m. before he knew it. It was the first time that Keith had been able to put Gina out of his mind.

Before going to sleep, Keith returned to Psalm 118:6. It read, "The Lord is on my side; I will not fear: what can man do unto me?" Keith reread the verse, liking this man, David, who had been inspired to write the words. He could relate to David because he too was a man who didn't seem to fear anyone or anything. But there were certain things that were beyond his comprehension, like Trey's illness. So what that scripture said to Keith was that he needed God on his side and on his son, Trey's, as well. As long as God was with Trey, Keith would not worry about the outcome.

People's words and predictions were nothing for God.

Keith knew that if nothing else, he could pray for his son. Feeling a little nervous, because he was still uncertain God would even hear his prayer, Keith slid to his knees. He did not have much to say, but he did say a few heartfelt words. "God, please send a miracle and save my son."

Chapter Fourteen

Why hasn't he called?

Maybe Keith saw the futility of their dead-end attraction and was keeping his distance. Gina hated herself for even obsessing over his not calling, but it was so unlike him.

Sitting in her computer room, Gina swiveled in the chair. She creased her brows and bit her bottom lip. It was perplexing. Perhaps Colleen was right. Maybe she was selfish. She couldn't fault Keith if he decided to move on. That was what she'd urged him to do on so many occasions in the past. She moaned. Deep in the inner recesses of her heart, she admitted that she didn't want Keith to get over her, not when she didn't have any realistic hope of ever shaking her addiction to him.

Gina held her chin while she stared at a blank screen on her iMac. Was it her unsolicited kiss in the elevator that had precipitated his sudden elusiveness? Maybe he'd found her brazen action despicable, considering the fact that her son was on his deathbed.

No, that's not it. That would be like the pot calling the kettle black. Since his arrival, Keith hadn't kept his hands off her. Gina remembered their passionate encounter in her kitchen hallway. She picked up a pencil and tapped her bottom lip.

No, it has to be something else. "Why won't he call me?" she groaned. She snapped the pencil in half. *Ugh.* She threw the two halves in the trashcan located to the left of the computer stand. "Get yourself together, Gina."

She opened the desk drawer, took out another pencil, and shoved it in the electric sharpener.

Michael had remained cool and distant. The two things had to be connected, Gina deduced. She could not feel settled in her spirit until she had answers. All day, throughout her entire visit with Trey, this issue had been at the back of her mind.

She knew that if anyone would tell her anything, it would be Keith. "But he's avoiding me."

That's it! She'd had enough! Her pressure level rose, and she snapped another pencil in two. Tossing it in the trash, she grabbed her phone and tapped in Keith's speed dial number. *He'd better pick up!* she thought. If he didn't . . .

A few seconds later Gina stormed out of the house, her cream linen suit wasn't warm enough for mid-September, but she was too heated to notice. She marched to her car and jumped in, slamming the door. She fumed the entire ten-minute ride to Keith's place.

Her heels clicked on the short path up to his door. Gina pressed the doorbell. She wasn't going anywhere until he answered. Keith swung open the door with an irate look on his face. He must have awakened moments before, because he was wearing only pajama pants. Keith's manner was that of a bear awakened from hibernation. She clutched her chest as her heart hammered. In his state of undress, he was eye candy, but she wasn't going to be distracted.

"Why haven't you returned my calls?" she asked, knowing she sounded like a harried housewife, but who cared?

Keith raised his eyebrows at her possessive tone, but he stayed quiet. *Good move.* He backed up. "Okay, calm the storm. I feel like I'm about to get struck by lightning. I was reading my Bible," he finally answered with a soft tone.

Gina's mouth hung open like she was a fish out of water. "Oh." She hadn't expected to hear that. Now she felt dumb, but she couldn't think of a comeback to save face.

Keith lifted one eyebrow and folded his arms in a gesture that was meant to make her back down. He was making his displeasure known at her unexpected visit. He shifted to stand on one leg, which showed off his well-toned muscles and six-pack. Keith did not have any hang-ups with his body, and why would he, when it was stuntman perfect?

With a huge swallow, Gina strove to hide her discomfort.

"What did you think?" he asked.

She wasn't going to even answer that one.

He continued. "I have an idea why you're so upset. You're used to me always being at your beck and call, and you're spoiled."

She watched Keith bite back a smile while she fumbled with her response. That dimple of his was messing with her senses. "I was worried when you didn't call me back," she hedged. Gina turned around and started to walk away from the still open door.

Keith reached out and snaked his hands around her arm and pulled her into the house. As soon as he closed the door, he whispered, "Seeing you is like fire. I wonder if you smell as good as you look." He planted a kiss full on her lips, nipped at her ears, and let out a low growl in her hair. "Yes, yes, you do."

Goose bumps popped up over all her body. In his arms, Gina couldn't contain her relief. There was no one else. She could feel Keith's desire and delighted in every moment. She was still the one. She acknowledged to herself that this was the true reason that she had come over here.

She ended the embrace and stepped out of his arms. With sadness, she admitted, "You're right. I'm spoiled and selfish."

"I know. I'm the same way when it comes to you."

Their eyes met. Gina had to get her lustful thoughts under control. She had another, altruistic motive for being here. "What's going on with Michael?"

Keith blinked. "I do know, but it's not for me to tell. Michael will open up when he is ready."

"So I am right!" Gina sighed. She pinned him with her gaze. "Do you think he suspects us?"

"No," Keith assured her. "If that were the case, I would've told you, and Michael wouldn't take that sitting down, believe me. He'd erupt."

She couldn't take it anymore. She moved farther into Keith's space.

He put his hands up. "What are you doing?"

She reached out and touched his flat stomach. His muscles flexed under her hands. She luxuriated in his sheer maleness. It was intoxicating. She stood on her tiptoes, kissed his neck, and inhaled his woodsy scent. What was she doing? She didn't recognize herself at the moment. She knew this was a temptation and that she should resist. It felt so exquisite that she lingered a little longer before finding the restraint to stop.

Keith smiled and tucked her under the chin to meet her gaze. "I can't," he explained.

"You don't want to?" she asked, batting her lashes.

"You know I want to. Please don't tempt me," Keith begged.

Gina nodded. Keith was right, but her heart wanted what it wanted. She reached over and played with his chest. Keith swung his arm and covered her hand to quell her movements.

"Gina, you're going to get me in big trouble."

Knowing that she was going too far, Gina stilled herself. She didn't know why she was behaving like a territorial animal. Usually, she tried to fight this attraction, but a raw craving had arisen from Keith's alleged abandonment, and she was staking her claim.

He doesn't belong to you. Gina ignored the voice.

Keith's cell rang, and he moved to answer it.

Gina was annoyed while Keith spoke on the phone, and she showed it.

"You'd better go," Keith warned after ending the call. "That was Michael, and he is on his way over here."

In a panic, Gina smoothed her clothes and then rushed out the door. It wouldn't do for her husband to catch her running out of his brother's house.

Chapter Fifteen

Two minutes.

That was how much time he had to throw a shirt on and compose himself before he heard the doorbell ring.

Michael entered the house and headed straight to the kitchen. Keith smiled in remembrance. Ever since they were boys, Michael had always hit the kitchen upon entering the house. This time was no different. Most times Michael didn't want anything. He liked browsing. Keith waited for Michael to get to the reason behind his visit.

Snatching an apple out of the fruit basket, Michael took several big bites, chewing fast.

"Slow down, bro. The apple isn't going anywhere," Keith teased, shaking his head. "You're such a big kid."

Michael waved him off. Keith started to say something, but Michael put a hand up in a silent request for Keith to wait until he was done with the apple. Once he swallowed, Michael lost interest in eating the rest of the apple and set it down on the kitchen counter. Keith noted Michael's nervousness and sat down on one of the stools, waiting for a valid explanation.

Michael opened his mouth to speak and then closed it.

Still trying to recover from the unsatisfactory ending to his visit with Gina, Keith was impatient. "Spit it out."

"With no donor in sight, I'm worried about Trey's chances of survival."

"I know. I am too." Keith nodded vigorously.

Michael coughed. Whatever it was, Keith knew it had to be difficult for him to say it. Michael was never one to hesitate when it came to asking for his help. "Well, as you know, I am in no position to help the situation."

Keith understood his brother's need to deflate his discomfort with humor. "Michael, don't put any blame on your shoulders," Keith advised.

"I'm becoming resolute about that," Michael responded. He looked at Keith with determination. "I need to ask you a favor."

Uh-oh. Keith didn't know how to feel whenever Michael asked him for a favor. It was bound to be preposterous or crazy or . . .

"I want you to give Gina a baby."

Out of the question. Keith almost choked from the enormity of Michael's request. He couldn't fathom his brother's reasoning at times. Who would ask his own brother to procreate with his wife?

Michael must have seen the look on Keith's face, for he was quick to explain what he had in mind. "You wouldn't have to do it the natural way. I was thinking more along the lines of artificial insemination . . ."

Keith picked up Michael's half-eaten apple and took a big bite. He needed time to think.

"Yuck. Can't you get your own apple?" Michael frowned.

Keith shrugged. He had to chew on something before he said what was most prominent in his mind. He knew that what Michael was asking was common nowadays, but he was flabbergasted at the clinical coldness of creating a child that way. Nevertheless, Keith could understand why his brother would ask. A child's life was at risk. His child.

Keith had other worries. Like, what if the baby resembled Trey? He could never explain that as a mere coincidence. If the circumstances weren't so dire, Keith would laugh at the irony of it all. He was being asked to father a child to save his secret love child. Keith was becoming sick of the lie. It was becoming more convoluted with each passing day.

When Keith remained silent, Michael ended the conversation by asking him to give it some consideration. Michael also made sure he mentioned how much Trey's life depended on Keith's willingness to fulfill his request.

Keith could feel the guilt pressing down on his shoulders. This was the moment when he could assure Michael that he had no problem sleeping with his wife. Why? Because he had already been there, done that. This was ridiculous. God had a sense of humor! Keith was living proof of that.

The truth shall set you free.

Keith opened his mouth to speak; however, Michael beat him to the punch.

"I wouldn't ask if I did not know that I can trust you. There's no doubt in my mind about that," Michael pleaded.

Keith shut his mouth and gritted his teeth to keep from blurting he should be the last person Michael trusted.

Bereft, Michael drove around for a while after leaving Keith's house. He wasn't cognizant of getting on the highway and stopping at red lights, for he was so caught up in his thoughts. Before he knew it, Michael was pulling into his mother's driveway.

Gerry was happy to see him, but he could see the concern etched on her face. "You look like something the cat dragged in." She held Michael's chin and took a good look at him. "You look troubled and gaunt. Are you eating?"

Michael shook his head. "No, and yes, I feel as bad as I look."

His mother herded him into the kitchen and then ambled over to the stove, where she was keeping a pot of curry chicken and white rice warm. She dished up a hearty plate and gave it to Michael. He sat down at the kitchen table and began to eat like he hadn't consumed a meal in weeks.

"It does my heart good to see you eat with so much enthusiasm." She chuckled.

Michael nodded, but his mouth was full of food, so he refrained from speaking. His mother remained quiet until he'd finished his meal.

"Talk to me," Gerry commanded once he'd wiped his mouth.

Michael put his plate and utensils in the sink and washed his hands. Returning to where his mother sat, he leaned over and grabbed her into a bear hug. Her small frame still provided comfort even at his age and with his bigger size. Then he started talking. Michael told her about the test results and explained that he was infertile. He told her how conflicted he was regarding his feelings for Gina. Michael even told Gerry that he had asked Keith to father a child for him with Gina.

After hearing that, Gerry put her hands up. "I can't wrap my head around everything that I'm hearing. When it rains, it pours." She paced the kitchen. "Son, I know you're hoping I'll have something to say, but I'm having a hard time digesting this news. Stretch out on the couch and rest your brain for a moment while I think about this."

Michael headed to the living room, took off his shoes, and did as his mother had suggested. With a small yawn, he closed his eyes.

An hour later, Michael woke up. He heard his mother on the telephone. He swung his legs to the floor. He roamed through the house before heading into the family room. On the floor were open photo albums. His mother must have been having one of her moments. Whenever she was stressed, she always took out the baby pictures. "I'm looking back at a simpler time," she would say.

A photo caught his eye. He leaned closer. It was a picture of Trey. He didn't remember this one. He removed the photo from the jacket and looked at it for several seconds. *Wait a minute. This isn't Trey,* he thought. He flipped the picture over. His mother always wrote the something about the picture on the back.

Keith, 1 year old.

Michael looked at the picture again. Keith looked so much like Trey. His heart denied it. Michael jumped up, and with shaking hands, he placed the photo of Keith next to one on the mantel that he was sure was of Trey. The resemblance was uncanny. It was eerie.

It can't be. No, there has to be another explanation.

"Michael, what are you doing?" his mother asked from across the room. Her careful enunciation of each word told him that his mother knew exactly what he was doing.

"Just looking at a picture of Keith, my brother. And Trey, my son. Or should I say, his son?" He faced his mother, but she couldn't look him in the eye. "How long have you known?"

She stepped farther into the room. Tears rolled down her face. "I didn't. I suspected when you talked to me earlier, and I wondered. I came to look at the pictures, but then I had a phone call and . . . I meant to put those away." She fiddled with her housecoat.

Disillusionment and hurt were etched on every contour of his heart. Michael broke. "I asked him to help me out by fathering a child with Gina. Little did I know that he'd already been there, done that. Imagine . . ." He tossed the picture of Keith aside and covered his eyes with his hands, giving his head a vehement shake.

The photograph was worth a thousand words.

"Aww!" he screamed. Blinding fury engulfed him, and he ran back to the living room, grabbed his shoes, and shoved his feet into them. As he headed to the front door, his mother tried to block his path, but he lifted her out of the way. She cried and pleaded with him to stay, but he was going to confront Keith.

His voice escalated as he vowed, "I'm going to kill him! He's going to pay for this. If it's the last thing I do. He will pay!"

Chapter Sixteen

Keith heard a crash. He couldn't ascertain the source of the commotion before he felt himself being tossed to the floor in the hallway outside Trey's hospital room. He felt pounding fists on his head before he used his strength to push his assailant to the floor.

He'd come to the hospital to sit with Trey. Gina wasn't there.

Pinning the attacker's body beneath his, Keith raised his fist to return the favor when he saw who it was. "Michael?"

"You know what this is about," Michael shot back before his huge fist landed on Keith's lower jaw.

Keith felt blood ooze from his mouth as his jaw hit teeth. He moved out of the path of Michael's flailing fists. He lifted his hands to ward off the blows and to try to defuse the situation. Michael was out for blood. He was not up for a conversation.

"Let me explain," Keith said, then retreated as Michael charged toward him.

A punch landed on Keith's left cheekbone, and his head swerved so hard from the impact that he had whiplash. Fury set in. Keith swung his powerful arms and made contact with Michael's right eye. Since Michael was incapacitated for a moment, Keith was able to grab him and haul him into the nearest elevator. Within the compact area of the elevator, much pushing and shoving occurred, but Keith's intent was for them to take this war outside. He pushed the button for the lobby.

"Quit it!" Keith growled. "Are you trying to get us arrested?"

Too angry for words, Michael didn't even give him a response. When the elevator reached the lobby, Michael dashed out and headed to the hospital entrance. As soon as the door swung open, Michael ran toward his car, activating the remote UNLOCK button as he went, and jumped into the driver's seat. Keith was right behind him. He opened the rear door before Michael could lock it and jumped in, even though Michael had already put the car in gear.

Michael's car squealed as he sped away, skillfully handling the car. Once he'd stopped at a red light, Michael found his voice. "I hope the whore was worth it."

Keith's wrath bubbled up, and he bounded out of the car. Michael had made the mistake of leaving his window open, and Keith used that opportunity to deliver a mind-blowing punch to his face.

Michael's head swung back so hard that he had whiplash, but he wasn't going to back down. "You want some of this!" Michael put the gear in park and jumped out of the vehicle.

Heedless of the green light, he shoved Keith with tremendous force. Keith harrumphed and pushed back. Michael and Keith became enfolded in a tight grip as neither man would give in to the other. They were fit enough to continue their onslaught for hours without tiring. They twisted with rage, arm in arm, backing up until they had crossed the intersection and smashed through a glass shop window.

The owner of the shop was flipping the OPEN sign to CLOSED. Keith saw that the poor man was frightened out of his wits to see two large men rolling on the floor, amid the broken glass. They had not been slowed down by the glass and seemed immune to the shards tearing at their suits.

The shopkeeper shouted, "I'm calling the cops!"

Michael took off running.

"I'm sorry," Keith said, his breaths coming hard and fast. He pulled out his wallet and tossed the shopkeeper a business card before taking off after his brother. This was not over.

"You can't have her!" Michael screamed. Keith saw that he was running toward the park, where their altercation would not raise any eyebrows. People at this end of town tended to mind their business.

"You don't deserve her!" Keith screamed back, closing in on him.

"She's my wife!" Michael taunted. He stood by the entrance to the park and crooked his finger. "Let's finish this."

Keith propelled himself to the park entrance and swung his head around. His chest heaved. Michael was nowhere in sight. He took several deep breaths. Leaning over, he rested his hands on his knees. That semi-fetal position was all Michael needed to jump on his back. With surprise on Michael's side and the force of his jump, Keith landed with a hard thud facedown on the ground.

"I never imagined that you would be the self-serving jerk who would do this to me," Michael roared while still on top of his brother. He pushed Keith's face farther into the ground. "There!" Michael said with deliberate cruelty. "Let me rearrange that pretty face of yours."

Keith pushed Michael off his back so hard that his brother hit his head on the ground. Then Keith stood to his feet, intending to put an end to this sorry debacle. Never in his life had he made such a spectacle of himself. Michael, however, was far from over.

He swung his leg to dropkick Keith to the ground.

Keith felt his knees buckle, but he did not fall. He turned and limped away from Michael. Michael hoisted himself to his feet and tackled Keith to the ground. Keith could not believe Michael's tenacity. He deflected a few punches before returning more of his own. His fists were bruised, and they stung, but Keith was no punk. He could see that Michael had injuries too, but he preferred the physical altercation to facing the pain of his betrayal.

Keith wanted to advise him that the stinging of his fists would never alleviate the pain of his heart, but he held his tongue. Michael was stubborn enough to try.

Keith managed somehow to push Michael to the ground. He yelled, "Michael! Can we talk?"

Michael's cell phone rang from his pants pocket. It was a miracle it'd survived the scuffle. He answered it. Keith sat on the ground with his head in his hands, listening to Michael's conversation.

"What happened? I'm on my way!" Michael hurled himself to his feet and started running in the direction of his car.

Keith became alarmed. It had to be about Trey. He pounded the pavement, trying to catch up to his brother. Michael skidded to a halt at the light where he had abandoned his car. It was being towed. Hailing a cab, he jumped in to head over to the hospital.

"Michael! Wait up!" Keith knew Michael saw him, as he was only a few yards behind, but his brother ignored him.

"Find your own way. Better yet, why don't you find your way back to New York!"

"You won't keep me away from my son. I have every right to be there, and if you think you can stop me, I'd like to see you try."

Perched on the edge of Trey's hospital bed, Gina heard rustling outside the door. Curious, she tilted her head to listen with keen intensity and had her eyes peeled on the door as Michael entered.

Gina rushed over to him and then suddenly stopped in her tracks, mute with surprise. She took in his disheveled and tattered clothes. "What happened to you?" she asked. "Don't you even think of telling me, 'Nothing,' again."

He shrugged away her concern. "It's nothing for you to worry about."

Gina burrowed her hands in her hair with frustration. She was going to go crazy if Michael kept being this way with her.

A moment later Keith ran into the room. He too looked a hot mess.

Gina's mouth hung open. "Have you and Michael been fighting?"

"That is an understatement," Keith replied as he shoved his shirttails into his pants. Both were ripped beyond repair.

"Are you two juveniles?" Gina said sternly. "What's going on? Trey's sick, for crying out loud." Keith held up his hand, and she paused. When no information was forthcoming, Gina grabbed his shirt. "Keith, what is it?"

Keith removed her hands and stepped away. "Not now, Gina. I can't talk about this right now."

Gina wanted to press the issue, but she felt the heat of Michael's gaze, which was pinned on her hands. Self-conscious, she rubbed them together. At that moment, Dr. Milliner entered Trey's room.

She didn't miss the severe glance the doctor gave both brothers, but his only words were, "I need to talk with you." He led all three occupants of the room out into the hallway. "It's imperative that we find Trey a donor. His immune system is weakening by the day. I've extended the search, and we have made several calls across the country. The option of his waiting until a sibling is born is a moot point right now. At the rate this disease is progressing . . ." Dr. Milliner trailed off.

Gina filled in the blanks. Trey's life was at stake.

She started crying. Reality hit her like never before. "My son, my son . . ." She clutched her chest. "I really believed that he would be okay. But he's not. He's not." She gulped and wailed, "My son is going to die." Tears poured from her eyes. She didn't bother to wipe them. They ran down her chest, soaking her blouse. "I'm going to lose my son. I believed . . ." Gina knew that she had been on an emotional roller coaster, but a huge part of her had clung to the hope that something miraculous would happen.

Now it appeared that was not the case.

Terror struck her, and her knees began to quake.

Overcome with emotion, Keith entered the hospital's chapel.

He needed to pray. He wasn't too sure if God was going to hear him after today, but he still had to try. Keith cried, begging for a miracle, until he was spent.

After talking to God, Keith decided to go into the waiting room. Dr. Milliner had stipulated only one visitor at a time, so only Gina had stayed in Trey's room. Michael was the only one in the waiting room when Keith entered.

Keith locked the door from the inside. Maybe now, with the recent turn of events, he could talk to his brother. "Michael," he said, entreating him.

"Don't say anything to me," Michael spat out with extreme bitterness.

"We have to talk. We're brothers. Don't make me a scapegoat because you're feeling hopeless because of Trey," Keith pleaded.

"Brothers." Michael uttered the word like it was a profanity. He marched right up to Keith's face. "You dare use that word? You are no brother to me."

Michael pushed hard against Keith's chest. He would've delivered a punishing blow had Keith not deflected the move. Keith remained poised. He knew Michael needed an outlet for the anguish racking his soul. At that moment, Keith was the ultimate target. Nevertheless, Keith was taken aback by the venomous derision in Michael's voice. It struck him hard, hearing the deep resentment in Michael's words. He never imagined Michael would feel such animosity for him.

Seeing that Michael was about to strike again, Keith grabbed his hand before shoving his brother clear across the room. Michael landed with a heavy thud on the wooden coffee table. The sound of his back whacking against the wood resounded around the room.

Michael's anger must have heightened his reflexes, because he was on his feet in an instant and was going back for more. Just then, the locked door rattled, interrupting Michael's plans. With their chests heaving, both men looked at the door, waiting for the unwanted intruder to move on to another room. But the rattling was persistent.

Keith moved to open the door.

A distinguished, well-dressed man of average height entered the waiting room. At first glance, he seemed young, but slightly graying temples and light crinkles around his eyes told Keith that the man was older than he had first thought.

The gentleman had an expectant gaze. "Ah, I was told that Michael Ward was in here. But perhaps I have the wrong room."

"No, you are not mistaken. I am Michael Ward." Michael extended his hand out of courtesy.

Keith noted the expression of shock on the stranger's face after he took a close look at Michael. He knew that with their torn shirts, missing buttons, and glass-scratched skin, both he and Michael resembled a pair of bedraggled dogs that had been dragged out of a ditch.

He stepped forward to introduce himself. "I'm Keith, Michael's brother." He tried to inject as much professionalism into his tone as he could muster. He wanted to sound like a gentleman, even though at the moment he looked like anything but one.

Michael grunted, showing open disdain for Keith's choice of words, but said nothing.

"I am Jefferson Alton, or Jeff for short."

Michael groaned as if he were in pain.

Keith ignored his brother. "And you are . . .?" he asked the gentleman, rolling his hands, a gesture intended to elicit further clarification.

"Gina's father."

Chapter Seventeen

This wasn't how she wanted to meet her father!

Furious was an understatement for how Gina felt. *Mortified* was the more accurate word to describe the emotions coursing through her body. There were other words swirling in her head that she didn't have the gall to utter aloud.

At this precise moment, Gina wished the earth would open up and swallow her whole to spare her the humiliation of Michael's latest escapade. She couldn't believe that he had had the audacity to locate her father without even consulting her. Then, of all the times for this man to present himself, it had to be when her husband and his brother were fighting.

Gina felt like slapping them both upside the head the way she would two recalcitrant boys. She looked over at her husband, who was standing in a corner of the waiting room with a woebegone expression on his face, and rolled her eyes, signifying her acute displeasure. With a slight hiss, she turned her head away.

Gina recalled how she'd barged into the waiting room, mad as a hornet and ready to confront Keith and Michael. She had been all set to give them a well-deserved tongue-lashing but had been stopped short by the almost comical expressions of horror on their faces.

With a sharp tone Gina had stated, "Well, I can see that you two were fighting. Somebody had better start talking fast."

Keith had reached over and had held on to Gina's shoulders with both hands. She'd braced herself for bad news. When Michael took a step forward, she'd held her hand up in a manner that was meant to convey that she would brook no argument. "I don't know what's going on, but right now it's about my son. Anything else between you two is insignificant."

Keith had then turned her shoulders gently so that she faced the other individual in the room. She'd jumped with fright. In her fit of temper, Gina hadn't realized that the three of them were not alone in the waiting room. She was a private person and wouldn't dare behave in an undignified manner in front of an outsider.

"Gina, this is Jefferson Alton," Keith had said.

Jeff had stepped forward. She watched him stare her up and down like she was a cool glass of lemonade on a hot day. No, that was not it. His scrutiny was filled with sentiment, but it wasn't lecherous. She couldn't put her finger on it, but Gina knew she'd never seen him before.

She rubbed the goose bumps popping up on her arms, uneasy about the gentleman's odd behavior. Why was he crying?

"Keith, please explain, because I'm freaking out." Panicked, she stepped away from the man, who was wreaking havoc with her senses. Her heart raced and her palms felt sweaty, but she didn't know why.

"I believe Michael should do the honors," Keith stated, and then he stepped back to give his brother the floor.

Michael moved forward with a forced grin on his face. She wasn't going to like this one bit. Taking her hands in his, Michael said, "Jefferson, or Jeff, is your father. I've found your father, Gina. And he has agreed to help our son."

Her mouth had popped wide open, and for several seconds she forgot to breathe. With incredulous eyes, she took in the stranger who was crying before her. She looked into the face of the man she had only envisioned. A surreal moment, for sure. Definite material for a syndicated episode of *The Twilight Zone*.

It was just too much. She pulled her hands out of Michael's grasp and slapped him hard across the cheek before fleeing through the open door.

"As usual, Michael," she heard Keith mutter as she fled. "You act without thinking, and then I have to clean up your mess."

Gina didn't go far. She stood, immobile, outside her son's door.

She had no plans to leave the hospital, but she needed a moment to compose herself. As a child, Gina had always dreamed about meeting her father. She had tried without success to picture what he looked like. Gina had imagined meeting him now, as an adult. She had a mental image of a distinguished guy meeting her at a five-star restaurant for a respectable and dignified lunch.

Not once in her thirty-four years had Gina pictured meeting her father in this manner. Never had she imagined that her father's first impression of her husband would be the one he had gotten today. Not that it should even matter what he thought, Gina supposed. After all, her father had been nonexistent her whole life, so his opinion shouldn't matter. But Gina admitted to herself that it did.

She wanted her father to like her and to be impressed with her husband and son. She wanted him to rue not getting to know her. She wanted her father to be filled with penitence. Now she could only begin to guess what was going through his mind. He might be thinking that leaving her was the best decision he'd ever made.

Gina gave a heartfelt sigh. Her life had too much tumult. Still, hope sprang within her. Jeff might be the miracle that her son needed. Nothing else mattered.

Gina saw Keith as he approached. "What do you want?" she snapped.

"Please don't aim the dart at my head. I was concerned and wanted to check on you. See if you wanted to talk." He arched an eyebrow at her.

Gina moved away from Trey's door and walked farther into the hall. "*Now* you decide you want to talk to me?"

"Gina, please don't be like that with me," Keith pleaded. He gave a dramatic sigh. "This is not my day."

His payback had arrived with a vengeance.

Keith was still reeling from his encounter with Michael. He knew he needed to fill Gina in, if she would listen.

"You knew, didn't you?" Gina accused. "You knew about Michael looking for my father and you chose not to tell me. How could you let him spring that on me like this?"

Keith raised his hands to still the darts from her fiery tongue. "I didn't know. Sweetheart, please believe me. I'm as taken aback as you are."

But Gina was way past the point of listening. "I would think you would've asked him to use a little more tact. I never once imagined I would meet my father like this!" she exclaimed.

Keith tried to embrace her, but Gina shrugged out of his arms. "No," she said. "Keep your hug. That is what you seem to do. You wait for Michael to mess up, and then you pounce . . . You swoop in to comfort and save the day."

Confused by her harsh comment, Keith stepped back. "Gina, you're emotional right now," he remarked in a low voice. "Please calm down a moment."

She lashed out at him and shook her head. "Don't patronize me, Keith. This explains why Michael has been secretive with me. I bet you he thought he was helping and doing something good."

"Isn't he?" Keith asked. He was glad for the chance to speak, because so far, Gina hadn't let him get a word in edgewise. He had to let her know Michael knew about them.

"Yes," Gina sighed. "He is. But I blame you for this."

"I'm trying to keep up with you, but I'm not following your train of thought." He scratched his head before asking, "You're blaming me?" Keith bent over to look her in the eyes. Without warning, he grabbed her and pulled her down the hall.

She tried to hold her ground, but she was no match for him given his superior height and weight. He kept dragging her until he had taken her into an empty lounge. He locked the door.

"I only know of one way to silence you, because you're not listening," he murmured.

Gina opened her mouth probably to berate him for manhandling her, but Keith crushed her in his strong arms and pressed his lips to hers.

She kept her mouth closed. But her will was like water vapor compared to Keith's. He was on a mission. Gina fought back, but he felt when she submitted. Her flailing arms rested on his broad shoulders. Her body caved into his, and the kiss deepened with intensity.

As soon as he felt her respond, Keith slung Gina out of his arms. Looking at her with satisfaction, Keith asked, "Are you still blaming me?"

Gina's wrath spiraled back with a vengeance. She gave him a look that said she wanted to slap that knowing smirk off his face. He returned her glare for glare. His look said, "I wish you'd try it."

"Yes," she spat as her chest heaved from her emotional upheaval. "I do blame you. You messed with my life and my marriage. You're always interfering, even when I don't ask you to. Yet when I needed you to interfere, you did nothing. So thanks a lot."

"You know, you're one infuriating woman," Keith raged. "You're the one who insisted I back off. You're the one who said we should pretend like nothing happened, and like a fool, I listened to you." He bent over until he was right in her face. "And as far as me messing with your life, I don't remember hearing you complain the two times we were together. In fact, I remember you begging me not to stop."

Gina's mouth popped open, and a huge blush stained her cheeks. "I . . . I . . . That's crass of you to mention that."

"Well, you're like a yo-yo, and it's downright confusing. One minute you want me and are pleading with me not to go, and the next you're throwing everything on me. *You* approached *me* two days before your wedding. Don't forget that."

"How can I forget?" Gina's sadness diffused his anger.

Keith took several deep breaths. He licked his now dry lips. "This is ridiculous. What are we even fighting about? We can't undo the past, no matter how hard we try."

She looked down. "I don't even know why I heaped all that on you. I feel scared that I had to meet my father this way."

"I understand. But Michael and I also had to meet him after having one of the biggest fights of our entire life. Trust me, Gina. I had no idea."

Gina was now curious. "What were you two fighting about, anyway?"

His heart pounded like a conga drum, but he had to tell her the truth. All the guilt that had been buried came back in full force. "He knows, Gina. Michael knows."

Keith words sank in. Though Gina understood, she played ignorant. "No. How could he? That was years ago."

"I'm trying to piece it all together myself, but, Gina, Michael knows we slept together all those years ago. Right now he hates me." Keith's voice broke after that comment.

Gina's body rocked back and forth as she grappled with the news. "He must hate me too."

"He's angry and hurt," Keith said in his brother's defense. "But I think he'll forgive you in time. He loves you and Trey too much to let you go. He'd be a fool to leave you, and trust me, Michael is many things, but a fool is not one of them. He knows he has a good woman in you, Gina."

Her eyes looked glassy. Keith led her to the nearest chair. "My legs feel like rubber. I can't believe it. Michael must think I'm the worst woman on the planet for sleeping with you. And he's right." She faced him. "He idolized you."

"I feel like we're on *The Jerry Springer Show*. Fall in love with you, and my life is now filled with all these twists and turns."

Gina snorted. "Oh, please, Keith. Do I have to remind you of your ex-fiancée, Eve? She was with you and was pregnant with another man's child."

Keith nodded but decided not to travel down that lane.

"Michael's a good man too," she whispered in a voice that showed she was still racked with guilt. "I don't know why I did that to him."

"Don't you dare place all the blame on yourself. Michael was no saint back then," Keith urged. "Let's not forget that he'd slept with Karen, and he had her living in his penthouse for months. So I'm not going to sit back and let you put a halo over his head."

"Yeah, but that did not give me the right to sleep with you, of all people," Gina countered. She put her head in her hands. "That must be killing him. You're his precious Keith, and I'm at fault for destroying your relationship."

Keith paced the room. "It's not your fault. I knew what I was doing. I pursued you because I had fallen in love. I was in the throes of something I had never before experienced in my life. And I, for one, have no regrets. Being with you has brought me the biggest joy in the world."

"Well, I have regrets," Gina revealed. "I had morals and standards, and I should've kept them. I should've resisted, but it seems as if every opportunity I have, I run into your arms. It's what I have done and continue to do. I've even used my son's life-threatening illness as an excuse to try to jump your bones. When did I become so selfish? I don't know myself anymore. How am I going to face him?" She buried her face in her hands out of self-recrimination.

He touched her shoulder. "Gina, you may be many things, but selfish is not one of them. This thing between us was—and still is—more powerful than either of us could manage. It was only a matter of time before we gave in."

"But I could have resisted," Gina replied as the tears flowed. "I could have, but I didn't. Michael didn't deserve this, Keith. We betrayed him. He trusted us, and we took that trust and smashed it to pieces. We're getting too old for this tawdry affair. It's time I think about my actions and the fact that there are serious repercussions for what I do."

"Watching you cry, I feel remorse hit my soul. Regardless of what you say, I know I'm the one who got you in this predicament. But there was nothing I could've done about how I feel about you. I love you," Keith said. "I love you, and I mean it with every fiber of my being. I can't regret that."

"I love you too, Keith," Gina rose to her feet. "But I regret it, Keith. I regret it with every fiber of my being." With that, she walked over, unlocked the door, and opened it. She stepped out of the room and closed the door with a decisive click. Keith flung his large frame into the chair that Gina had vacated. He felt great pangs of remorse over losing his brother's trust. He wondered if he should have confessed it all. Should he have told Gina he was Trey's father? Yes he should have. But she was so upset and mad that . . .

No, Keith thought.

The truth would've further complicated matters.

The truth was bringing him heartache right now.

The truth had taken away everything he held dear in his heart.

Keith could not take any more truths. He knew that somehow once he'd reasoned things out in his mind, Michael would forgive Gina. After all if it weren't for Michael's affair with Karen, Gina wouldn't have slept with him. Also, Michael was the father that Trey knew.

But where did that leave him? Did loving his son meant he had to give him up?

Chapter Eighteen

"So what happens if I'm a match?" Jeff asked.

Michael stood next to him inside Dr. Milliner's office.

"If you're a match, there are options for being a transplant donor," the doctor said. "You can either undergo an allogeneic transplant, where the bone marrow is taken from the back of your hip bones. The second option is what's known as leukapheresis. You'll be given shots over five days to help your stem cells move from your bone marrow into your blood. Then your blood will be removed using an IV line in one of your veins."

After that lengthy explanation, Jeff gave Michael a reassuring pat. "We'll begin tomorrow."

Jeff's eyes looked glazed, and Michael attempted to put him at ease. "Don't worry if most of this goes over your head. I'm sure the doctors will give you step-by-step instructions."

After Keith and Gina's rapid departure from the hospital waiting room, the task of putting Jeff at ease had fallen on Michael's shoulders. He'd succeeded, with a lot of finesse and charm.

After the conversation with Dr. Milliner, Michael offered to take Jeff to a nearby diner so they could talk at length.

"I don't know how much pain you'll be in, and your recovery might be challenging," Michael warned once they were seated in a booth and had ordered from the menu.

Jeff said, "Painful or not, I'll do all I can to help my grandson. I'll get tested tomorrow to see if I'm a match for my grandson." Michael saw his eyes soften as he repeated the word *grandson*.

"He's precious," Michael told Jeff. Then he returned to the matter at hand. "Before all that, though, Dr. Milliner will put you through an extensive physical and blood work, because he has to make sure you're fit and well enough to do the transplant. But once you're cleared—and I'm speaking that into existence—Trey will start chemotherapy and continue it for two weeks to destroy all his bone marrow so he's ready for new marrow . . . yours."

"Wow. I'm impressed with your knowledge. Poor Trey. He has a tough road ahead of him," Jeff said. He sounded sympathetic. Michael saw him shudder.

"Yes, he does, but I have faith. I know in my gut that you're the donor. I would stake all of my businesses on it."

"Well, when you put it like that, I'm obliged to believe you. My daughter is lucky to have you," Jeff said, praising him.

Feeling a strong urge to ask Gina's father the burning question most prominent in his mind, Michael resisted and decided to bide his time. Michael wanted to know the reason why Jeff had been absent from Gina's life, but he'd leave that conversation for Gina.

Thinking of his wife, Michael felt the old resentment rise, but he made sure to show his pearly whites. "I feel the same about her. She's a good woman. She cares about others. In the first year of our marriage, she spent a lot of time volunteering and helping needy high school kids." The lie rolled off his tongue, but then he realized that he had spoken the truth. He was shocked when he perceived his genuine love for and faith in Gina. This revelation strengthened Michael's resolve. He needed to remain committed to his wife, his son, and his marriage.

It would be difficult, and he wasn't about to pretend otherwise. He could forgive Gina, but he knew he'd never allow himself to love her with the same intensity as before. From the moment he'd put that ring on her finger, he had been faithful and had kept his vows. He lived every vow he'd made that day, but she had failed him.

While he and Jeff were eating dessert, Michael called his car service and arranged to have Jeff picked up outside the diner in twenty minutes and taken to his hotel. His ever-efficient secretary had secured five-star hotel accommodations for Jeff with specific instructions. The hotel staff was to cater to his father-in-law's every whim and would be well compensated for this. Michael intended to ensure that Gina's father was treated with style.

After paying the bill and escorting Jeff to the waiting limo, Michael hopped into his car and drove. Now that he was alone with his thoughts, he dumped most of the blame for Gina's infidelity on his brother. After learning about Karen, Gina had needed a shoulder to cry on, and Keith had taken advantage.

He turned at the light and glided onto I-285 for the short ride to Suwanee.

Michael's heart burned when he thought about his brother, whose actions were unbelievable and despicable. Keith had violated the man code, the brother code, and the friend code. *You cannot eat from the same pie. Bite from the same fruit. Eat from the same plate . . .* It was just not done. That was understood.

Punching the steering wheel column, Michael knew that somewhere underneath all that hurt, he still loved his brother, but he didn't want to see his face anytime soon—if ever. He couldn't see his brother without thinking about Gina in his arms . . . in his bed . . . and who knew where else?

Michael pulled into his driveway. He saw that Gina's car was parked in its usual spot in the garage. He sat behind the wheel, hesitating. He did not want to see her. He did not want to look at her face, knowing her deceit.

Michael twiddled his thumbs, lost in his thoughts. A part of him wanted revenge in some way. He wanted to make Gina pay. He wasn't sure if he could feel any natural warmth toward her, and he wasn't trying to pretend. There was a numbness around his heart because of her betrayal, and he didn't see that defrosting anytime soon. He knew for certain he would not trust her around Keith. He was going to sever that bond between Gina and Keith for good.

Michael supposed that it was due time for him to experience true heartbreak. He had caused a lot of it in his heyday. He didn't believe in karma, but this sure felt like it.

Michael got out of the car and slammed the door shut. He bent over and rested his head on his car. It hurt to even go inside the house. He didn't want to face her. He heard his front door open and turned his head to see Gina standing in the doorway. He read the uncertainty on her face.

"Gina," Michael whispered. He crooked his finger for her to come to him. He watched her take careful steps toward him. Her gait was uncertain, but she came with a brave look on her face. With every step, his heart broke. How could he begin to get her to understand the pain that wrenched his soul? He had to try.

"Why Keith? Gina, why him?" Michael uttered with a ragged, pain-filled voice.

"I . . ." Gina trailed off. She could not look him in the eyes.

"I was a dog. I know that. I can understand why you felt the need to pay me back, but why Keith?" Michael demanded in a guttural growl.

Gina wrung her hands. The words were stuck in her throat. She could not drive a knife in his heart by acknowledging her intense love for Keith.

"Tell me the truth," Michael said. "Do you love me at all?"

"Yes," Gina answered. "I do love you, Michael. I didn't mean to hurt you. But that was before we were married. Keith and I . . . I didn't see the point in telling you. It's behind me."

Michael looked at her as if he didn't buy any of what she was selling. Heck, she was having a hard time convincing herself, but Trey needed his parents united.

Gina waited, watching her husband process the information. He turned on his heels and walked into the house. Gina stood rooted in the same spot. Michael was hard to read. She didn't know what he was thinking. Michael turned suddenly and stretched out his hand toward her. With hurried steps, Gina joined him and placed her hand in his. The two walked into the house together.

Once they closed the front door, Michael turned to face her. His face had an inscrutable expression that made her knees shake. She had never seen Michael look like this. For the first time in their relationship, Gina saw the ruthlessness that Michael reserved primarily for business matters. Scared, she gulped and waited for Michael to talk.

"You will not have anything more to do with Keith," he said. "Not a word ever again."

"Yes, Michael." She was too frightened to disagree.

"Trey is *my* son," Michael said, emphasizing the word *my,* as if he felt the need to make that clear. He looked at her, expecting some sort of response. "Did you hear me? Trey is *mine.*"

Gina looked at him, experiencing a little confusion, but she was too penitent to ask for clarity. She was not sure where he was coming from, but she nodded her head in acquiescence. Gina was so glad that Michael was giving her another chance that she did not dig too deep for the reasoning behind his words. She was willing to eat crow.

"Good. That is all I intend to say about that. We will never speak of this again." Michael stalked off without another word.

Gina found her tongue and raced after him, confronting him in the living room. "But . . . don't you think we should maybe get therapy or something?"

Michael stopped in his tracks. His expression was unyielding. "We don't need therapy for something that has already been resolved. You'll stay away from Keith. Understood?"

"Yes." Gina was too terrified to offer another retort.

She wanted to ask if he was going to patch things up with Keith, but she held her tongue. Michael was giving her another chance. Gina was grateful for his forgiveness. She wouldn't let him down again.

Gina headed into their bedroom, undressed, and slid into bed. She felt the need to climb under a warm blanket to ease her shaking. Her teeth were chattering because she was so scared. Gina knew that things with Michael would never be the same. But she was the guilty party. She would have to pay the penance for her crime. Gina figured that she was going to pay for a lifetime, because that was how long it would take for her to get over Keith.

After Gina went upstairs, Michael strode into his study and closed the door. As he fixed a quick drink, he acknowledged that he had been tough on Gina. He knew that he had decided to forgive her, but thinking and doing were two different things. He needed time for the hurt to heal. But time was a commodity. Trey needed both his parents, and Michael was going to do everything to keep it that way.

As far as Michael was concerned, he was Trey's father. He wasn't giving up his son, biological or not. He viewed Keith as a sperm donor—a means to an end. He was the one who'd been there for all of Trey's milestones, not Keith. He was the one who'd found Jeff, the man who would save Trey's life.

Michael was glad that Gina had concurred with him on the issue of Trey's paternity—or so he thought—because he couldn't see Keith not telling her the truth about Trey. He was glad she had agreed that Trey was his, and he was glad that Gina was his. He was not going to give Gina up, because Michael knew that Keith would step into his shoes in a heartbeat. Keith wouldn't condone Trey growing up in a single-parent home. And he loved Gina too much to sit on the sidelines while she reared her son alone.

Michael wouldn't let that happen. He wasn't going to move out of the way for Keith to get the kid and the girl.

Michael smiled a vindictive smile. It appeared that for once, he was going to beat his brother at something. At the biggest game ever played. Love.

Chapter Nineteen

Michael had been waiting for him. He knew he'd come.

He wouldn't be Keith if he hadn't. His brother didn't care if it was midnight. He was here to get "his" woman. Michael knew that stance. Keith had entered his house like a man on a mission—a man who wanted it all. He wasn't surprised. He had expected this from his brother— had been waiting for it.

"Have you decided?" Keith jumped right to the point as the two brothers stood face-to-face in the study.

"I should think that's obvious," Michael taunted.

"Gina!" Keith called. When he didn't hear an answer, he called again. "Gina!"

Michael watched Gina approach Keith from out of the shadows.

"So is that it, then?" Keith asked.

"What do you mean?" Her brows knit. She wasn't following the choppy conversation.

"Are you staying with him, Gina?" Keith spelled it out.

Michael feigned boredom and walked over to the minibar to pour a drink. But he was all ears.

"Gina, this is it. This is our chance," Keith declared. "I don't want you to think too hard. I need you to follow what's in your heart. So, tell me, are you staying with him?"

Gina found the words. "No, Keith, I'm not doing this. I've got too much going on. Michael's my husband. I love him."

Keith stepped toward her.

Michael felt the pulse in his head pound. He urged himself to maintain his cool demeanor. He did not want his brother to see him as anything but confident.

"Gina, the truth is out. It has set us free," Keith pleaded. "Don't you see? We can be together. Go get your bags. Why are we even having this lengthy debate? You must've known I'd come. You should've been waiting."

Michael grunted so Keith would know he'd better back off, but his brother ignored him. He refused to accept that she had chosen to stay. Michael smiled to himself. Keith must think that Gina knew he was Trey's father. Well, he wasn't about to rectify that assumption.

He saw Gina's reaction to the desperation in Keith's voice. She took a step toward Keith. Oh, no, he wasn't having this. He moved to stand next to Gina, staking his claim, marking his territory.

Keith's jaw clenched, and he walked right up into Michael's face. His brother was so close that Michael could feel his breath on his face. They were like two lions circling each other and waiting to pounce. Michael didn't care. He relished the mental tug-of-war. Welcomed it, even.

"I don't want this. I'm not an animal to be bartered between both of you." Gina exhaled. "Keith, Michael is my husband and the father of my son. We're married. There's nothing else to say." Michael saw her push against Keith's chest, but he wouldn't budge.

I'm not moving, either, Michael purposed. She turned to face him and engaged him in a stare down. Michael didn't back down. He knew Gina would choose him. As seconds passed and his confidence grew, Michael grinned. He felt triumphant and gloated in Keith's direction. He felt so good that he wanted to do the victory dance from his college days.

"No, Gina. You're wrong," Keith argued. "This is our chance. I don't care anymore. Gina, choose me. Choose us. We are right for each other. Nothing else matters."

"No, Keith," Gina yelled. "Trey matters! I have to consider him. Trey needs his father. He needs *both* parents."

Above her head, Michael and Keith's eyes met. Understanding dawned in Keith. Neither of them had told Gina the truth. Keith opened his mouth.

He's about to confess, Michael thought. His pulse quickened. His brother was about to tear his world apart.

Keith began, "There's something I've got to say. I thought that I was doing the right thing, but—"

Michael opened his mouth. However, before he could formulate the words, Gina raised one hand. "No, Keith. I have told you before, and I will say it again in front of Michael. I'll remain with my husband."

Keith sighed. "Gina, you don't understand. There's something that you don't know."

Michael experienced a moment of fear, because Keith was determined to tell her the truth. He knew it was time for drastic measures. He'd give Keith an eyeful. He grabbed Gina and kissed her. He ran his hands along her body and opened his eyes to stare at Keith.

Keith caved. He looked away.

Triumphant, Michael ended the kiss and demanded, "It's time for you to leave."

To his relief and surprise, Keith complied. However, before he reached the door, he stopped. Keith turned to look at Gina. "This is it for me. You're the one I want. You're my everything. I love you. I need you. Sweetheart, please. I've never loved like this in my life."

Gina swallowed her pain. Her regret was evident. "No, Keith."

"Leave my house," Michael demanded. "You've worn out your welcome."

"As much I want to pummel you to the ground, little brother, this is between Gina and me. I'm not leaving without her." With a locked jaw, Keith stretched his hands out, beckoning her to make a choice.

Chapter Twenty

Gina had rushed to the hospital early in the morning so Gerry could go home and rest. Her head throbbed from a lack of sleep and from crying. After Keith left the house last night, her heart had screamed that she should've left with him. But in the light of day, Gina was sure she had made the right decision. She could make a good life with Michael, and she refused to pine for Keith for the rest of her life.

Gina entered Trey's room, intending to be there when he woke up. She stopped short, surprised to see Jeff sitting there. With last night's showdown, she had simply forgotten about him. In her defense, though, it was not like she knew him. *Okay, that isn't nice,* she thought.

But it was true.

What does one say to a father one didn't know existed?

"Where's Gerry?"

Jeff stood up. He looked her square in the eyes. She took a step back when she saw eyes so similar to her own. It was spooky—but sort of comforting. He glanced at his watch before answering her. "She left five minutes ago. Trey's fallen back to sleep. Gina, let's take a walk."

Gina debated his offer for a moment before nodding her consent. She led the way. The two took the elevator down to the courtyard.

Jeff began, "I never knew about you, Gina."

Gina's eyes widened. She turned to face him and grabbed his arm. "What? I don't believe that."

"I mean, before Michael contacted me, I had no idea I had a daughter."

"But . . . I thought . . . That's not what my mother told me." Gina felt like she had sucked in a roomful of bad air. She walked a few steps away from him as she strove to compose her thoughts.

"You thought that I had deserted you? No wonder . . ." Jeff trailed off. He too looked stumped, like that notion had never entered his mind. He wandered over to a nearby wooden bench and plopped down. After a moment's hesitation, Gina joined him.

"No, Gina. Had I known, I wouldn't have been an absent father. You'd best believe that. Regina and I didn't have children of our own, but how I wanted them. I wanted them. And to hear that I have a beautiful daughter and a grandson . . ." His voice broke, and he scrunched his lips to contain his emotions.

Tears dimmed her eyes, but Gina was focused on one word. "Regina?"

Jeff twisted his body. This time he couldn't look her in the eyes. "My wife of forty years."

"Forty . . . years." Gina couldn't prevent her harsh intake of breath. She understood what Jeff was trying to tell her. She covered her mouth with her hand.

Her father took her hand in his. "Yes, Gina, I was married—and young and stupid—when I met Lucille. Your mother didn't know that at the time. Our affair went on for a year before I told her the truth and she broke things off."

"Wow." Gina found it all hard to grasp. She shook her head. Okay, so he wasn't a deadbeat, but he'd been a cheat. She squirmed. That didn't sit well with her, even though she'd been a cheat too.

"My mother didn't tell me much about you. I think it pained her to talk about you. All she said was that you didn't want me. So as I got older, I didn't press the issue. Why didn't she tell me that you were married, and why didn't she tell me that you didn't know about me?" Gina eyed him with doubt. His explanation seemed too convenient, considering her mother wasn't here to clarify the matter or defend herself.

"I don't know her reason, but I can try to fill in the blanks." His voice took on an airy tone as he went back in time. "I still remember what she was wearing the day we broke up. She had a flower in her hair, and though it was late September, she had on a jean skirt and a bright yellow top. She had asked me to meet her, as she had something important to tell me." He turned to face Gina with a sad smile. "I now realize Lucy wanted to tell me about you. Well, as it happens, I never gave her a chance. I insisted on speaking first." He looked away. "I told her about my wife, Regina, and that I intended to end things with her and make my marriage work."

"So, let me guess. Heartbroken, she never mentioned me." Sarcasm dripped from her voice.

"Yes, that's what I'm saying, though I can tell from your tone that you don't believe me. Your mother was mad that I was married and hadn't told her. Lucy was independent, and she had a lot of pride, so she wouldn't have told me about you." He sighed. "But I can assure you that had I known about the pregnancy, there was no way I would've abandoned her—or you. Maybe she didn't want me to be with her because of an obligation."

Gina could believe that. It would have been just like her mother to decide to raise her child on her own. Maybe that was why her mother could never speak about her father. Had she died loving Jeff? She'd never married, so that seemed plausible.

Of one thing, Gina was certain. Her mother had been in love once in her lifetime. "I've had a love I know I'll never find again," Lucy had said on many occasions when Gina had pressed her about dating.

Gina crossed her arms. Still, a part of her blamed Jeff Alton. She'd grown up without a father. No explanation could change that.

But he was here, and she knew he was willing to be a donor for Trey. She was grateful for that. She cleared her throat. "Thanks for being here for my son. We should go and check on him. I imagine your results should be in soon."

Jeff nodded and gave her hand a small pat, signaling that he would let the matter rest.

Keith was sitting with Trey when Gina and Jeff entered the room. She greeted him with civility, but her eyes drank in the sight of him. She'd made a mistake. She had. Then she looked at Trey. No, she hadn't. She'd done the right thing for her child. He needed his parents—both of them.

Michael and Gerry walked in five minutes later. All the occupants of the room stood on pins and needles. The tension in the room continued to build. But then Doctor Milliner entered with the good news.

Tears of joy and laughter filled the room. Exultant, Gina clapped her hands. God had sent a miracle. Jeff was the match needed to save her baby's life. A grandparent as a donor wasn't common. But who cared? He was a match! Trey was going to live! He was going to live!

Jeff pulled out his cell phone to call his wife at home and update her on the news. "Baby! I'm a match! I'm a match!" When he ended the phone call, he announced that Regina was delighted and would be en route to Atlanta within hours. Michael then offered to pay for her flight from Phoenix and take care of all the arrangements. Jeff was more than willing to foot the bill, but Michael was adamant.

Gina herself was skeptical. At the most discreet moment, she pulled Jeff aside—she couldn't think of him as her father yet. She wasn't sure if she ever would. "How did your wife react to your pulling a grown daughter out of the woodwork?"

Jeff couldn't quite look her in the eyes.

Gina tugged his shoulder. "Tell me."

"She was furious. She felt hurt and betrayed. She left the house for two whole weeks. I was beside myself with worry, but I'd married a praying woman, and I had never prayed like that in my life. I prayed round the clock and sought God's face. Then, at the end of the second week, I heard the door open. Regina had returned. You don't know how I praised God. Her first words were, 'Start talking,' and I told her everything."

Curious, Gina tilted her head. She didn't know her father was saved. Was this how saved people handled things? Come to think of it, everybody around her was getting saved.

Without knowing her thoughts, Jeff answered her question. "Oh, it wasn't easy, let me tell you, but she loved me enough to forgive me. We did do counseling—as old as we were." He smiled. "And my pastor told me about myself, but Regina packed my suitcase and sent me up here. Now, forgiveness is a process, mind you, but we'll be all right."

Gina couldn't fathom Regina's apparent love and understanding. She found herself eager to meet her stepmother, who, according to Jeff, was "ecstatic to meet her." *If that doesn't beat all,* Gina thought. She thought about Michael. If only he were so forgiving . . . But his second chance came with a hefty stipulation.

Jeff left soon after that for his consultation with Dr. Milliner. He would need more blood work and an even more in-depth physical examination to make sure he could indeed donate.

Two weeks. Gina clasped her hands with glee. In two weeks her son would be delivered, thanks to Jeff, who, she could see, already loved his newfound family and grandson. She didn't realize that God deserved the thanks, as this had been His doing and His answer to many prayers.

Her eyes locked with Keith's. Gina could see unshed tears in his eyes. He came over to her, filled with relief and jubilation, and embraced her. She sniffed. He smelled so good. Hugging him was like returning home. Gina felt a bolt of electricity surge through her veins. Keith felt it too. He hugged her a little tighter.

"I don't like it, but I guess I understand your decision," he whispered in her ear.

You'll stay away from Keith. Michael's warning haunted her. He'd left to talk with the doctors, but she pulled herself out of Keith's arms, nonetheless. Something told her that despite Michael's exuberance, he wouldn't tolerate her bending the rules.

When she didn't say anything, Keith left the room.

Standing there, Gina was not okay with her decision. She knew without a shadow of a doubt that she shouldn't have let Keith go. She should've grabbed on to his love with everything she had. But now it was too late.

Chapter Twenty-one

Keith made a beeline for the chapel. He raced inside and fell to his knees. "Thank you, God. Thank you for saving my son."

He felt a small hand touch his shoulders. Gina. She'd come to him. Had she heard him? He spun around and saw his mother standing beside him. Keith swallowed his bitter disappointment and cracked a smile. Gerry sat on the bench and Keith joined her. His mother hugged him, and Keith held on to Gerry for dear life.

He had gained a son.

But he had lost his life.

He had nothing left.

"It's time for me to go home," Keith declared. "I'll go after the surgery, once I'm assured that Trey will make a full recovery."

"I didn't tell him, son. Your brother found out the truth on his own, and I'm glad he did."

He'd wondered about that. "How did he find out?"

"I had taken my photo albums out. He saw your baby picture and put it together after that." Gerry then asked him, "Did you know you were Trey's father?"

"No, not until Michael told me he was infertile. I felt so blessed to know Trey was mine. I should have told him the truth then. I hesitated. But the truth had to come out, and when it did, I thought . . . I thought this was finally me and Gina's chance, but she chose him."

Gerry shook her head. "As she should. I wish that you'd move on. What kind of spell are you under? You have to get her out of your system."

"Yes, but she's the love of my life, and Trey is my son. *My* son. How can you even think to ask me to turn my back on him?"

"If you love him, you can't do this. The time isn't right. You're going to confuse that little boy."

Why not? "I'm going to tell her, Mom. She has a right to know. I've never lied to her, and I don't see the need to start now."

She grabbed his arm and pleaded, "I'm begging you, Keith. Listen to me. Gina's not the one I'm worried about. No good can come of this. I'm not saying never to claim your child, but in time. Not now, when he's fighting for his life. He's going to have a rough recovery ahead, and he doesn't need any kind of confusion or to see his family fighting." Choked up with tear-filled eyes, she added, "That's what parents do, Keith. They do the best for their children."

Keith shook his head. "You're asking for too much, Mom. Would you do it? Would you turn your back on me or Michael?"

She didn't answer his question but asked him another instead. "How much of this is about you and Gina, and how much is about doing what's best for your son? If you love him, leave tonight. Since you know he's going to be all right, say good-bye to Trey and *move on*. I'll be here to keep you posted. I'm going home to freshen up, but I'll be back tonight."

Her words stung Keith's heart. His mother felt she was right, but his heart rebelled, telling him that it was very wrong.

An hour after she left, he still grappled with conflicting emotions as he sat alone in the chapel. Looking upward, he wrung his hands and sobbed, "God, what should I do? Tell me, please."

God was silent.

No. Keith gulped. He couldn't do it. He couldn't deny his child. His heart bled like someone had plunged a knife in it and twisted it.

Standing, overcome with emotions, he swayed, feeling faint. He exhaled. No, this was too much. His mother meant well. She had said what she thought was best, but in this instance, she was dead wrong. He didn't know why she'd even encourage him to perpetuate a lie—it was so unlike her. But maybe she was thinking about Trey. Well, so was he. He used his hand and swiped his face clean. He had made up his mind.

With unsteady feet, he headed to the elevator to go see his son.

When he neared Trey's door, he saw it was cracked open. He placed his hand on the door to swing it open even wider, then froze. Michael was in there with Trey. He could hear their voices, which were crystal clear, and he wasn't above eavesdropping.

"I'm scared, Daddy," Trey said in a weak voice. "And I don't like this place."

"I know, son. I know you're scared, and guess what? Daddy's scared too. But we're men, and we're going to be tough. I'll be here with you, I promise you."

Keith hated to admit it, but Michael was saying the right words. He heard Trey's coughing fit and, from his vantage point, saw his brother wipe Trey's face and mouth with such tenderness that his heart moved. He second-guessed himself, wondering if he shouldn't just leave well enough alone. He hesitated until the next words he heard sealed his choice.

"I'm so glad you're my daddy. You're the best daddy ever," Trey said, lifting his arms to hug Michael.

"I love you, Trey. You're the best son any father could have."

Keith put his fist in his mouth to muffle his sharp cry at those words. On leaden feet, he inched his way back to the elevator. With every ounce of willpower he possessed, he left the premises, knowing his son was in good hands, but how he hated it.

Gerry had told Gina the news of Keith's impending departure. Keith was leaving in the morning.

She was ready for bed, but instead of sleeping, she paced back and forth in her bedroom.

Keith is leaving. Keith is leaving. Keith is leaving. The single thought bounced over and over in her mind.

No. No. No. The words reverberated in her head.

She pulled her hair and groaned. He couldn't leave her. He couldn't leave her. He could not leave. He was her . . . her all.

Determined to sleep, Gina dove under the covers. She tossed and turned. Sleep teased but eluded her. Her mind refused to rest. All she could think about was that this was her opportunity. Michael and Gerry were both at the hospital. It was now or never.

Gina sprang up and squatted in her bed. Her heart compelled her. She had to go to Keith. She swung her feet to the side of the bed. She was destined to be with him.

Without allowing second thoughts, she rushed to change out of her pajamas and into the clothes she'd worn earlier. She threw a light jacket on and raced over to Keith's home.

She pressed the bell. "Keith, open up. Keith, please."

The door swung open and Gina stepped back in shock when she saw Keith. He'd been crying. He looked awful. He looked broken. "What's the matter with you?"

"I knew you'd come," he whispered and snatched her into his arms. He kissed her full on the lips, right there in the driveway in plain sight. He kissed her with the exuberance of a man drinking a tall glass of cold water on a hot summer day.

She couldn't control her response. Gina kissed him back with passion before reluctantly ending the kiss. Her chest heaved from his onslaught, but she needed answers. "Tell me what's wrong," she demanded.

He didn't answer but grabbed her hand to pull her inside his house and slammed the door. Gina jumped. Her senses were on full alert. She was very cognizant of the fact that she was alone with Keith.

With a growl, he pulled her against him and held her as if he weren't ever going to let her go. Then Keith cried. He cried as if pain wrenched his soul. Gina patted him, but no matter how much she asked, he wouldn't say anything but "Oh, Lord, no . . . no . . . I can't. . . ."

"Keith, I love you." Gina felt compelled to tell him what was in her heart.

"I love you too," he returned. "I love you and Trey so much, it hurts." Dried tears streaked his face, and fresh ones followed. He took her hand and placed it over his chest. "Feel how my heart beats for you. Gina, you've got to know . . . " Keith trailed off. He didn't or couldn't say more.

With her own water-filled eyes, she copied his gesture. "As does mine."

He opened his mouth, maybe to insist she stay with him. She placed her index finger over his lips. "Don't. Let's have tonight, please. I need you. Trey's going to be all right, and I want to celebrate this moment with you."

She saw his struggle before he nodded. He was grappling with something, but she didn't know how to help. He honored her request and placed a light kiss on her neck. Like a crescendo, it built into passion. Keith muttered endearments and his tears blended with hers as he loved her like he never had before. It was as if he couldn't get enough . . . couldn't give enough . . .

Is he saying good-bye?

She dismissed that thought as her ardor rose. Surely this meant he would stay. But this wasn't the time for conversation. Their bodies were talking a different language, and together they travelled to a blissful place and for a moment found peace.

Gina fell asleep in his arms, spent and satisfied. But when she awoke, Keith was gone.

Chapter Twenty-two

The present day . . .

"Showtime, Pastor Ward." His assistant, Natalie Henderson, knocked before opening the bathroom door to poke her head in. "You're up in five."

"Thanks, Natalie," Keith replied with a quick, unguarded smile. "Just finished getting my face camera ready." He'd chosen to wear a black Armani suit, a crisp white shirt, and his yellow tie with miniscule red polka dots. It was a good thing the building was air-conditioned, or he wouldn't be able to stay dressed this way in the June heat.

"Pastor, you look more like a soap opera star than a preacher," Natalie commented. Anticipating his response, she shut the door, thus dodging the washcloth he tossed her way.

Keith shook his head. He'd been told that his good looks made it hard for people to believe that he was saved. Those trite comments never failed to baffle him, because nowhere in his Bible did it say salvation was solely for ugly folks. Were they saying saved people were ugly? The devil had been one of the most beautiful angels in heaven, so that mind-set was preposterous.

Keith had needed salvation. It sounded like a cliché, but he didn't want to know where he would be if he hadn't accepted the Lord in his life. Yes, he'd had money—the house, the car—but he'd been lacking. Until he had found the only One who could give him peace.

Now that he'd been set on a new path, Keith lived each day with contentment and fulfillment. His smile expanded from his heart to his face as he thought about the transformation he'd undergone. His conversation, his priorities, his entire life had changed for the better.

Over the past three years Keith had shot up the spiritual ladder at Zion's Hill, just as he had excelled at everything in his "previous" life. And what was remarkable was that there had never been even a whisper of any scandal. No woman could call his name.

He lived his life to please God, and though he was charming to the ladies in his congregation, he took every precaution to make sure he didn't lead any of them into thinking he was interested.

Because he wasn't.

The members of the board hinted all the time that he needed to be married. "It's not good for you to be alone," Minister Phillips had advised him over and over.

"You need a wife," Deacon Broderson said at least once every week. He also never failed to introduce Keith to every single and successful church sister who he thought would make a good potential helpmate.

Keith tolerated the other men's feeble attempts at matchmaking. Little did they know that there was no need to worry about him falling prey to any woman around him, even though there were many. He avoided the miniskirts and the coy glances. His heart had been captured eight years ago, and by the look of things, it was in no danger of being released.

It was not as though he hadn't looked or hadn't tried. It was that he hadn't met the woman who could replace what he had. His mantra from Song of Solomon leapt up to him. "Many waters cannot quench love, neither can the floods drown it." A truer statement had never existed. Distance and time had done nothing to heal the puncture made to his heart when he had loved and lost.

Gina.

Keith closed his eyes at the mere thought of her name. He breathed in, tilted his chin upward, and visualized her as he'd last seen her. Unbidden, images he had tried to suppress taunted him . . . tantalized him as if it were mere hours ago, instead of years. He knew this was the enemy at work and rebuked him.

Jesus, help me. Keith called on his Savior. "I can't continue like this, Lord," he said aloud. He massaged his temples. Grace was not enough. He needed strong deliverance. Taking deep breaths, Keith kept uttering that blessed name until his heart rate slowed. He felt the storm blow over. The torment racking his mind, body, and heart subsided. Grateful, Keith expelled a sigh of relief.

He leaned into the mirror and turned his head from side to side. His haircut looked tight. Opening his mouth, he ran his tongue over his perfectly aligned teeth and licked his full lips. His cheeky dimple, which couldn't resist popping out during the most inopportune times, also made a brief appearance.

Viewers were perched by their television sets, waiting for the inevitable peek at his indentation—the reason why Keith had shaved. The execs had nixed his idea of growing a groomed beard, ignoring his argument that his dimple detracted from the Word of God.

A sharp rattle came from behind the door. "Coming," Keith called. He finished his ministrations and strode into the adjacent office to grab his worn Bible—an item the producers had begged him to get rid of. He tapped the worn leather. The Bible might be dilapidated and torn apart at the seams, but he wouldn't let it go. He could find all the passages with ease, and it had sentimental value.

Keith opened to the first page, and his finger outlined Gina's beautiful cursive. He planned on keeping this

Bible for life. But, he conceded, he might have to retire it to his office at home.

Opening the door, Keith walked out and saw Natalie, or "the Hawk," as he called her, sigh with relief. Her heels clicked as she scurried toward the podium.

On the way to the pulpit, he swallowed as his past threatened to creep its way back into his mind. *Why today?* He was a changed man, ransomed by the blood of Christ. Jesus had washed away his terrible sin. He was now new. God had forgiven him for what he had done. And one day he would be able to do the same for himself.

Keith banished the guilt back to the sea of forgetfulness and silently recited his pick-me-up from Psalm 103. *As far as the east is from the west, so far hath he removed our transgressions from us.* Keith repeated it until he no longer felt like the hypocrite he was. As he sauntered up to the podium, he waved at the cheers and praises going forth. The choir burst into song.

Keith greeted the other ministers before sitting down. He couldn't fathom how God had brought him out of the quagmire called sin to this place, Yankee Stadium, and to this seat among the most influential ministers in the country during this evangelical crusade.

Keith sat in his designated seat and swayed to the sounds of the choir. Closing his eyes, Keith felt himself getting caught up in the praise and began clapping his hands. Keith smiled his first genuine smile of the day and looked around the stadium. His eyes roamed over the thousands who had gathered. And as impossible as it seemed, he locked eyes with someone in the crowd.

He saw me. From her seat in the huge stadium, Gina felt a moment of panic when Keith spotted her. She bit her thumb and exhaled.

How could Keith have spotted her in this crowd? His seeing her was like finding a needle in a haystack. She had worn a basic black suit and had bought a broad-rimmed hat to obscure her face, but Gina should have known better. It had always been like that with them. Time and distance hadn't changed that. The sheer magnetic energy that they gave off when in each other's presence was enough to light up a few cities.

Losing her composure, Gina reached into her purse to get her handkerchief. Beads of sweat formed across her upper lip and brow. She blotted her face. She chanced another sly peek at Keith. His gaze was still pinned on her.

She squirmed under his intense scrutiny. Lifting one eyebrow, she tilted her head, which was pointless, since Keith could not see her furious gesture, which was telling him to stop staring. Fidgeting, Gina felt like all the television cameras and lights were aimed at her. She bent her head and closed her eyes to compose herself and gather her wits. She remained in this position while the choir sang.

Before the choir concluded, she took a chance and looked his way. Keith was still staring. Feeling the heat from his intense perusal radiating in her direction, she fanned herself. He was going to arouse suspicion if he kept looking her way, she thought in exasperation. But Gina knew from experience that Keith was his own man. He didn't care.

Not knowing what else to do, she stood and began inching her way down the row, using the pretext of going to the restroom. As she passed, people harrumphed and rolled their eyes, as they had to turn their legs, but Gina was not deterred.

She had to get out of there. Pronto.

Gina picked her way through the maze of hands and feet until she reached the end of the row. *Almost there. Don't look his way. Don't spare Keith Ward another glance.* She walked ramrod straight before she caved, daring to steal another fleeting look his way.

Keith was still looking—entranced.

With one foot forward, Gina willed herself to continue moving toward the exit sign. *Skip the bathroom.* She was going to keep walking. She had to get out of there.

Then he spoke.

Gina stood transfixed as his voice resonated throughout the stadium. She held on to her heart, willing it to remain unmoved by the smooth timbre of Keith's voice. Near the exit doors and out of sight, she leaned against the wall and listened, taking in everything Keith said. His sincerity and genuine fervor for God were evident in every word he spoke.

Tears flowed from her eyes. How she loved him so. Gina admitted that to God. *Did you hear me, God?* she thought.

Enthralled by Keith's passionate, meaningful words, Gina stayed rooted until his sermon ended. A devout usher offered her a tissue and then asked, "Do you want to go up for prayer? I'll be glad to escort you."

Choked up, Gina shook her head in dismay. How could she ask God for something she knew she couldn't have? She wanted Keith. Still, after all these years. She always would. She still couldn't have him.

She looked at the huge diamond on her left hand. It had the finest clarity and cut, but to her it felt like a weight that held her down, body, mind, and spirit. Michael's ring was a constant reminder of what she could not have. Overcome, she stumbled out of the stadium. She had allowed herself this excursion, being too weak to resist the temptation of seeing Keith preach the Word. But that wasn't why she was here. She had been given a task, and she couldn't leave until she had completed it.

Snuggled underneath a huge blanket on the king-size bed, Gina heard the doorbell and swung her right arm over her face. "Go away."

Her eyes were puffy from crying. She hadn't been able to sleep, because every time she closed her eyes, she saw him. Keith Ward. Seeing him earlier that day should have been a reprieve, but it had only added to her anguish.

The unremitting peal of the doorbell continued.

Cross and disgruntled, she bolted out of bed and stomped barefoot to the door. She had tossed her suit on a lounge chair in the bedroom and was clad only in her bra, chemise, and underwear.

Gina stood on tiptoes to look through the small peephole. She swung open the door with emphasis. Her mouth gaped open at the sight of the person standing there.

"You knew I would come," he said before entering.

Gina stood transfixed as Keith entered Michael's Park Avenue penthouse suite. He was still wearing the sharp black suit he'd delivered his sermon in. The only thing that was different was his tie—he'd loosened it. Was he coming undone, or did he need to be comfortable? Either way, she wanted to make it all better. Keith headed straight toward the living area. With its soothing beige and mint-green walls and its plush leather couches, Gina had found the room peaceful until his entrance. He paced like a tiger in a cage. His presence enveloped the entire room, making it feel like a tiny closet.

Thrown off guard, Gina held on to the locket, which she had never taken off. It was a gift from Keith.

Gina stared.

Keith stared back.

Their eyes feasted on each other like they were ravenous wolves beholding the first meal after days on the hunt.

Keith looked amazing. There was something even more attractive about him now. Was it God? Was it the spiritual change?

Chapter Twenty-three

Stop staring, he told himself.

He stared.

He couldn't help it.

Gina had not aged. She looked younger than her thirty-seven years and was as appealing as ever. The only thing different about her was her hair. Gina's replica of Halle Berry's hairstyle emphasized her beautiful cheekbones. She had colored her hair with varied shades of brown, which suited her bronzed skin. Her skin, Keith remembered, was ever so soft as a newborn baby's and just as unmarred.

Smiling, Keith realized he had forgotten how short she was. But her height did nothing to hinder the strong, confident woman. As always, her chocolate eyes beguiled him.

An unknown force inevitably swept them into each other's arms. Keith grabbed Gina, kissing her as if he were dying of thirst. Their lips became synchronized, remembering what it felt like.

His hands rediscovered her body.

Gina moaned, and her hands circled his waist.

Keith devoured her lips, while his fingertips developed a life of their own. It had been three years since his lips had touched hers. It had been three years since he had had any woman in his arms, and it felt good.

With expert fingers, he reached under the confines of her chemise to undo her bra strap. She arched her body. Keith bent his knees to place a light kiss on her navel.

Gina whispered, "Yes," urging him to keep going.

Keith's passion-filled eyes glossed over the room and skimmed the Bible on one of the end tables. Something about seeing the Bible gave him a momentary pause. The thought took root, permeating the clouds and bringing him to his senses.

Rationality returned. His conscience was restored.

Keith froze.

Gina turned her head to see what had captured his attention.

He stood upright. "We can't. I can't do this. I'm a servant of God." He turned away. "Get dressed." He felt her small hand touch his back.

"I love you," she told him before walking towards the bedroom.

When she returned dressed in jeans and a shirt, Keith said, "I'm a pastor. People look to me for guidance, to be a light. I won't let you be my Delilah." He referenced the biblical character that had brought down Samson, a great judge and man of God.

"You're still a man," Gina retorted.

Pain filled his voice as he admitted, "I can't shake it. God help me, at times I feel like a hypocrite, preaching the word while knowing that given the chance, I would be in your bed."

"Doesn't God understand? Won't He forgive you?" Gina asked. "Isn't that what you preachers' messages are all about?"

Keith didn't want to answer those questions, but he had to. It wasn't okay to play with God's grace. He tapped his chin as he gathered his thoughts. "Yes, God forgives, but He doesn't approve of willful sinning. If we sin, He's provided His Son as our advocate. However, as scripture says, we cannot continue in sin so that grace may abound."

He saw her confusion and elaborated in simpler words. "In other words, we can't sin on purpose, with the plan to ask for forgiveness. The more we sin, the more we need God's grace, so we can't take advantage of that, nor take Him for granted."

Seeing that she understood, he turned the tables with a burning question of his own. "How's Trey doing?"

Gina stepped back, with her hands at her throat. Her body shook upon hearing Keith mention Trey's name. "Trey's the same precocious, active boy you remember, although he now has a slight British accent from attending school in England. He's been in remission, which is good."

Keith's eyebrows arched. "Yes, I've been getting updates from Dr. Milliner. Each time I hear he's okay, I lift up a prayer of thanksgiving."

She fiddled with her collar. "Oh, I didn't realize you were keeping track. You could've called me or something . . ."

He nodded. "I wanted to, believe me." He took a tentative step toward her, and she swallowed. He continued. "But you changed your number. Then you left the country. I had no idea where you were, or I would've come for you and Trey. I wasn't going to take no for an answer. I pressed my mother until she filled me in about Michael's building projects and expansions in England, so I figure I'd wait it out. I thought I'd be waiting months, not three whole years."

She stammered, "I d-didn't change my number . . . Michael . . . Michael . . . well, he insisted. He fell in love with London. We have a large flat there. I've been back since March . . . about three months." She paused for a moment. "I already stopped by to hang with Colleen a couple of days ago, to celebrate our birthdays." She wiped her hands on her pants, a dead giveaway that she was circling the truth.

She decided to divert his attention back to Trey. "Trey's seven now, and far beyond his years. He's been reading since he was three years old, if you recall, and he's acquired an extensive vocabulary since then." Her chest puffed with pride. She pointed to her shoulders. "He's about this tall now. He reminds me so much of you."

Keith tilted his head at her words. "Does he?" His face brightened like a thousand-watt bulb. "Is he with Michael?"

"No, he's staying with my father." Gina prayed that Keith didn't detect her nervousness because she was lying through her teeth. Trey was not with her father as she'd said. She strove for normalcy, but her heart was in her throat. Lucky for her, Keith focused in on her father—a much safer topic.

Keith lifted a brow and queried, "Oh? I'm glad you two managed to develop a relationship. How's Jeff doing?"

"He's fine." Gina meandered her way to the window. "Both he and Regina have been a godsend for me. Trey loves them."

Keith ambled over to stand next to her. In a congenial tone, he asked, "So what brings you to New York?"

"I came to talk to you about Michael. He needs you."

Keith bent to peer into her face. "Michael hasn't spoken to me in three years. He didn't even reach out to me when he left the country. I had to hear about that secondhand. Prior to that, we had never gone without speaking for even three days."

Gina could hear the distress in Keith's voice. She knew she was the reason for their split, and it rankled. Every day she had to live with the knowledge that she was the one who had come between them.

Keith invaded her personal space. He was so close that his breath teased her ear. "I haven't seen you in three years," he said, touching her face. "Do you have any idea what that was like for me?"

"Hell?" Gina said. She knew because that was how she had felt when she had awakened to find an empty bed that day three years ago. She had cried for days, not caring who saw. Then, during Trey's lengthy recovery, Gina devoted more of herself to her son. She remembered wiping Trey's mouth, which had been filled with sores, and recalled how his feet and hands had turned black. He became her lifeline for facing another day, although his being in isolation for thirty days had been a gruesome trial. Her efforts had paid off. Trey was thriving. Her relationship with Michael was what suffered.

"Yes!" Keith said. "I came back to New York desolate and out of my mind with grief. I had given up everything that meant something to me." Keith's phone rang. Looking at the caller ID, he said, "I'm sorry. I have to get this."

Gina watched Keith as he spoke on the phone. She knew from the urgency in his voice that their visit had concluded. She stared as Keith swiped his iPhone to disconnect the call.

"I have an interview with BET, and I'm behind schedule."

"Go ahead," Gina said. "I'll be here for a couple of days." *Or as long as it takes to convince you to come back with me.*

"I'll be back tonight," Keith told her. He pointed his index finger at her. "Don't go anywhere."

Gina remained silent until he left the apartment. Keith needn't have worried. She was not going anywhere without him. Michael had given her strict orders not to return home without his brother. If she returned without Keith, Michael would not allow her to see her offspring again. He had made that crystal clear.

Chapter Twenty-four

"Pastor Ward, where have you been? You told us fifteen minutes. You've got a nighttime special with BET. What is more important than that?" Natalie was fit to be tied.

Keith gave the Hawk a sideways glance as he swooped into the limousine that was waiting for him at the curb. He decided to ignore her ramblings. Besides, he was used to it, and truth be told, it was what he paid her for, to keep him on schedule. He looked at his watch. They had plenty of time to make the interview. He closed his eyes. Gina sprang to his mind. Keith would return and see her, but this time, he'd be focused. His ardor would take a backseat tonight. Something was not right, and Keith needed to know what was going on.

He spoke to his mother often, and she'd never given him the impression that anything was amiss with Michael or Gina.

But Gina was miserable. It was written all over her face. Her mannerisms were that of a woman under duress, and he knew a lonely woman when he saw one.

Throughout the interview, he laughed, he entertained, but at the top of his mind was, *What's eating at Gina?*

As soon as he was done, Keith raced out of the building and into the waiting limousine and directed the driver to take him back to Michael's high-rise. Now that his head was clear, Keith realized her sudden reappearance in his life wasn't by accident. She was in town for a reason, and he wasn't going to let up until he knew why.

The rush hour traffic had died down, so Keith made it back to Gina's in record time. He used his key card, which Michael had never taken from him, and entered the elevator. Within minutes, he was again pressing the doorbell.

Gina opened the door. She'd changed her top to a light summer sweater. Keith took off his dress shirt, tie, and dress shoes. He removed his belt next. He felt better already in just his white undershirt and pants. He could unwind.

He felt Gina's eyes on him as he made himself comfortable. He knew he was a fine specimen of manhood. Age had done nothing to diminish that, or so the ladies said. The slender patch of gray that lined his temples only increased his appeal.

Gina exhaled.

Keith basked in her feminine appreciation. He was a minister, but it still felt good to be seen as a man. However, he wasn't going to get sidetracked. He had been on the right track for too long and had pledged not to disappoint God, or himself.

"So, tell me all about how you ended up here, Pastor Ward," Gina said. "I'm dying to know about your career change."

Keith sniffed the air. He smelled food and gravitated toward the kitchen. Seeing the pots and pans on the stove, Keith lifted the lids. "Mmm."

Gina laughed. "Men and their stomachs." She waved at him. "Help yourself. I cooked dinner for you in case you were hungry."

"How thoughtful, and yes, I am." Keith found the necessary utensils and helped himself to some of the scrumptious feast Gina had prepared. He offered to dish up a plate for her, but Gina passed. She wasn't hungry and said she preferred to watch him enjoy his meal.

Declining the use of the table, they went into the living room. Keith headed for the armchair and rested his plate on his lap.

While eating, Keith spoke about the past. "Well, needless to say, after I left you, I was heartbroken—"

Gina broke in. "I didn't understand that. I didn't get how it was easy for you to love me, then leave me."

Keith stopped and looked into her eyes. He took a deep breath. He knew desire when he saw it. *Behave yourself,* he cautioned himself. *Keep the conversation going.* "You want to know why I left after our night together?"

"Yes." It was obvious from her tone that this was something that had plagued her. He knew that she must have awakened to find him gone and felt despondent. He hadn't even said good-bye. He had vanished.

"I knew that you wouldn't have been able to live with yourself if you'd run off with me," Keith remarked. "That's not you. You're not made that way."

"In retrospect, I guess you're right, but I was mystified and hurt to know that you had just up and left." Her little voice pierced his heart. "I mean, I kept busy, volunteering at the hospital, reading to the children—Michael and I even started a foundation in Trey's honor—but that didn't dull the pain. You left."

He explained in a gentle tone, "Gina, I had to. You even told me you chose Michael. Trey chose Michael. Would you have changed your mind, or would you have suffered from the Lot's wife complex?"

"Huh? I'm lost."

"You know, the whole 'looking back and regretting' thing."

"Oh," Gina said.

"So I came back to New York a broken man," Keith said, continuing his story. "And for the first time in my life, I didn't know what to do with myself. Here I was at the pinnacle of my career, a senior partner in one of the most respected and prestigious law firms in the city, but when I opened my door and entered my home, I realized that I wasn't happy. I felt empty and hollow. I was a wreck."

Gina remained silent, but he witnessed her eyes welling up with tears.

"So I called my job and resigned."

"What?" Her mouth hung open. "You've never struck me as the type who'd take such a risk without a concrete plan."

Keith laughed in agreement. "Well, I did! I was out of my comfort zone, but I knew that I'd gotten all I needed from my job. I didn't hesitate for one moment."

Gina was stunned by his bravery, and told him as much.

"My confidence in my decision lasted a month. I started to second-guess myself and wondered if I should crawl on my hands and knees and beg for my job back."

She cracked up at his words. "You're so descriptive. I can visualize you doing that too."

"It reached the point where I was sitting and twiddling my thumbs. I had nothing to do. Then I started reading the Bible you gave me. At first, it was because of sheer boredom, but the Psalms and the profound truths in the verses fascinated me. I started on what I call a Bible fast. I ate, drank, and slept with my Bible. I feasted on Proverbs. I was taking notes and studying. It was great, Gina."

Gina lifted her hands toward him. "Your enthusiasm is contagious. There's such joy reflected in your voice, and I can feel it bubbling over. Listening to you makes me a little envious. I would love to feel that exhilaration. Compared to your exuberance, my life feels . . . stagnant."

"This joy I have comes from God. His words were my lifeline. I soaked them up. I mean, I would put the Bible down, but it was like the verse said, I began to hunger and thirst after a better and more fulfilling life. I was doing well until I came across Romans 10:9 and 10:00. Is there a Bible here?" Without waiting for her response, Keith sprinted into the master bedroom to hunt for a Bible.

Gina shook her head at his brazenness. *I guess he's made himself quite comfortable in Michael's home.* But that was nothing unusual. Keith had done the same thing years ago, when she'd first invited him into her home when she was single and living in Queens, New York. She'd taken a phone call, and during that time Keith had taken the liberty of going into her bedroom. Then he'd fallen asleep in her bed. She grinned at the memory of his nerve.

He returned, triumphant, with his find, jolting her out of memory lane.

Gina watched him leaf through the pages with the assurance of someone who knew what they were doing. She felt a brief pang of envy due to the fact that Keith knew so much about the Bible. Her Bible back at home was gathering dust on the mantel. She couldn't recall reading it more than twice.

"Here it is!" Keith exclaimed. His voice filled with strong conviction while reading the scripture.

While she listened, she felt the words hit her heart. She tried to remain settled in her seat, but the Word had hit its mark. Feeling a need for space, Gina jumped up off the couch and walked into the kitchen to get a glass of water.

Keith didn't pick up on her discomfort and continued with his soliloquy. "Those words sank into my consciousness and seeped deep into my heart, where I held all my hurt, anger, and disappointment. I dropped to my knees and began to holler. I talked to God and placed everything on the table. I acknowledged my sin and asked God to wash me. I asked Him to change me."

She did not even try to hide the tears this time. She grabbed several tissues and wiped her eyes. Keith wanted to stop the tears.

"No, Gina, don't cry. That was the most joyous experience of my life. I felt a peace come over me and a calm feeling that I had never known existed. It's a miracle how you can start your day one way and end it another. I climbed in my bed that night a changed man."

She lifted one eyebrow, remembering the intensity of his passion earlier that day.

He chuckled, with a sheepish grin. "I know. You're my exception, Gina. I've been a good boy otherwise."

"I beg to differ. You were definitely a man earlier," was her cheeky rejoinder.

Keith's dimples widened at her response, but he felt compelled to add, "Please don't think I'm a hypocrite."

"I don't see you that way, Keith. We have something that's hard to shake."

Keith nodded his head in agreement. "For me to deny our mutual attraction would be like denying my very existence."

"Continue," Gina said. She wanted to hear the rest of his testimony.

Keith returned to his story. "God's Word became a delight to me. I decided to find a church home. I read in the book of Genesis that God rested on the seventh day, so I combed the Internet and researched further scriptures in Hebrews. I concluded that Saturday was the day of worship for me. I'm not knocking anyone else's path to Christ, though. But the fact that Terence and Colleen also went to church on Saturday helped with my decision."

Keith told her that he'd visited several churches before he found the Pentecostal church. They rejoiced and worshipped and talked about the Holy Spirit. Keith told Gina, "When I stepped through the doors, I felt right at home."

At that time, the church had only about one hundred members at most. As soon as he was baptized, he started sharing the Word. He didn't know what it was, but he had a pressing desire to tell everybody about Jesus and His grace.

Pastor Nicholson saw his zeal and made him an evangelist. He continued to minister. His experience as a lawyer was an added bonus. Keith used the church to provide free legal services and to share the good news. His efforts paid off. He'd been shocked when only a year and a half after being saved, he was ordained a pastor.

Now Keith was on national television.

Gina had visited church a few times when Colleen invited her, but she'd also been on a Sunday. "Does it matter what day you go to church?"

Keith looked at Gina. He strove to reassure her. "I've been asked this question a lot. Gina, our main focus should be about Jesus and his enduring love for us. Romans says that we have to accept Him as Lord and Savior to get eternal life. He died for our sins and was resurrected. That's what is most important."

Gina nodded her head in agreement. Keith was so right. He looked so sure about Jesus. His testimony rang with sincerity. Keith's church now boasted close to three thousand members and was featured on BET news.

Gina was impressed. "I, for one, am not surprised you jumped to the pinnacle of leadership in the church. You were always successful at whatever you did. I'll never forget the Marshall case and how you saved Penny from a lifetime in jail. So, now with God behind you, I can see how you'd end up on television."

Keith smiled and confessed, "Well, BET asked me to consider taking a half-hour slot, and after prayerful consideration, I decided to take the job. And the rest, as they say, is history. I owe it all to God."

Gina whooped and clapped her hands for joy. She was overjoyed that Keith had found contentment with his faith. The only area lacking seemed to be in his personal life. "The only thing missing from your life is a wife and children."

Chapter Twenty-five

Keith choked on his water. He looked Gina square in her eyes, "Gina, when you've had perfection, you cannot settle for anything else."

Gina felt warm under his praise. "But it must be lonely," she objected. Gina fiddled with the locket on her necklace.

"I won't lie to you. It is lonely at times," Keith affirmed. "But I'm determined to wait for the one who is right. Let me point out that loneliness doesn't mean I'm alone. However, the board is eager for me to settle down and put the females out of their misery. But I'm not going to up and marry anybody because they feel I should."

"I understand their plight, Keith. You're too charismatic, and your good looks are distracting. They want to spare you from getting caught up in the wrong situation with those young girls and their nubile bodies . . ." She trailed off.

Keith shook his head. "I'm set on this. I'll marry only the woman I can see myself with forever. You're the only woman who has given me that picture, so I know it's possible. I'd rather remain single until I find that again." He reached out and took her hands in his. He stunned her with his next words. "Gina, you're the only woman alive who could ruin me. I'm a weakling when it comes to you. There's no worry about me getting caught with my pants down with another woman—and I mean that in a figurative and literal sense."

She gulped. There was no response needed for his heartfelt declaration. Gina decided to tackle the reason for her visit. "So I bet it shocked you to see me after all this time."

Keith flowed with the conversation shift. "I was flabbergasted. You were the last person I expected to see in the crowd."

She licked her lips. *Here goes.* "I came to see you, Keith. I had to because, to be honest, I didn't have a choice."

She saw the effect of her mysterious words. Keith's interest and instinctive concern had been stirred. With kind but curious eyes, he moved closer to Gina and prompted her to keep talking.

"Michael sent me," she confessed.

"Michael?" He looked perplexed. That was not the answer he'd been expecting. "Why would Michael send you? Why wouldn't he come instead?"

"That's what I cannot figure out or understand myself," Gina replied. "I've been trying to guess his motives, but I have no clue what goes on in Michael's head. He is not the same person anymore."

She'd piqued Keith's curiosity with her woebegone intonation. She knew what he was going to ask before he even asked it. "What do you mean, Gina? Is he hurting you?"

"No. Well, not physically," Gina hedged. Her body tensed up with discomfort.

"I see your hunched shoulders and clenched fists. Now, I'm concerned." He held her. "Gina, you can tell me anything. I think you know that by now. You can trust me as I trust you, without question."

Nodding, she took a deep breath. "It's not what he does. It's what he says and how he says it. Michael has become disingenuous, and I know I can no longer trust him. I know I violated his trust, but I didn't think he would make me pay for it for the rest of my life. I was so convinced we were at a good place . . ."

Keith's chin dropped. "That does not sound like my brother. He was always so quick to forgive, and he never held a grudge."

"Well, the Michael you know has changed. He's bitter and cold and . . . different. I can't put it into words, but I know it and I feel it."

"Have you spoken to him about it?" Keith asked. He had a sneaky suspicion about what was eating away at Michael, but after all this time Keith wondered if he should let sleeping dogs lie.

The truth shall set you free.

He heard the thought. He remembered the last time he'd been given that warning. He had not heeded it then, and he didn't heed it now. Though the Spirit urged Keith to clear the matter up, he kept his mouth shut.

He knew Gina would be hurt and furious over his deception, but he couldn't tell the truth. He couldn't tell her he was Trey's father. He couldn't tell her about Michael's infertility. It was something he felt Michael should man up and do.

Gina sighed and returned to the matter at hand. "Michael sent me here to get you. He was most persistent about that. For my sake, I hope you can come back with me."

Keith heard the desperation in Gina's tone and surmised that though she wasn't saying so, Michael would make things unpleasant for her if he did not return with her. "I don't relish being Michael's pawn, but for your sake, I'll go. I'll book my flight."

"Michael took care of all the arrangements, and he gave me an open-ended ticket for you," Gina replied while reaching over to grab her pocketbook. She started scouring through it for the plane ticket.

He felt anger toward his brother rise within him when he saw the visible relief on Gina's face and her desperate search for the plane ticket. Her gratitude was evident.

She fixed him with an anxious gaze. "I know it's short notice, but can we leave next week?"

"Yes, I can arrange my schedule." Though he agreed, Keith felt uneasy. "Gina, is there more?"

She nodded her head in the affirmative, but he could tell she wasn't ready to tell all. "Yes, but I can't talk about it now. Please understand."

Keith stood, ambled over to the windows of his brother's penthouse suite, and looked out. He felt anger. The old demons of guilt attacked his being. It was his fault that Gina was now in misery. He was the one who had to have her. Caught up in his thoughts, he ground his fist into his palm.

Gina must have felt compelled to walk over to him and make a physical connection. She placed her hand on his arm. Keith turned to face her. He didn't try to disguise the torture riding his senses. She lifted her hands to smooth his brows, and then placed her palm against his cheek.

Keith closed his eyes and leaned his head into her hand, much the way a pet would seek comfort. He felt the warmth resonating from her hand ease the thoughts running rampant in his head. She moved her hand and put both hands on his head. Keith opened his eyes.

Their eyes locked. She shivered from the impact and broke contact.

Oh, no, Gina. Grabbing her hand, he pulled her into him to comfort her as one friend would another. He could tell when her fears dissipated. Her shoulders relaxed and her stiff posture loosened. He didn't know what Michael had up his sleeve, but he knew without question she would be safe as long as he was there. He'd make sure of that.

***

After Keith left, Gina returned to the window to people watch and take in the night scene. She reflected on Keith's conversion experience. There was such a light in his eyes, which drew her in.

The shrill ring of the suite's phone startled her out of her reverie. She scurried over to answer the call. As expected, it was Michael. He'd called the apartment phone to make sure she was there. Gina rolled her eyes, even though she knew her husband couldn't see her.

"Hello."

"Hello, wife," Michael chirped on the other end. "How are things?"

Gina sucked her teeth and mumbled under her breath but kept up the farce. "The weather is beautiful, and I've settled in."

"That's good," Michael said. "Was the car service acceptable?"

"Yes," Gina answered, hating how their conversation was stilted and awkward.

"What about the penthouse?"

"Everything's fine, Michael. The renovations you had done are impeccable, exquisite," Gina sighed. "I've made contact with Keith, as you ordered. Are you still in England? I miss Trey and . . . I miss Trey." She had to be careful with her words.

"Glad to hear you've gotten in touch with Keith," Michael said, ignoring her question.

But Gina wouldn't be swayed from the topic foremost in her mind. "Are you coming home?" she asked again.

"I told you I've scheduled the flights. We're leaving for Georgia tomorrow. Stop acting like I'm a kidnapper."

But you are, her insides screamed. It had been three months, and she was a desperate mother at her wit's end. "Well, let me talk to him."

"All in good time," Michael said.

His "All in good time" grated on her last nerve.

Frustrated, she hung up the phone in his ear. She hoped he liked the sound of the dial tone. It was better than telling him what she wanted to say. The phone rang again. However, this time she ignored it.

Gina pondered her life. When had things between Michael and her soured? He had been so forgiving of her past affair with Keith, and for the first few months, they'd been in heaven. Then, overnight, he'd changed. He'd packed them up and moved them to a whole other country, away from family and friends, away from Colleen—away from Keith. Which was pointless, since distance wouldn't fix what was in her heart.

Gina didn't know if he had realized he could never get over her sleeping with Keith and thus shut down. Gina had been deceived into thinking Michael had given her another chance. He had convinced her, but how wrong she had been.

If pressed, Gina could not articulate exactly how Michael had changed. He was jovial. He laughed at the right times and made good conversation, but that all changed at bedtime. Then Michael would become cold and unfeeling. He would turn away from her if she took the initiative and pursued intimacy between them.

Gina cried herself to sleep constantly, feeling undesirable and unwanted. The worst part was she had no idea why. She had asked Michael over and over why he'd turned against her, and he declined to answer. She couldn't pinpoint when it happened, but something had gone wrong somewhere. She believed something was eating away at him, but he refused to tell her. She had done everything she could think of to rattle him. But he never caved.

She strolled over to the window. She couldn't help but think of the great times she and Michael had had together back when they were dating. He'd been so charming. But Michael had transformed into a monster. It wasn't that he abused her. In fact, he'd never laid a hand on her. But, somehow, from his tone and mannerisms, Gina discerned that she could not trust him.

After months turned into over two years of torment, Gina had resigned herself to accept what she could not change. Colleen had been her sounding board and had told her that she was praying about it, but Gina had not seen any fruits from her labor yet.

Sometimes, Gina considered severing the ties between them for good. But Michael was a magnanimous and doting father. He had been the best thing for Trey during his recovery. She could sacrifice her happiness for the moment.

Then, out of the blue, Michael did the unimaginable. He took her offspring hostage. He sent her back to the United States alone—using the separation to manipulate her into doing whatever he wanted. *Who did that?* she thought. Gina furrowed her brows.

Well, maybe *hostage* was too strong a term, but Michael had not given her a choice. Instead, he had bought her a plane ticket and commanded her to persuade his brother to return with her on the pretext of mending fences. Gina suspected Michael had a hidden agenda, but she had no idea what he had planned.

Thinking about her husband, she felt chills run up and down her spine. She rubbed away the goose bumps springing up on her arm.

Michael was being downright creepy.

She ran her hand through her pixie cut. It was her sole act of defiance. Michael loved her hair long. She'd chopped it off to get a reaction. Instead, he'd recommended that she color it.

Gina sighed. Of course, she'd complied.

That was the scary part. Gina felt she had become a pawn in a higher scheme, but she couldn't figure out Michael's angle. Gina had tried without success to encourage Michael to contact Keith himself. But he'd been adamant about following his plan.

Michael completed his call with Gina, satisfied with the outcome. He was pleased she'd made contact with Keith. As he'd counted on, his brother was still hung up on his wife. Michael smiled.

So far so good.

Keith's obsession with his wife had become useful, and Michael anticipated using it for his benefit. His brother would pay.

Chapter Twenty-six

Keith and Gina landed in Atlanta on time. They'd enjoyed first-class seats and a special treat in recognition of the coming holiday, Independence Day. They had been afforded a small measure of privacy since first class was practically empty. In fact, there had been only one other person in the section, and he appeared to be in his own world.

Keith urged Gina to use this occasion to relax. As she'd rested her head on his shoulder, he basked in the simple pleasure of being in her company. It had taken him a couple of days to clear his schedule. He hoped he would be able to resolve things with Michael and prayed they could rebuild their former relationship.

He missed his brother with a fierceness that surprised him. As he got off the small aircraft, a sense of nostalgia encircled him. He couldn't help but remember the last time he had been with Gina in Atlanta. It had been for her birthday, but it had turned into a vigil for Trey. Though he'd been back since for two mega gospel conventions, it had still been almost a year since he'd last set foot in Atlanta.

In hindsight, Keith welcomed the experience he had with Gina, because it precipitated his learning about Christ and accepting Jesus as Lord and Savior. He quietly uttered the words, "I can do all things through Christ, which strengthens me," and felt a calm reassurance assuage his fears.

Gina gave him an odd look.

"I'm whispering a scripture for fortitude. I'm not a madman," Keith assured her.

"I'm glad to hear you're apprehensive. I was wondering if God had made you invincible. Nice to know you're still human."

Her words were preaching words. He couldn't let that slide. "I'm a Christian, not an alien from outer space. I still have feelings—as you know—but it's how I deal with them that's different. I'm a human. I'm flawed, but I serve a perfect God." Keith couldn't hold back his praise. "Hallelujah. Thank you, Jesus, for salvation."

Gina glanced to the left and the right as a light blush grazed her cheeks. Keith didn't care. He wasn't ashamed of God.

Keith followed Gina to long-term parking. She disabled the alarm system on a red Range Rover. He gave a small whistle. Her tastes had improved since he'd last seen her.

"Thanks for the luxury ride."

She rolled her eyes and hoisted her small frame into the driver's seat and started up the engine. Keith bit back a smile and jumped into the vehicle. Gina expertly maneuvered the vehicle out of the space and then tore out of the lot.

As he watched her drive, Keith acknowledged that he was worried about her. He knew she was being manipulated by his brother, but Keith didn't have a clue what Michael was holding over her head, and he hated being in the dark. However, no matter how he coaxed and prodded, Keith hadn't been able to get anything out of Gina.

This only heightened his concern, because it wasn't like her to be close-lipped with him about something. It had to be big. He uttered a prayer while she navigated through the city and into the suburbs. His eyes widened when she pulled into the driveway of a sprawling mansion in Alpharetta.

His eyes roamed the flamboyant structure before him. It spoke of so much opulence and grandeur that Keith couldn't contain his surprise. He looked askance at Gina, who shrugged her shoulders.

"Your brother's choosing," was all she said.

Keith followed suit as she exited the vehicle and walked up to the house. She'd left the keys in the ignition. A gentleman, who, Keith presumed, was a caretaker, got in the car and drove off.

Keith knew his brother was wealthy, but Michael had never flashed his money so ostentatiously before. He knew without any doubt that this wasn't Gina's doing. She had exquisite taste and style, but she had always been restrained and conservative. These upgrades were a clear indication that his brother had changed. He was overcompensating for something that was lacking.

Gina opened the door and greeted an older Latina woman. She introduced Keith to Melinda Diaz and instructed her to show Keith into the great room. Then she excused herself to freshen up.

After being escorted into the great room, Keith took a seat in one of the chairs and waited for her to return. He remembered a time when he would have made himself at home already, but Keith was all too aware that this visit was altogether different. He felt uncomfortable and sat stiffly in his seat until Gina returned.

When she reappeared, she took him on a quick tour of the house. As he looked around and took in his surroundings, Keith remained silent. But on the inside, thoughts were racing through his head. This was not a home; it was a massive monument with all the glitz and luxuries one could desire. The house lacked warmth.

Keith did not see Gina's stamp anywhere. In fact, she acted like a real estate agent who was giving a tour of a mausoleum. Her voice lacked any real pride or enthusiasm. As he listened to Gina ramble on, he had to prevent himself from grabbing her and shaking life into her. Her entire demeanor was monotone and resigned. This was not the same woman he'd encountered in New York a few days ago.

Keith came to a halt. "Gina."

She stopped and turned to face him. She looked at him and then avoided his questioning eyes.

Keith reached over and turned her face toward him. He couldn't keep the pity from his eyes and voice. He glided his thumb down her ear and trailed a path to her neck. "This is a nice house, but where is your touch?"

He knew she saw and despised his pity, but she'd never admit it. Instead of answering his question, she scoffed, "What do you mean? Michael hired the best of the best to turn this place into a showpiece."

He agreed. "I agree with you. It's a showpiece. But is it a home?"

"Ouch," was all she said, followed by an awkward laugh. She declined to answer him further. Keith wished she would open up and tell him the truth. She was spared having to utter another word, as at that moment they both heard Michael calling for her.

"Come on. Let's go get this over with," she said, offering Keith a hand. He put his hand in hers, but discomfort filled him.

Gina dragged her feet like a woman heading to the guillotine instead of toward her husband. She held Keith's hand until she was at the door of Michael's study. Then she removed her hand from his.

Taking a deep breath, Keith entered the room to see his brother.

Michael had been anticipating Keith's arrival. He had planned this meeting down to every single iota and now wanted to see his plan come to fruition. He could admit a small part of him wanted to patch things up between himself and his brother, but the greater part of him couldn't. He had constant reminders every day of his life of Keith's transgressions, and the bitterness covered his heart and overtook his good judgment.

Even if he wanted to, he couldn't mend things now. He had gone too far to turn back now. He'd been ruthless about damaging his relationship with Gina. It felt satisfying to see her face blanch with pain. He'd approached his marriage like he did his business ventures, and he was reaping the returns from his investment.

Gina was faithful to him. She fulfilled every demand and wish like a devoted employee. She stayed in the marriage because she'd grown up in a single-parent home and hadn't liked it. She didn't want her son to have to experience that. Her guilt was the second reason. He didn't know why she still blamed herself for his accident, but that didn't stop him from using it against her.

The problem was every now and then his conscience kicked in, and Michael would admit to himself that he wanted a wife. He wanted his old life back, with Gina by his side. However, he would dismiss his momentary pang of regret each time. Gina and Keith had ruined his ideal life, and they had to pay.

Keith greeted his brother. "Hello, Michael." He extended his hand. Was that supposed to be a peace offering?

"Keith." Michael choked on the word. His brother still looked handsome. Michael looked over at Gina, who had remained in the doorway. He saw the color in her cheeks and knew Keith was the one who had put it there. He made a fist. He resented it, but he could keep up the charade a little longer. It would be all worth it in the end. He would have the last laugh.

Michael reached out and gave his brother a hug. He had to make Keith believe he wanted to reconcile things between them. He closed his eyes and allowed himself to savor the moment. He knew Keith had fallen for his act when his brother returned the hug.

When the brothers parted, Michael saw tears in Keith's eyes. He looked over at Gina and saw she was also teary.

Oh, this is too easy. It was all he could do to keep from laughing out loud. Michael's smile was as insincere as it was wide. "I'm so happy you're here." He extended his hand toward Gina, who walked over to him.

He enfolded her in his arms. Michael kissed her full on the lips. It was all for Keith's benefit, but he knew she would comply because he had something she wanted. "Go to our old house," Michael whispered in Gina's hair. He gripped her hair during their seemingly tender embrace.

Heedless of the pain, Gina laughed with relief. "I didn't know you still owned that house. I thought you sold it before we moved to England." She gave him a genuine hug of gratitude before excusing herself.

Michael could see the blatant curiosity as Keith watched the exchange, but his brother refrained from his character-istic bluntness. Gina had bounced out of the room without sparing Keith another thought, which was fine by him.

"So where's Trey?" Keith asked.

"They're at the other house. You'll see them soon," Michael replied. He turned his back to Keith and trudged over to his desk to pick up a pen, which he proceeded to twirl in his hands.

"They?"

Michael could've kicked himself for his blunder. He'd forgotten his brother was still an attorney at heart and didn't miss much. He fought for nonchalance and made sure he maintained a calm tone.

"Yes. We hired a nanny." Michael hoped he had covered the slipup well, although all would be revealed in due time. When Keith nodded, he felt relieved to know his brother had fallen for it hook, line, and sinker.

I hope he knows I didn't buy that. Keith wasn't fooled for an instant. He had questioned enough witnesses to know when someone was lying or holding something back, and his brother was guilty of both. Michael's posture and the nervous twirling of the pen in his hands were a dead giveaway. Nevertheless, he had come to mend fences, not to stir up anything, so he shrugged his shoulders and allowed the matter to rest.

The two brothers spoke about general topics and fell into a brief camaraderie of sorts. Keith relaxed his stance and berated himself for reading more into things. His brother seemed the same as always. Though things with his brother and Gina appeared tense, it might not mean anything.

Michael finished giving him the tour Gina had begun. Then he showed Keith his room. It was the very last bedroom in the east wing of the house. Michael and Gina's bedroom suite was in the other wing. Keith was glad for the distance between them, though it was of no surprise that Michael had arranged things that way.

Michael excused himself on the pretext of getting some work done. Keith was glad for the time to shower and read his Bible. He chose to read about Jacob and Esau and their reunion. The two brothers had been at war with each other because Jacob had stolen Esau's birthright. He enjoyed reading this passage of scripture because it was somewhat like his and Michael's situation. He only hoped this truce lasted.

Keith fell to his knees by the side of his bed and prayed a fervent prayer for his brother and his family. He prayed and thanked God for all that He had done. At the end of the prayer, he stood and called his mother. He promised to see her before he left Georgia. Gerry cried tears of joy when she heard her sons were renewing their bond.

Keith then called his assistant, Natalie, to check on things. She sounded excited to hear from him, and then she mentioned his impending interview.

Keith burrowed his ear deeper into the phone. "What interview?" he asked.

"What do you mean, what interview?" Her voice sounded acidic through the phone.

Keith turned down the phone's volume several decibels, because she was now screeching.

"It's been on Twitter all day. Your interview with CNN. Isn't that the reason you flew to Georgia?" Her patience was wearing thin.

Keith's heart hammered in his chest. He tapped his chin with his index finger. Something was not right here. He had no clue what Natalie was rambling on about.

"Turn on the TV!" she said. "CNN is talking about your upcoming interview."

Keith picked up the remote to the television hanging on the wall above the dresser, clicked the TV on, and changed channels until he found CNN. Sure enough, she was right. The line remained quiet while he listened in. The announcer declared there was going to be a televised event about him, his brother, and their sordid past.

Michael. It all made sense now. His brother was behind this. Keith was sure of it. His brother's saccharine grin flashed across Keith's mind. Michael was knee-deep involved in this.

"I've got to go," Keith said, rushing to get off the phone. He was going to confront his brother. He walked out of his room. His insides churned with each stride he took down the long hallway. This was not a pleasant reunion to bury the hatchet. He'd been set up. He knew it. He needed only to know the how and why.

Keith raced through the house and found Michael in his study. His brother looked as if he had been anticipating his arrival.

"So you heard about the interview?" Michael swiveled his chair back and forth.

"Yeah," Keith responded. He stemmed the urge to snatch his brother out of the chair. He wanted to wipe that look off his face. "What's going on? Our relationship and affairs are private. Anything going on with us or with my personal life is not something I want publicized on a national scale."

"I know you value your privacy," Michael announced. He tapped his fingers on his desk unconcerned. "But the good people deserve to know a little more about the big-time preacher they're all swooning over."

"No." Keith shook his head. "Michael, don't do this. For myself, I don't care, but consider Gina's feelings if you air your dirty laundry like this for all to see."

"I have!" Michael shouted.

Keith walked around the desk and stood in front of his brother as understanding dawned. "You won, Michael. Gina's your wife and the mother of your son. You have her!"

"No, no, I don't," Michael snarled. He jumped out of his chair and looked at Keith dead-on. His chest heaved up and down from his pent-up emotions.

The doorbell rang.

Keith watched Michael compose himself and witnessed his slowly widening smile of satisfaction. "Yes, my dear brother. You're cornered, and there is no finagling your way out of this one. Pastor Keith Ward cannot back out of this interview, or he will be faced with the salacious tongue wagging and speculation of the media."

"I thought you loved, Gina," Keith said. He put a hand out to touch Michael's arm. "This is going to destroy her. I'm not doing this."

"I *loved* her." Michael shot back, shrugging off Keith's hand. "But then . . . Let's just say I had an epiphany I couldn't live with. And, yes, you're doing this, or Gina suffers, believe me. All I need to do is make one phone call." He took out his cell phone to show he'd follow up on his promise.

"What are you talking about? Are you blackmailing me?" Keith demanded. He arched an eyebrow, but Michael was done talking. He felt a frisson of fear flow through his body. Whatever ace Michael held up his sleeve was potent and damaging. But he was worried for Gina. This would humiliate her, and Michael knew it.

Michael's demeanor conveyed that he didn't care one iota. If anything, his sardonic grin showed how pleased he was with himself. Keith only hoped Michael had considered the ramifications of his actions.

Where's Gina? He pulled out his cell phone and called her on speed dial. She'd given him her new number while they were in New York. He had to give her a warning. She didn't answer. Gina was about to walk into a hornet's nest, and he wasn't going to be able to rescue her.

The truth shall set you free.

Keith pursed his lips, filled with doubt. He knew at that moment that there was only one entity who could make it right, somehow. His humanity felt frail at the moment, so Keith sought help from God. He needed to rely on God to see him through.

Chapter Twenty-seven

Gina parked her car and raced up the stairs to her old home. She wished she'd known this was where Michael had taken her children. Her heels clicked on the paved steps as she headed to the front door.

He was cruel, but most of his vindictiveness was confined solely to her. Gina should've realized Michael wouldn't place them in any real jeopardy. He was a terrible husband but a wonderful father—well, to Trey.

When Michael first approached her about going to visit Keith, she'd refused. She remembered the moment well. Her body had gone into shock, frozen with fear. "Where are my children?" Gina had spat with fire in her eyes. She told herself, Michael had gone too far this time. She advanced on him, determined to scratch his eyes out. The way she felt, she could have done serious damage.

"I wouldn't if I were you," Michael had returned with an eerie calm.

Gina had heeded his advice but struggled to control her temper. She was tired of Michael and his ridiculous demands. He'd demanded a nanny. She conceded. He'd decided to have Trey homeschooled. She conceded. But Gina would allow only so much.

"If you don't comply, I will make sure you never see your children again," Michael then threatened.

Gina's throat had closed in, and her hand circled her neck. Her eyes popped open wide. "You wouldn't!"

"Try me," Michael urged. He looked menacing as he advanced on Gina.

Gina tried to call his bluff, but Michael had her cornered. He knew she was not about to play any games involving her children. "Where are my children?"

She loved her children too much not to cave. Why was she even still in this marriage if Michael had no qualms about taking advantage of her? she wondered. *Guilt.* That was why. Her guilt ate at her enough to make her remain in their sham of a marriage. She also wanted her children to have their father in their lives. *But at what cost?*

"Somewhere safe," Michael returned. He had folded his arms and refused to offer any more information on the matter. Unsure and full of fear, Gina's resolve weakened, and she'd given in.

Her orders had been to go to New York and arrange a meeting with Keith. But Gina had not been able to resist going to see him preach. Keith agreed to return to Georgia with her, and Gina was glad her mission had been successful.

Her hands shook now as she unlocked the front door. The smell of popcorn assailed her as she entered the house, but she couldn't hold on to the smile that crossed her lips. Trey loved popcorn.

Marisol Meares, the nanny, was sitting on the living room rug with Trey.

"Mommy," Trey squealed and ran into his mother's arms.

Gina felt tears come to her eyes at the sight of her son. She kissed his head and face and squeezed him over and over again. "I missed you."

"I missed you too," Trey replied, wiggling free from her onslaught and returning to the action figures he'd been playing with. She noted that he wasn't wearing his typical play clothes. He was dressed in a little navy suit.

"Trey, baby, why are you all dressed up?"

"I'm going to be on TV!" he exclaimed.

Gina looked askance at Marisol. Her facial expression showed her confusion.

"Mr. Ward told me to get the children dressed because there is an important press event at your home this evening."

Gina held her tongue. She had no clue what was going on. Michael neglected to tell her anything, and she knew he had done it on purpose. She felt her heart begin to pound. Michael was up to something. Gina had a feeling that after tonight, her life was not going to be the same. "Where's Epiphany Joy?"

"She just woke up from her nap. I finished styling her hair and getting her dressed. She ran to get her bunny," Marisol answered with a little smile.

Gina heard the patter of little heels clinking on the tile and began to smile. She bent down and opened her arms. *Thank God.* Her babies. She hadn't known if she would ever see them again. "There's Mommy's girl."

Epiphany squealed and clapped her hands. Her curls bounced from her enthusiasm. "Mommy's home."

"Yes, baby," she affirmed. "I'm never leaving you again."

Chapter Twenty-eight

You're a man of God. You can't punch your brother in the face, especially since it would end up on national television. Keith told himself that over and over. It wasn't working.

He ached to knock that stupid look off his brother's face.

Keith shifted in his chair in the great room. He fiddled with his tie. He was nervous, and it showed. He'd already wiped his brow several times. He looked over at Michael, who gloated as he prepared to make his television debut.

He would have left without a care if it hadn't been for the fact that Michael had threatened him. Gina was on her way. Keith knew he would not leave her to face this farce on her own. He was powerless to stop Michael from putting on this spectacle for the nation to see, but he could at least attempt to shield Gina from whatever Michael had up his sleeve.

Before he knew it, the cameras were rolling. Keith willed himself to relax and answer the questions. The reporter, a woman named Lauren Goodman, whom Keith had seen many times before, was unreadable, but she did seem to enjoy Michael's charm.

The young reporter was eating up every moment as she did the rudimentary introductions for the viewers. She basked in Michael's attention. Keith gritted his teeth and hoped it all would end before Gina returned home. He kept his eyes peeled on the door.

In a flash, the interview shifted. Keith watched the woman before him transform into a barracuda. It was obvious Michael had prepped her with a lot of private information. Lauren had started off with basic questions about their youth. Michael recounted stories, some of which even made Keith laugh. Then, after a couple commercial breaks, Lauren zeroed in for the kill. She showed a clip of one of Keith's sermons. It was his message on Paul's conversion.

As soon as the clip ended, Lauren attacked.

"Pastor Ward, I'm having difficulty equating the man I see on the screen with the man sitting here before me."

Keith forced a smile on his face. "What do you mean?"

"I did some investigating, and I heard raving reports about your integrity and your devotion to God. Not even one breath of scandal was linked with your name."

Keith was getting an idea of where this was going, and gave his brother a pointed look. The smirk on Michael's face told Keith all he needed to know. Yet he labored on and remained cool. "Lauren, I think I know where you are going with this, and I refuse to make any further comment."

Lauren looked right into the camera and bluntly taunted him, saying, "Listeners, I imagine the good pastor has something to hide."

"Keith . . . " Michael interjected, in a tone that was laced with contrived sincerity.

Keith saw the crocodile tears fill his brother's eyes and had to prevent himself from rolling his eyes. Keith watched the cameraman zoom in on Michael's face.

Michael patted Keith's arm in a gesture meant to show his support and assurance. "It's okay to talk about it. I've forgiven you, and that's what matters."

Keith pursed his lips in anger. He took a moment to drink from the glass of water on the side table while he gathered his thoughts. He couldn't believe Michael was going to go through with this spectacle. What was his purpose? What did he seek to gain? Keith knew he couldn't have more than a moment's silence on the air, so he spoke. "Don't do this, Michael. Think of Gina." Keith watched the emotions cross his brother's face. He could see Michael begin to second-guess himself and start to waver. Maybe he'd gotten through to him.

Lauren perked up and called for a quick commercial break. As soon as they were off the air, she worked on reminding Michael about the favor she'd done for him in arranging this interview. "Mr. Ward, I've moved mountains to get you this time slot. Don't back down now."

"I know you think you have something here," Keith said, addressing her and not giving Michael a chance to answer. "You're after a story you think will make your career. This isn't about anything else."

Lauren touched Michael on the arm. "I'm after the truth."

"Michael, please let's end this right now," Keith said, pleading with his brother to back off. But he could tell from his brother's posture that Lauren had won the battle. Keith could only stand by and watch the events play out.

As soon as they returned from the break, Michael started talking. He talked about Keith and Gina's betrayal. He spoke about Trey's illness and finding out he wasn't Trey's biological father. He told of his decision to forgive his brother once he found out Keith was the actual father.

Keith remained silent as the interview went on. He felt relieved that only five minutes remained on the clock. He could not wait for it all to be over. He was going to give Michael the beat down of his life. Keith thanked God that Gina had missed this.

He thanked God a little too soon. From the corner of his eye, Keith saw Gina enter the room. Her mouth was agape as she listened to Michael's words.

"It took everything in my power to forgive Gina and Keith after what they had done to me, but I did it. Even after finding out I was infertile and the child she had carried wasn't mine, I loved her enough to forgive her."

Keith heard a huge intake of breath. Gina's gasp filled the room. Her shocked eyes met Keith's, and she gripped Trey's hand.

Keith lifted one of his hands to signal to her to remain calm, but Gina looked like she was about to have a coronary. Her eyes mirrored her shock at the truth. He could see the disbelief and the anger building.

"Why didn't you tell me?" she screamed. "How could you . . ." She closed her lips tight, tapping her heels. While he read her facial expressions, the cameras recorded every visible reaction for the nation to see.

"But that's not the only reason why you called the interview today," Lauren said, prodding Michael.

Keith watched the reporter's body arch with anticipation, as if there were more. A part of him wanted to snatch her out of the chair and shake her, but Keith knew that wasn't an option. He couldn't understand how someone could get an obvious high off of someone else's misery.

But he knew people like her. Lauren Goodman wasn't thinking about pain; she could only see dollar signs and her big break.

Keith couldn't imagine anything else Michael had to say that could trump that last revelation. However, it was evident Michael was far from finished. Keith saw him lick his lips before giving someone a signal.

"Yes, I think it's time to mend the fences, because I haven't spoken to my brother in three years. But in order to do that, because he's a public figure, I felt it was important that the truth be revealed to the nation." Michael looked Keith square in the eyes. "All was forgiven until I had what I now refer to as an epiphany."

Michael's words were cryptic. Keith and the other occupants in the room looked quizzical, that is, except for one person, who reacted with surprising vehemence.

Hearing Michael's last statement, Gina sprang into action. She rushed over to her husband from behind the scenes, where she'd hidden herself from view. "No!" Her plea resonated through every television screen across the nation.

Enthralled viewers would pause and replay that emotional moment over and over again. They would witness the raw emotions and distress on Gina's face. But right now, Keith reacted, not caring about anything but Gina. He reached over to grab hold of her hand.

Michael plodded on, as if his wife hadn't begged him on national television not to continue. With stubborn resolve, Michael crooked his finger, signaling for someone to come toward him. Keith watched Trey's timid gait as he came forward. Tears rolled down Keith's face as he beheld his son, whom he had not seen in three years. He looked adorable and so brave in his suit.

He saw a little girl run forward. *What a cutie,* he thought. He kept his eyes glued to her. She ran over to Gina and disappeared in the folds of her dress. She must have hidden herself earlier. He tilted his head and studied the little girl, trying to figure out who she was. She looked so familiar, yet he knew with certainty that he'd never seen her before. Keith now forgot about the cameras. He looked over at Gina.

"Gina?" he said.

But Gina was speechless. Her eyes were wide with fear. She stammered, "I . . . I . . ."

"Keith," Michael said, chirping up like the cat that had caught the proverbial canary, "Let me introduce little Epiphany Joy. My wife's second child and your daughter."

Chapter Twenty-nine

A shocked silence spread around the entire room before pandemonium broke out.

Gina used those moments of confusion to snatch her children and leave the house. She didn't know how she managed to escape the throng of reporters who were encamped outside her house. She drove a few miles before pulling over to the curb. She took a moment to breathe and to think. She could not go to her usual spots. Where could she go? In an instant, Gina knew. Her decision made, she put her car in gear and took off.

Keith ached to go after Gina. But he decided he wouldn't leave the interview, because the viewers might think he left disgraced. He didn't want his actions to turn them against God. God had delivered him, had given him a new life, and he was going to stand on His promise. What he'd done was shameful, but he had to face his past and try to salvage his future.

Thoughts of his daughter swirled around and around in his head. He closed his eyes and tried to picture the little girl, who had already captured his heart. He was surprised to discover how fast his heart could expand.

He felt the air in the room chill and saw Lauren squirm with discomfort. The crew had paused in midair to take a commercial break. Their orders had come directly from the network. Keith applauded that move.

Lauren's cell phone vibrated just then. She rushed to answer it. He could hear her boss hollering through the phone about potential lawsuits and slander. "Do you have proof to back up your story?" he heard her boss yell.

His own phone was ringing, but Keith sent the call to voice mail. He angled his ear to hear Lauren's response.

"I don't have any physical proof, but I believe Michael Ward. He has no reason to lie to me, and nothing to gain. Why would he make something like this up?" she persisted in a shaky voice. When she licked her lips, Keith knew she was worried.

The voice on the line screamed, "You had better be right about this, Lauren, or this will be your butt!"

The cell phone on the other end clicked off, and she jumped. When she walked over to them, Keith could see that her hands were shaking. Her cockiness had been replaced with distinct humility. She gave Keith a pointed look. "I didn't realize you have so many friends in high places—both literally and metaphysically."

When the cameras started rolling again, Lauren switched gears and threw Keith's brother under the bus. "Michael, you've made serious allegations here on live national television," she began. He could see Michael shift in his chair from apprehension when she asked, "Where is your proof?"

Michael hedged for the first time that evening. Keith knew she'd sprung that on him, deviating from the script. Lauren was now about saving her hide. "'I'm not able to have children." He had the good grace to look embarrassed. "My doctor can back that up."

"Okay, but I have to cover all my bases. Michael, what proof do you have to show that Pastor Ward is the father of your children?"

Michael didn't answer her question.

Keith found perverse pleasure in watching his brother face the heat. He was of a mind to let Michael stew in the hot seat, but that wasn't how God operated. Keith knew that God had been urging him to face the truth, but never did he imagine that he would have to do it in front of millions and on a bevy of Internet websites. Keith shuddered at the thought.

Lauren turned away from Michael to face Keith with a sharp gaze. "Pastor Ward, you're a man of God, and your viewers trust you to be open and honest with them. What do you have to say?"

Before he responded, Keith uttered a silent prayer. He needed God to give him the right words to say right now. Keith did not have any time to prepare a statement. This was live television. Keith knew that he would have to speak from the heart. A sudden commercial break gave him a small respite, and he chose that moment to pray. Keith asked God to give him the right words. He looked over at Michael, who appeared to be having second thoughts about his rash actions. But any regret disappeared once Michael realized Keith was focused on him.

"I only spoke the truth," Michael uttered defensively. Keith saw him look over at Lauren, who had left her seat and was once again on the telephone. Keith read his body language and facial expression. Something was going on with those two.

Keith's cell phone buzzed. He had set it to vibrate. Keith saw that Natalie was calling—probably to proffer a plan for damage control or to advise him to get an attorney. Keith sent the call to voice mail and turned his phone off. He was going to rely on the best Advocate of all, his Savior, Jesus Christ.

Keith smirked with derision. "Wow, Michael. She's classy." Sarcasm and disgust dripped from his tone. He had figured out that Michael and Lauren were more than what they appeared. He discerned that they were lovers.

Hearing the censure in Keith's voice seemed to only strengthen Michael's resolve. He taunted, "I don't care what you think. I'm past the point of caring about your opinion. It doesn't matter to me at all. As a matter of fact, from my perspective, the interview was a resounding hit." His disingenuous tone angered Keith, but he knew how to handle his brother.

"No weapon that is formed against me shall prosper. And every word that rises against me shall be condemned." Keith paraphrased Isaiah 54:17 with passion.

Michael was unfazed by the Word of God, which broke Keith's heart even more. How had he let himself stay away for so long? The people he loved were unsaved. If they died today, they wouldn't enter paradise. He was the one who was supposed to lead them, and he had failed them all, even his children.

"Keep your scriptures for yourself. You're the one who needs them," Michael muttered. Then his emotions took over. "Mr. Holier-Than-Thou, right now your career as a preacher is in the toilet. You are nothing but a hypocrite."

Keith hunched his shoulders as the full impact of Michael's words hit his core. He felt like Michael had read his mind. He did feel like a hypocrite. It hurt to hear his brother say the words, because his brother's venom reminded him of his failure.

Lauren ran over to her seat, as they were going back on the air. Keith could tell she was disturbed by the tension between the brothers. He watched as she gave Michael a quizzical look. He only shrugged. Keith, of course, wasn't about to volunteer any information.

As soon as she received her cue, Lauren said, "We are live on the air with Pastor Ward and his brother, entrepreneur Michael Ward." Turning to Keith, Lauren stated, "Pastor Ward, you were about to address all of our listeners."

Keith squared his shoulders and looked directly in the camera.

Chapter Thirty

As soon as the interview ended, Keith shot out of the chair. He had only one destination in mind. He grabbed the keys to Michael's car and rushed out the back door. It took some maneuvering, but he was able to leave Michael's house and head over to the other house without anyone on his trail. Keith was banking on the fact that Gina had taken refuge there.

Once he got to the house, Keith reached for the spare key that was still hidden in the hanging potted plant by the front door. Letting himself in, Keith walked through Michael and Gina's former home. It was as he remembered. But he was out of luck. Gina and the children were nowhere to be found.

Keith walked into the living room. He had a vivid recollection of Trey watching television and dancing to the beat of a popular kid tune. There were toys strewn all over the floor, evidence that his children had been playing here before they were summoned to the dreaded interview.

He sat on the floor and picked up the toys. He held them to forge a connection with his children.

His children. "I have two children."

He couldn't wrap his mind around that fact. He had not one, but two children with Gina. Keith tinkered with the Elmo toy and pressed the button to make it giggle. A sudden overwhelming feeling of sorrow for the opportunities he had missed engulfed him. Keith bent his head and cupped his face with his hands. Grief engulfed him, and his chest heaved from the impact of unshed tears. Then he wept for the time he had lost with his children, which he could never regain. Pain pierced his heart as he conjured up a mental image of the two little people he had helped create.

"They have no idea who I am," Keith cried. His voice boomed in the empty space. Sucker punched by emotion, he wailed, "My children. Trey. My daughter." Keith looked upward. "Lord, I made a big mistake. A big mistake. How can I fix this? I should've claimed my son. I shouldn't have left Trey with Michael." Keith sank backward until he was laid out on the floor. He acknowledged with sorrowful regret that he'd made a grave error by leaving Trey. "I should've told the truth." He fisted both hands and emitted a guttural cry. Keith rolled to his side and bent his legs. His suit was crushed, but he didn't care. "I thought it was for the best." He gulped. "But I was so, so wrong."

He'd taken the coward's way out. He hadn't wanted to face the truth then, which would've set him free. He would've been with Gina and his children all these years. Together.

Keith thought of the interview. The truth had been exposed for millions to see, and Gina was furious and hurt.

He'd just texted his mom his location when his cell phone rang. Of all people, it was Terence. He pushed the ANSWER button.

"Hi, Keith. Colleen and I wanted to check on you to encourage you and offer our support."

"Thanks. Is Gina with you guys? I've been trying to reach her, but she's nowhere to be found." He prayed to hear the word *yes*.

"No, and Colleen is mad with worry. Did you know about Epiphany?"

Keith sighed but hid his disappointment. "I had no idea, or I wouldn't have done the interview. Michael threatened me, saying that if I didn't do it, Gina would pay. I think he must've compelled her not to tell anyone."

"Yes. Colleen was shocked and hurt. I can't believe Michael exposed your dirty laundry on national television."

"I don't understand the vindictiveness of waiting years to carry out a plan of this magnitude. Michael bode his time, then lured me back here under false pretenses. I thought this was about mending fences. Instead my life is now ripped apart."

"Let me put you on speaker," Terence said. "Colleen wants to talk to you."

Keith's stomach twisted. He imagined Colleen was going to rip him apart for his deception. He heard the faint static before she came on the line.

"Keith, I know how you love Gina. I wanted to share with you that though things look dark, God will see you through this. One good thing is that the entire truth is out and now you can find peace—no matter the outcome."

In spite of everything, Keith had to let out a word of praise. Her words were confirmation of what God had been telling him. He voiced his deepest concern. "I can't even imagine Gina forgiving me for not telling her I was Trey's father. I tried years ago, but I should've insisted. I don't think she's going to be lenient or forgiving when it comes to her children."

Colleen didn't try to sugarcoat things. "Gina loves you, but she'll be overprotective of her children. In time, I think she'll forgive you, but what's more important is that God has already forgiven you. He's got you. Just trust Him."

The couple prayed with him, and Keith rejoiced in God for sending comfort his way. He placed a call to Gina again, but it was to no avail. She had turned her phone off and retreated to parts unknown.

With no recourse, Keith entered into a season of prayer. He needed God's forgiveness and guidance. It was comforting to know God would never reject him. Keith poured his heart out until he had nothing left to say. He even prayed for his brother and asked God to help him forgive Michael.

Keith accepted blame for the whole ordeal but then gave the entire burden over to God. He knew he was going to have to face the world, but Keith would rebuke any worry or fear. He was protected in the hands of Jesus and felt secure with that knowledge.

When he finished praying, he felt peace and contentment wash over his being. He knew that no matter what, God was going to take care of him. Now that the truth was out, Keith would rely on God to turn his wrong into something good and make it right.

He knew God had the power to overturn his mistakes and disappointments and transform them into blessings.

An hour later Keith sprang to his knees at the sound of the doorbell. He stretched to his full height and rushed to the front door. He looked through the peephole to see his mother standing outside. He undid the locks to let her enter. Gerry stormed in and grabbed him in a tight hug.

"Oh, son, I'm sorry. I didn't know about Epiphany. When Michael called me to tell me to tune in, I was hoping for a reunion. I told my friends and the neighbors, but now I wish I'd kept my mouth closed." She wrung her hands and stormed into the living room. "I dropped my bowl of mint chocolate chip ice cream. Glass is still all over the floor, but I had to get here."

"Me too. I thought this was about bygones being bygones and moving forward. Instead, I'm Internet fodder and a YouTube sensation."

Keith saw Gerry slouch. "I have another grandchild." She held her heart and looked at him with tearful eyes.

"How could Michael have kept a child from me—from you? I'm shocked and appalled at his cruelty." Gerry's shoulders shook. Keith moved to hold her. She said, "Three years . . . three long years."

Gerry's crying tore at him. "That explains why he moved them to England. That's how his scheme worked."

She pulled herself out of his arms. "What hurts is he was gloating on national television. He looked pleased with himself. That's what I don't get. Where did I go wrong?"

"It's not him," Keith said, surprising them both. He realized the truth behind his words. "His actions are the result of the buildup of all the pain, hurt, anger, and jealousy I caused. Michael has allowed his anger to consume him, so he's become vindictive."

"That's no excuse. I fear for him," Gerry confessed. "All this malice is going to eat away at him. I don't know what is going to happen once the dust settles and the repercussions of his actions hit home."

"I'll be praying for him. I did him wrong. Now, I didn't feel this way earlier, because then I wanted to strangle him for all this mischief and manipulation. But there is power in prayer. Only God can heal him and mend his ways."

"I love you, son," Gerry stated. "I'm proud of you."

Feeling a moment of self-pity, Keith snorted. "You may be the only person who feels that way now. After the interview, I'm going to be labeled a hypocrite."

"You're not a hypocrite, Keith! You're human!" Her tone changed. "I did tell you to stay away from her. 'Move on,' I begged." She shrugged. "But I guess that's water under the bridge now, eh?"

Keith broke into a sob as the weight of his actions pressed down on his shoulders. He thought he'd cried enough, but his emotions were still raw. "You're right. I didn't listen, and I've made a mess of things, Mom."

"Yes, you have. But that is what it means to be human. From a child, you were always so perfect, and I admit, it was intimidating!" Gerry confessed with a slight chuckle.

Keith lifted his eyebrows in shock from his mother's revelation.

"I used to watch your brother strive to be like you, but no matter what he did, you did it better. Whatever you put your hand to; it was like the Midas touch. Football, swimming, basketball, law were so effortless for you. You succeeded at everything you did without even trying. I see now that it was because you were highly favored. Keith, it was all a part of God's divine plan for your life."

Keith crooked his head. "I've never seen it that way before."

"I have never seen anything so clearly in my life," Gerry observed. "Gina was a necessary part of your life. She was the one area of your life that wasn't pleasant. Your betrayal is what precipitated your walk with the Lord. He used your sorrow and pain to reach you. If it hadn't been for that experience, you might never have seen the need for the Lord. You wouldn't have reached the thousands of souls who tune in to hear your message."

"God is amazing," Keith responded. "He used something so despicable to bring about good. It's like when Samson killed that lion and its guts became a nest for bees to make honey."

Gerry laughed. "You live, breathe, and talk the Lord, Keith. Every step you take is about Him. You're not a hypocrite."

Keith smiled at his mother's insight. He felt rejuvenated. "When did you become such a believer?"

"Since I started listening to my son preach the Word on television."

Keith opened his mouth as the implications of her words sank in. "Mom, what are you saying?"

"I accepted the Lord as my Savior two weeks ago," Gerry admitted.

Keith whooped and grabbed hold of his mother. "Why didn't you tell me before?"

"I don't know," Gerry said with a blush and splayed her hands. "Maybe God had me save the news for this moment, when He knew you'd need to hear good news."

Keith couldn't help but smile. "How did I luck out with you for a mother?"

"It wasn't luck, son. It was God."

Chapter Thirty-one

"Oh, Michael," Lauren purred, replete with passion. She twisted her body and snuggled under the covers. Michael prided himself on being a tender, considerate lover, but tonight he had been like an animal. If he were honest, it was because he was trying to exorcise the guilt he was feeling.

He hadn't been as unaffected as his mannerisms bespoke. He was hurting. He was angry, and he thought he had every right to do what he did. Michael knew his vengeful nature had alienated everyone he treasured. He had irrevocably damaged his relationship with Gina. His mother was also going to be hurt and disappointed in him. Michael had even felt pain at the sight of his brother's discomfort.

When he sat there and listened to Keith's impassioned address to the viewers, Michael admitted to himself that he'd been moved. His brother was a gifted speaker. His sincerity and grief were apparent.

Michael felt a strong pull to help his brother, but he resisted the urge. He'd gone too far to turn back and admit his error. He jutted his chin. Keith was paying for everything. Even now, Michael knew he was using Lauren only as a means for overcoming his grief and guilt. He had to admit he welcomed the ball of anger churning inside him. It gave him a sense of freedom to do whatever he wanted. He relished not feeling anything and not caring what anyone else thought.

He felt like a king and enjoyed watching Gina rush to do his bidding. Yes, there were times when he battled with his conscience, but selfishness won out every time. He had to look out for himself, even if it meant he would end up alone.

Trey's trusting face came before him, ruining his enjoyment. Michael felt a sharp pain pierce his heart at the thought of hurting a seven-year-old. He loved his son and wanted to protect and nurture him. But his need for revenge won out. Every time he second-guessed himself, Michael had only to think about Epiphany—the product of yet another betrayal—and his heart would harden.

Try as he might, Michael couldn't love her as a father should. Epiphany was like another slap in the face to him. Michael just couldn't drum up any tender feelings for the little girl, who looked so much like Gina that it hurt.

She'd been another blatant reminder of his infertility and his failure as a man. Epiphany had been the result of Keith once again being the better brother.

He welcomed the resentment, for it fueled his vengeance. Gina hadn't favored the name Epiphany, but he'd insisted on it. Epiphany aptly suited the situation. Gina had given in, but she had also included Joy in the child's name, which further rankled, for his Epiphany was her Joy.

"You're ignoring me." Lauren pouted.

Playfully, Michael slapped her exposed leg. "You're one woman who is hard to ignore, Lauren. You're smart, beautiful, and a pleasure."

Michael watched his words take effect as Lauren basked under his knowing gaze. He reached over to caress her, willing himself to feel more than what he was feeling. It was like the anger had wrapped around his heart and devoured every other emotion. It left him feeling dry and dissatisfied. But he was powerless to extricate himself from the pit he'd dug, and then jumped into, with both arms held high.

Spotting a used rubber on the sheets, he reached to dispose of it, but Lauren swatted his hand. "Let me," she offered. "I think there's another on the floor. I'll toss them both."

Michael nodded his assent and went to shower.

It will take time, Michael reasoned. This wad of pain that had desensitized him and turned his heart cold would recede with time. He was now free to be the man he was before, and he'd reaped the fruits of his hard labor.

He'd planned and schemed, and his efforts had paid off.

His endeavor was, for all intents and purposes, a resounding success.

Then why did he feel so empty inside, and why was he alone? To those questions, Michael had no answers.

Chapter Thirty-two

He'd stick to the plan.

Natalie pretended to wait for him in the back of the building. She told him she'd "leaked" information regarding his arrival. Her manipulations were a success, because photographers had swarmed the rear of the complex. They were waiting with cameras in their arms, eager to capture the winning shot of the man who had created millions of hits on the Internet.

Keith peeked out the window and saw the reporters waiting to peck at him like hens. He saw the car service limo pull up and the camera flashbulbs go off. He urged his driver to pull up to the front of the building.

With a brisk pace, Keith entered the building, knowing he had mere seconds before the group of photographers recognized his decoy. He made it inside before the flash of a lens was mirrored on the glass door. He maintained his composure and kept his face straight. He was not trying to help anyone make thousands of dollars off his distress.

Like he had many times before, Keith looked at his iPhone, checking to see if Gina had called, texted, or something. His screen was blank. With a sigh of resignation, Keith put his phone in his pocket.

He'd been trying, without avail, to find Gina. It had been four long weeks since that horrible interview, and still there had been no word from her. Keith had called Colleen several times, but Colleen had not been in contact with Gina, either. She too had left countless messages, all of which had been unanswered.

He rubbed his head. He didn't know what to think. It was not like her to be out of contact with her friend for so long. But he had to trust God that Gina and his children were safe in God's hands.

Keith entered the elevator and whispered thanks to the Lord that he was alone in the elevator car. He rode up to the top floor to get to his meeting with Ned Winthrop. He could feel his heart hammering in his chest. Ned Winthrop was the head of the broadcast station. There could only be one reason why he'd been summoned now. It was D-day.

Today was the beginning of the end of his televangelist career. Keith was surprised it had taken the bigwigs this long to call him in for a perfunctory dismissal. He knew his shows had been yanked off the air following his scandalous interview. It all seemed surreal to him, but Keith knew this was no nightmare. It was real, and it was his life.

Keith didn't realize how much he had valued the television show until this moment. He knew there were souls out there whom he'd been able to lead to the Lord. Keith could only offer up continuous prayers for them. He hoped his folly hadn't been a stumbling block to those converts.

That thought had accounted for some sleepless, guilt-racked nights.

Keith walked out of the elevator with a confidence that belied his nervousness and headed toward the main conference room. He ignored the curious stares from the various staff on duty.

He was not afraid of their faces, but he did not want his old self rearing its head, because of any possible negativity. He gave a brief knock, signaling his arrival, and opened the door. All the chief executives were present.

Keith was not concerned about any of the individuals in the room save for Ned Winthrop. Ned was a keen businessman, and over the years, he had become one of Keith's chief supporters and even a friend. Keith's gaze traveled to his.

At that moment, Ned's face was unreadable. Not even his days as an attorney could help Keith ascertain what the older gentleman was feeling. He felt a sharp sense of shame. He didn't want this man's disapproval. He cared about what Ned thought of him as a person.

It is what God thinks that matters.

The thought washed over Keith and calmed his being. He needed not to fear losing a mere human's respect. What mattered was what God thought of him. He knew that God loved him, and he straightened his spine. He would not fear any repercussions from men. God had already washed and cleansed his sins. He had sinned only against God. He would not fear the wrath of men.

The minute felt interminable as Keith sat while Ned scrutinized him. He knew it was impossible, but Keith felt as if the other gentleman was looking deep into his soul.

Keith resisted the unnatural urge to fidget.

Then Ned dismissed all the other occupants of the room.

Keith watched in silence as all the executives and producers departed the room. They were dying of curiosity, but no one dared question Ned Winthrop. When Ned Winthrop requested something, you moved to see that it was done.

Keith repressed the urge to smile at their speedy departure. He was also grateful for the one-sided glass, which allowed him to see them outside in the hallway but did not permit them to see what transpired inside the conference room. Ned had paid a fortune to have the room designed that way.

Once the door closed behind the last executive to leave the room, Ned shot to his feet and wandered over to the window to look out at the skyline. Keith watched him put his hand on his chin, in deep thought.

Anxious, Keith marched over to stand beside the man. He hoped that invading his space would give him a hint that he should get to talking. Keith also took in the view.

Ned chuckled at Keith's obvious impatience. He imagined he would be pulling his hair out if the situation were reversed.

"Do you still love her?" Ned asked.

"Huh?" Keith was unprepared for that question.

"Gina Ward," Ned said.

Keith creased his brow in confusion. "I fail to see what importance . . ." His speech faded away when Ned turned to face him. "Yes. I love her. She's the only woman for me."

"Hmm . . ." Ned nodded.

That's it? Keith wondered, perplexed. When Ned remained silent, Keith decided to take matters into his own hands. "I see that this is difficult, so I want to take the time to thank you for the opportunity. I also want to apologize for letting you down."

His quiet sentiments captured Ned's full attention.

"Keith, sit down."

Keith complied, but he was losing patience. He wished Ned would get on with it.

Ned looked him square in the face. "There has been an overwhelming response to your on-air debacle."

Keith nodded. He had expected the fallout to be tremendous.

"The station has been bombarded with e-mails, phone calls, and thousands of pieces of snail mail. We have a small cubicle that is overflowing with letters from your viewers. Your name has gotten more hits and blogs than even the biggest scandals of the past decades."

Keith raised his eyebrows in surprise. He had expected an outpouring, but nothing close to that magnitude. He opened his mouth to utter yet another apology, but Ned suppressed any comment.

"I think it's brilliant."

"Wh-what?"

Ned gave a little laugh. "You heard me right, Keith. It goes without saying that your future shows will be canceled."

Keith's shoulders hunched with disenchantment. He felt like he was on an emotional roller coaster. He could've uttered words in his defense, but he remained silent. The Spirit held his tongue.

"But I've got something else in mind," Ned continued. "I took the liberty of reading a few of the letters. There was hate mail, but the majority of the letters were from those people who did not know salvation was possible to them. They were sharing their life stories and asking if God still loved them."

Keith lifted his eyebrows but said nothing.

"That's when a new idea began to form." Ned clapped his hands. He jumped with excitement and came to sit next to Keith. Still jubilant, Ned reached over and pounded him on the back in commiseration.

Keith shook his head, still not understanding. He was missing a clue or something, because he wasn't following. Or Ned was nutty, and he hadn't known it or seen the signs. Because how could he be so delighted with this mess?

"Six months," Ned stated. He glanced at his watch and jumped to his feet. "I have to head down to address the press. Keith, this is great news."

"Spell it out for me, Ned, because I think I am missing something," Keith said.

"*Second Chances*," Ned offered. "I'm launching *Second Chances with Pastor Keith Ward* in six months. This episode will soon be a distant memory. People love you. They like looking at you. They want to hear from you."

"You're offering me another show?" Keith's mouth hung open in amazement.

He saw Ned's nod.

Keith repeated the question verbatim. He wanted to make sure he had heard right. "You're offering me another show?" He was filled with total disbelief. This could not be happening. He should have been fired, but instead he was being offered another more lucrative position. How did that happen?

God.

Keith uttered a silent "Hallelujah."

"Well, of course," Ned said on his way out the glass doors. "You'll have a prime viewer slot, and the salary package is generous." The older man pointed to a manila folder resting on the table.

Keith took the hint and walked over and opened it. It was a contract. There was also a letter.

"I swiped one of the letters, which I think you should read." With that, he was out the door to meet the press.

Keith stood still for a few seconds before whooping for joy. "Thank you, Lord. Thank you, God."

Only God could have done this. It was a divine miracle. God had turned his mess into a message. Keith perused the show proposal and the contract. His hands shook with amazement at God's awesome power. He knew this was the hand of God at work.

The letter was the last thing that he read. It was typewritten on parchment paper.

Dear Pastor Ward,

I have never considered myself religious, but I'm wealthy and well respected. When I was only twenty years old, I fell deeply in love with my step-mother. She was only a few years older than me. We had an affair of the heart, until my father found out. It goes without saying that he was furious. Especially when he discovered that Penelope was pregnant with a child. My son.

(Yes, I have a child, Victor, whom no one knows about and who is also successful in his own right. He is the kind of son anyone would be glad to claim.)

Needless to say, my father kicked me out of the house and told me he never wanted to see me again. I worked and studied hard until I made it. I am now at the top of my game. Once I became a success, I returned home, thinking I had finally earned my father's forgiveness. He refused to see me. Not even when he was ill did he change his mind. Even though I paid for the best medical care, he still could not forgive me. Then he died.

He died ten years ago without us ever reconcil-ing. It is an untenable pain. It is unbearable and heart wrenching. After his death, Penelope came to me. I rejected her. I was too filled with past guilt to even think I deserved to be with her. Then I saw that interview. I realized that God loved you no matter what you had done. I realized that if He could forgive you, then maybe God could forgive me.

Right at home, I prayed and I cried. I released all the past pain and hurt in my life. I have been supporting my son financially and had never felt worthy to be a part of his life. This is all about to change. I have reconciled with Penelope, and I now

have a son to call my own. God has given me a
second chance with the love of my life.

We are going to be married in two months, and
I would like you to perform the ceremony. It would
be a sincere honor if you could attend.

Your friend,
Ned Winthrop

Keith's eyes popped open when he deciphered the scrawled signature.

Ned had written the letter. Ned, his boss, had written that letter. No wonder he had never married. Keith had never wondered about Ned's married state. He had assumed that Ned was too busy to care about having a family.

Both he and Ned had more in common than he'd realized. They had both nursed broken hearts over a woman they could not have. No wonder they had bonded on a more personal level.

Ned, though, was not going to end his life this way. He was going to get his girl. Keith chuckled to himself with admiration. *Go, Ned.*

He reread the letter, filled with awe at how God was using his sinful life to bring Himself glory. *Go, God.* Keith folded the letter as if it were fine gold. Then he saw Ned's bold scrawl at the bottom.

P.S. Go get your woman and shred this when you
are done with it.

He saw the door open in slow motion. Keith shoved the letter in his pocket.

Natalie peered in. "Well?" She needed to know what was going on.

"See for yourself." Keith remained noncommittal and handed her the manila folder.

His assistant reached for the folder, saying, "I hope they at least gave you a sizable severance package."

Keith was touched by her loyalty but said nothing. He couldn't wait to see her face when the truth was revealed. He watched the anger leave Natalie's expressive face. She gave a yell of elation. She raced around the table to give him a tight hug. Her happiness was evident.

"You could've told me!" Natalie punched his arm, signifying that all was forgiven.

Keith laughed. He could see the wheels in her head already turning. The Hawk was back.

Natalie reached to fix his tie. "Mr. Winthrop sent me to get you. He wants you penitent for the press."

Keith was touched by her loyalty. "Natalie, you're a godsend. I mean that."

Her eyes glistened with tears, and she fudged a response. "Please, I know it. You will too when you see the raise you'll be giving me."

Keith laughed as she swept through the door. Before he left the conference room, he headed over to the shredder. He fed Ned's letter into the machine and waited until it became a distant memory.

With quiet determination, he walked out of the room and shut the door on his past, already anticipating his future.

Chapter Thirty-three

"Thanks, Frank."

Michael ended the call with his attorney. He was glad to hear that his package had reached its intended destination. Gina had received the divorce papers and the settlement agreement.

Michael knew where Gina had been staying for the past months. He'd given Frank the task of locating his wife when he realized that Gina hadn't sought refuge at Colleen's house. It had taken a couple weeks for him to find her. He didn't know where she'd been before that. Fortunately for him, Gina had opted to drive to her father's house. By nature, she was a private person and didn't let too many people get close, but Jeff was different. He was her father, and he had saved her son's life.

But while Michael knew that Gina and her father had gotten closer over the years, he hadn't considered that she would seek Jeff out for help. He was impressed with Gina's brilliance. His wife had chosen a good hideout from the press.

From experience, Michael knew it was only a matter of time before the bloodthirsty media hounds tracked her down. Nothing remained hidden for long in this age of broadband and wannabe private eyes. Someone would wag their tail. It was only a matter of time before a nosy neighbor spilled all for a couple of bucks or a "fifteen seconds of fame" stunt. Gina and Keith were hot news right now. Their life was better than reality TV.

The Internet was all a buzz about the romance. Millions wished that Keith and Gina would reunite, marry, and live in bliss forever. It was like a saga equivalent to Scarlett and Rhett's.

Michael realized he was pushing it with that analogy, but that was how he felt. And he had become the bad guy. He couldn't quite figure that out. He did have his share of empathetic, ticked-off husbands in his corner, but they were the deadbeats and dregs of society. To the middle and upper class, he was despicable for putting his children through the ringer on national television.

His brother was getting unbelievable press and sympathy. Michael attributed it to Keith's good looks and charm. People looked at that face and were willing to give him another chance. To the world it seemed he could do no wrong.

Gina had also generated a lot of Internet blogs and discussion. Women were curious to know the woman who had two brothers panting after her. The men wanted to know if she was ready to date again.

The whole lot of them disgusted Michael. It was like people didn't have anything better to do than get into other people's business. He chose to forget that it was his own actions that had precipitated this intrigue about their private lives.

But at least Keith had paid. Michael consoled himself with that little bit of news. He had relished watching the press conference where it was announced that Keith's show had been pulled off the air. It wasn't even in hiatus. It had been straight-out canceled.

Do not pass go. Do not collect two hundred dollars. Do get off the air.

Michael laughed at his dry wit, but his grin faded when his laughter sounded hollow in the empty house. He walked into his study and sat down in the imported leather swivel chair. It was a nut-brown color, which appealed to the senses. Michael ran his hand across the spotless desk. His housekeeper, Nancy, had done an impeccable job. Michael could see his face shining back at him, but he wasn't sure he liked what he saw.

A small droplet ran down the right corner of his eye and hit the desk. Michael used his hand to wipe the small bit of water. It left a smudge on the otherwise pristine shine.

Why was he crying?

Michael had no idea why more tears were threatening to come. He walked out of the study and inspected the house that he'd bought. He'd turned it into a showcase with amenities, which his friends admired with envy.

But it was empty.

Regret tasted like bitter bile in his mouth.

He walked up the long, winding staircase and turned right. Without knowing his intent, he ended up in Epiphany's room. From the canopy bed to the pink pillows and window treatments, Epiphany's bedroom was a princess's showroom.

Michael wandered over to a picture of Gina with Epiphany and Trey on the nightstand, which had caught his eye. He picked up the small frame and studied the faces smiling back at him. The significance of his absence in the family photo was not lost on him. After Epiphany, Michael had kept himself aloof from the family. He had refused to be involved in any of their family outings. Now the feeling in the pit of his stomach could only be attributed to deep, poignant regret.

Michael couldn't fathom why he felt this sharp pang. He didn't have paternal instincts toward Epiphany. He had severed any semblance of a father-son relationship with Trey. Though it had pained him, he kept Trey at arm's length.

Michael acknowledged that Epiphany was innocent and did not deserve his apathy. The child was endearing and beautiful. She had an angelic face and a sweet disposition. Everybody loved her. Everyone but him.

Michael stalked out of the room and closed the door. He rushed down the hallway to his own quarters. He found no comfort there, either. After he took in the large, empty bed, he did an about-face and stomped back into his study to down his agitation with a drink. He needed to drown this funk.

He heard the doorbell chime but made no move to get it. He was already on his second drink when Lauren appeared in his doorway.

"Mikey, I have been calling your cell phone."

Michael lifted an eyebrow but said nothing. He asked, "What're you doing here?"

Lauren gave her hips a suggestive wiggle. She was wearing a little teal dress that was meant to stimulate the senses. He looked at her with a speculative gleam in his eye.

Lauren pranced toward him with a breathy "I've missed you, and after your performance the other night, let's just say I'm back for more." She blushed.

"I can't promise you anything more than this," Michael confessed.

Lauren nodded her head with understanding. "Trust me, I have no expectations. I know what this is," she said, gesturing with her hands between them. "I'm a reporter. I know how to be aloof and straightforward."

Michael smiled. He would be hard-pressed to admit that he was hurting. He blinked to hide the pain he knew was in his eyes. Truth be told, he was glad Lauren had come. He didn't want to be alone.

With a groan, Michael snatched her into his arms and kissed her. He hadn't gotten out of his chair, so Lauren was bent over him at an odd angle, but she was not complaining. She seemed to welcome his manhandling. It was impersonal at times, but it was hot.

A moment later his hands squeezed her calves tightly. "That's going to bruise," she whispered. "But don't stop. I like it."

A discreet cough brought both participants to a screeching halt.

Familiar with the intruder, Michael bounced out of his chair. He turned away for a moment to adjust his nether regions and to gather his wits. Then he turned to face his mother. "How did you get in here?"

Gerry held up a key. "I know where you have your spare." He saw her upturned nose in Lauren's direction. "Well, this is an all new low for you."

Stung by the barb, Lauren felt her mouth pop open. Michael signaled to her to remain quiet. She regained her composure and plastered a wide smile on her face. With a confident sway, she sauntered over to Gerry and introduced herself.

"I know who you are," was his mother's frosty response.

Knowing his mother's temperament, Michael knew he had to intervene, or Lauren would be flattened. He rushed over to hug his mother and hoped he would be able to smooth things out. Gerry remained stiff under his embrace.

Michael stepped back. He looked over at Lauren, who was still standing there, stupefied by the stare down to which she had been subjected. The temperature had dropped several degrees.

"Lauren, I'm sorry, but I need to speak with my mother."

Lauren reached up and whispered in Michael's ear, "I'll be waiting upstairs. I have all night." In a brash move, she stuck her tongue in his ear.

Michael shivered from the feel of her wet tongue. It was downright erotic. He couldn't blame his mother for bristling at Lauren's audacity.

Lauren took her own sweet time to stroll out of the room and could not resist winking at Michael's mother. Her taunt did not go unrecognized.

As soon as she was out of earshot, Gerry said, "You've found yourself a barracuda. Somehow, this woman has sunk her claws into you, and she has no intention of letting go."

"Are you here to lecture me on my taste in women?"

His mother clenched her fists. "No, but I'm reminding myself that I'm now a saved woman, and saved people don't stomp on people and give them a beat down. I don't like the fact that you already have another woman in your house—and, from the look of things, your bed."

Michael arched an eyebrow. "Why are you here?"

His mother slapped him hard across the cheek.

Michael's mouth popped open. In stunned denial, he stormed, "What did you do that for? I thought you were saved. Saved people don't slap people across the face." He rubbed his cheek to ease the sting. He ran his tongue across his teeth and tried to inject humor into the situation. "I'm making sure my teeth are all intact. Thank goodness you didn't punch me. You would've drawn blood."

Gerry didn't laugh. "That was for keeping my grandchild from me. And if you want to talk about being saved, the Bible says something about turning the other cheek. I must comply with the Word." With the element of surprise on her side, she delivered a slap to his other cheek.

Chapter Thirty-four

Michael reeled from the impact. He looked at his mother, wondering if she had gone off the deep end. Michael retreated to the other side of the room.

"That was for what you did to your family," she said, rubbing her hand. She looked up toward heaven and whispered, "Sorry, Lord, but he had it coming."

Michael found his tongue. His defenses kicked in. "You dare talk to me about family! What about Keith and what he did to me and my family?"

"Leave Keith out of this for now," Gerry commanded. "This is all about you and your malicious behavior." Michael tried to interject something, but she put her hand up. "I'm not through yet. You went on national television without any regard for two children who adore you. Gina and Keith betrayed you, and it was awful, but what you did was contemptible."

He hung his head. His mother's words were like darts, and his heart was the bullseye. She had hit the mark. Tears rolled down his cheeks. "I know that you must hate me," Michael began, "but I wanted Keith and Gina to pay." With slow steps, he moved behind his desk and sat down. Deflated and filled with shame, he put his hands on his head and slumped in his chair.

"Congratulations. You've achieved your goal," Gerry retorted. She lowered her body into one of the chairs across from him. "Now, I have a question for you. Was it worth it?"

Michael shook his head in the negative. "I saw them."

Gerry looked quizzical.

Michael leaned back in his chair and closed his eyes. He clarified his statement. "I saw them that last night before Keith left Georgia." He stood on jerky feet and walked over to the minibar. Mindful of his mother's presence, Michael picked up two bottled waters. He handed one to her and opened the other. Then he took a seat in the chair next to her.

He went on. "Keith had stormed into our home, demanding that Gina make a choice. She chose me—and her family. Then, after that, her father was a match and Trey's transplant was a success."

Gerry moved her hand in a circular motion that signified that she didn't need the backstory. She wanted Michael to get to the crux of the matter. "I need to know what happened to transform you into this vindictive person I don't even recognize."

"If you recall, you and I were at the hospital that night," Michael stated.

Gerry nodded. "We'd heard the good news about Jeff being Trey's match."

"Well, I had done some deep soul-searching," Michael confessed. "I remember sitting there in Trey's room and watching him sleep. I figured it was time to let the past be the past and move on. I wanted to make things work with Gina."

Then his tone changed. His next words were difficult to express. "So I decided to leave Trey and go make amends with my brother. Life was too short, I told myself." His emotions were raw as he relived the moment. "I jumped into my car and drove over to his house. I had this speech planned about how we were brothers and should let bygones be bygones. Besides, it had been three years since he slept with Gina, and it had been just one time, as far as I knew." Tears rolled down his face. His body jerked with pain.

Gerry held her heart before she lifted her hand to stop him. "If this is too much for you, maybe—"

Michael stopped her. "No, Mom. I think this is the best thing. I need to get this off my chest." He had a half bath in his study and ran into it to get some tissues. *Great.* The tissue box was empty. Improvising, Michael unrolled a wad of toilet paper and blew his nose. He washed his hands before unrolling a generous amount of toilet paper for his mother. He had not missed her tears.

He returned to his chair after handing his mother the toilet paper and continued his story. "But when I neared Keith's home, Gina was already there. I saw them together in Keith's driveway. They were so enraptured with each other, that neither one of them saw me. I watched as my brother snatched my wife and kissed her."

"Oh, Michael," Gerry responded with sympathy.

"I felt my hands itch to . . . do something, but I counted to five. I told myself I would give Gina a chance to set Keith straight. You see, Mother, I thought that the feelings were all one-sided and that . . ." His voice broke, and he was unable to go on with that. He figured his mother could read between the lines.

Gerry put a fist in her mouth to keep from crying out. She understood his pain.

Michael started again. "I watched them go inside." He gulped. "Fool that I am, I sat there, expecting and hoping that Gina would come out the door. Hours passed, Mom. Hours before I got the hint that she was where she wanted to be."

"Oh, son." Gerry could take no more. Moved by compassion, she enfolded him in her arms.

"It was obvious that Gina loved Keith," Michael said after Gerry sat back down. "Why didn't she love me?

What did Keith have that I didn't?" His facial expression changed. He saw Gerry shiver from the coldness in his eyes. "I returned to the hospital, and it took all the strength I possessed to return home in the morning. I faced Gina, and she looked devastated. I thought it was guilt, but then you called and told me that Keith had left. No, Gina did not feel guilt. She felt heartbreak."

With nervous energy, Michael hoisted himself to his feet and walked away from his mother. His back was now turned to her, but he kept talking. "I was so angry. But I had a plan, so I made love to my wife and pretended that all was well. I think a part of me hoped that nothing had happened with Keith." He laughed in self-deprecation, then stated, "I almost lost my sanity when Gina came to me with the news that she was pregnant. She expected me to be overjoyed at the news. She said it was a new beginning. For her, it was joy, but it was my moment of epiphany. That's when I decided to make them both pay."

Gerry interjected, "Oh, Michael. You named your daughter Epiphany."

"Yes, Epiphany was the indisputable proof of Gina's infidelity. Because I knew she wasn't mine. And Gina stood there, smiling in my face, when she was a deceiver," Michael snarled. "She felt joy, while I resisted the urge to . . . to . . . ."

"Don't say it, Michael," Gerry pleaded. She covered her ears, not wanting to hear that yes, he had contemplated murder.

"Give me credit, Mom." Michael smiled. "I wouldn't physically hurt a woman."

"No," Gerry whispered. "But you could hurt her emotionally and destroy her reputation, Michael. That's what you did."

"Yes," Michael admitted without an ounce of regret for his actions.

"You feel you were justified, don't you?" Gerry quizzed.

"Yes," Michael confessed.

"That's where you went wrong, Michael. You took matters into your own hands. Now you are the one who has lost out on a beautiful wife and family."

"Yes." Michael answered.

"If it's any consolation, I don't think your brother or Gina set out to hurt you on purpose. They tried to fight it. I think it was something that was bigger than both of them. You can't help who you love, can you?"

"No," Michael concurred.

"But you can help who you hate," Gerry concluded.

Michael had no response.

Silence filled the room.

The silence was deafening.

Chapter Thirty-five

It had been three months since she'd last spoken to Colleen.

Gina sat in the formal living room and held a novel in her hand, but later she wouldn't be able to recall anything about what she'd been reading, because her mind was on her friend—one who had to be worried sick about her. She'd lit a scented candle, and the smell of Mia Bella's Chili Vanilli permeated the room. Putting her feet up, Gina fidgeted until she was in a more comfortable position on the plush white Italian leather chair.

Family pictures lined the walls, and even their AS FOR ME AND MY HOUSE, WE WILL SERVE THE LORD: THE ALTONS celebration plaque made their home inviting and welcoming. Her father and Regina had taken the children out to the park, so she'd grabbed the opportunity to have a heart-to-heart with her friend.

She put the novel down, picked up her cell phone, which sat on the table next to the leather chair, and dialed. Her fingers quivered, because she knew the person on the other end of the line would be upset, but it was time. "Hello, Colleen." she greeted.

"Gina, is that you? Girl, where have you been? I've been worried sick! I'm so glad you called, because I needed to hear your voice. So what happened?" Colleen said, her speech rushed. She then fired off more questions so fast, Gina didn't have a chance to respond.

She heard the relief and worry in her friend's voice and smiled. "I'm doing okay. I'm staying at my father's house here in Phoenix. Before that I was at Kelly Olson's home . . . Kendall's mother. You remember the baby I met at the hospital? Well, I stayed with them for a couple weeks. I racked my brain for a place I could go where no one would find me. So I called my dad to ask if I could come here with my children. My head and heart were all in a mess, and I needed some time," she explained, rambling.

Jeff and Regina had installed a play area in their backyard, complete with a sandbox. Trey and Epiphany had enjoyed many hours playing in the Arizona sun. Though it was October, they were experiencing temperatures in the low nineties. Watching them had given Gina countless hours of joy. More than anything, she was fortunate to have a family to call her own. For that, Gina could be grateful to Michael. He had arranged for her to meet her father, and since that meeting, she had developed a close relationship with her father. She would always treasure that. But before her father, there had always been Colleen. Colleen had been her constant, and Gina could hear the hurt underlying her concern.

"You knew I was here," Colleen pointed out. "I wanted to be there for you."

"I know," Gina said. "But, Colleen, I needed to get away, and I knew your house would be the first place anyone would look for me. That's why I drove to Kelly's. No one, not even Michael, would've thought to look for me there."

Colleen's sigh echoed through the line. "I understand. What matters is that you are okay."

Gina heaved her own sigh of relief. "Thanks. I need you."

"What's up, girl? You know I'm here for you," Colleen assured her. Then her emotions took over, and she began to praise God. "Thank you, Jesus. Thank you that my friend is safe." Gina listened while Colleen offered up some heartfelt praise. "I had to get that out of the way first," Colleen explained. "Terence took the girls over to his mother and the bishop for the weekend. So I can devote all my time to this conversation, without any interruptions."

Gina nodded, though Colleen couldn't see her. "I know you're wondering about Keith and how he could be the father of my child—make that *children*."

"Yes, and then some," she heard her friend say. "I wish I was there for the explanation, but I can't wait, so get to it, Gigi. How is Keith Trey's father? You slept with him months before you married Michael. I did the math, and that's not adding up."

Gina gulped. She closed her eyes and shook her head. There was so much she had to say. "A couple days before my wedding I invited Keith to my home. You remember when he announced he was going to move to Atlanta?"

"Yes, but—"

Gina interrupted, pacing the room. "He asked me to choose him, and then, when I told him I was marrying Michael, he marched to the door, intending to leave. It was so final. So . . . I don't know. My heart couldn't take it. I remember screaming to him not to go, and then the next thing I knew, we . . ." She needed air. She took the cordless phone with her and opened the front door to go outside. She whispered, "We slept together."

"Two days before your wedding!" Colleen's yell came through the line. Gina didn't have to see her face to know there was shock registered there. "Gigi, that's just scandalous. But why am I even surprised? I knew when I saw him kissing you like there was no tomorrow not even an hour before you were married. I knew I should've called a halt to it then and there!"

"But you know how stubborn I was," Gina said, remembering. "I thought I was doing the right thing."

"I know," Colleen replied, commiserating. "But marrying Michael was a big mistake. I can almost understand his fury—almost."

"I get that he's mad, but he had no right to involve our . . . I mean, my children." Gina didn't disguise the venom in her tone. Michael's manipulations and underhandedness had got under her skin. The fact that she'd put up with it for so long was something she couldn't understand.

"Speaking of which, how do you hide a child? Gina, that doesn't seem real to me. For you to keep something so monumental from me hurts. I love you as if were my sister, and I'd never do something like this to you."

Shame engulfed Gina as she acknowledged her participation in Michael's deception. She strove to explain. "I'm sorry, Colleen. You're right. I did a terrible thing, but please know I had no intention to hurt you. At first, I didn't realize that was Michael's intention. When I first found out I was pregnant, I was ecstatic. I decided to share my news with Michael before I told anyone. But when I did, that's when everything changed. He urged me not to tell anyone—not even you—until after the three-month mark. Then he packed us up and moved us to London—"

Colleen interrupted. "Okay, but what about the other six months?"

Something bit her on the leg. Gina exclaimed, "Ouch! I got bit by a mosquito." She reentered the house and perched on the couch. "That part was all Michael. He threatened me, telling me not to tell a soul, or I would regret it, and I believed him. He didn't even tell his mother. You don't know how he sounded, how he looked. I felt trapped, like I had to do as he said." Gina curled her feet under her and adjusted her body until she found a comfortable position. She added, "Epiphany would love your girls. She's three now, and though they're five, I'm sure they would play well together."

"I see."

Gina could tell that Colleen really didn't. She felt a small headache coming on. But she continued. "This is a lot to digest. I mean, what are the odds that you sleep with someone three times and you get pregnant twice? I don't even get that. I wish you were here. . . But, anyway, Michael made sure I kept her out of sight. I'm surprised it was easy to do. I think Michael realized that we couldn't keep this sham going much longer once we returned to the States. Gerry lives in Atlanta, and there was no way we could keep it hidden. I mean, Trey was bound to talk about it. It was an effort having to remind him not to mention Epiphany. It was all a nightmare." She lowered her voice. "What's creepy is that Michael had this all planned. He intended to humiliate me and his brother in the worst way possible."

"It sounds like it. Whew!" Colleen answered. "This is some crazy *Flowers in the Attic* stuff. I tell you, Gina. You've got drama. Is there anything else I need to know? Because I don't know how much more I can handle."

Gina gave a shaky laugh. "No, I tell you, this is the whole sordid tale." She then dropped her bombshell. "On another note, Michael sent me divorce papers yesterday."

"What! So Michael knew where you were this whole time? That . . . that jerk!" Colleen raged. "Don't tell me that, because I'm going to call him and give him a piece of my mind."

"I've no clue how long he's known where I am. But I'm not surprised he found me. Michael knows people and knows how to get things done. He's ruthless," Gina said with an edge in her voice.

"Have you signed them?"

"No. Not y-yet," Gina replied, faltering.

Colleen must have heard her hesitation. "Gina, don't tell me you are having reservations."

"It seems so . . . final."

"Gina, I've known you long enough to know you tend to suffer from cold feet. You've always dragged your feet when it comes to making important decisions, because you have such a fear of the unknown. You were a quivering bride. You were a bumbling mess when it was time for motherhood. So it doesn't surprise me one bit that you're feeling butterflies when it comes to your divorce."

"What?" Gina's mouth hung open. Colleen had read her like a book. Gina twirled her right foot. Her mind wandered. She needed a pedicure. Her purple toenails were chipped.

"Lord, give me patience. Gina, you get jittery."

She heard Colleen's aggravation and forgot about her feet. She tucked them underneath her again and pulled her floral skirt over her knees. "It's that I'm scared. I don't know what is going to happen."

"You sign the papers, and then the judge signs off on it. I presume that you are not contesting it." Colleen's sarcasm was palpable.

"Colleen, I know that. It's that I hate the idea of having to go to court and all that."

"Gina, you are a millionaire. Or did you sign a prenup? Stop thinking like you're a teacher and hire an attorney. That's what you pay them for. You won't have to do anything. You can more than afford it."

Gina sighed. Colleen was right. She hated the idea that her marriage had failed. But Gina knew that it was over. There was no repairing what was broken.

"It was never right in the first place," Colleen assured her friend, as if reading her thoughts.

"I didn't sign a prenup, and I do have money stashed. I know I'm not in church, but that doesn't mean I don't think about that 'no man put asunder' line in the vows," Gina admitted. Then she said, "I guess I also should've been more mindful of the adultery clause."

"Gina, just because you're not a Christian doesn't mean you don't have standards or values. I know you well enough to know that. However, you've forgotten about the 'what God hath joined together' part," Colleen replied. "God wasn't in this union. Not from the get-go. It was going to fall apart at some point because the foundation wasn't right."

Gina felt relieved. Colleen's words were liberating. Now all she needed to focus on was her kids. She shifted gears. "The children are doing well, considering."

Colleen chuckled. "They have a resilient, stubborn woman for a mother. I, for one, am not surprised. Trey and Epiphany Joy will be fine. Get them into counseling," she advised.

"I'm going to go sign those papers this instant, with you on the line." True to her words, she strode into her bedroom and pulled the divorce papers out of the nightstand. Then Gina picked up her pen and signed the papers in one big swoop. Colleen remained on the line while she folded the documents and put them in an envelope. She'd messenger them to her attorney in the morning. "Thanks, Colleen. You're a good friend."

"I know an even better friend," Colleen said, her voice softening.

"Yes, I know." Gina rolled her eyes. She knew that Colleen would not give up until she had converted, water baptized, and filled with the Holy Ghost. But after being exposed to the entire nation, she felt unworthy. She was afraid to show her face in public.

"This is the time for you to put your life in God's hands. They're big enough for you and all your problems. You have made a mess of things on your own. Gina, when are you going to realize that you need God to take over and set things right?"

When their call ended, Gina thought and thought about Colleen's question. Maybe God could set things right in her life. She used to think that she was all right, but now Gina was not so sure. She had made a mess of her life.

She couldn't even imagine how she could see her way through the mire in which she had become entangled. She tunneled her fingers through her hair in frustration. Expelling a huge breath of air, Gina could not understand how her life had become a soap opera.

She was married to one man and in love with his brother, who, as it turned out, in a sick twist of fate, was also the father of her children. It was like a bad episode of *The Maury Povich Show*. She could hear Maury's voice in her head. *Michael, you are not the father.*

How was she going to explain this to her children? How did she tell her kids that their uncle was their father? That their father was their uncle? Thinking of this must-have conversation made her ill, but what was the alternative?

Chapter Thirty-six

"So, who is our daddy, Trey?" Epiphany looked at her brother, expecting an answer. Sitting in the big sandbox in the backyard, Epiphany had her back turned to her mom and did not hear her approach. Trey was too busy digging in the sand and putting it in his bucket to note his mother's arrival.

"Uncle Keith is our daddy," Trey replied with the nonchalance of a seven-year-old. He sounded important, self-assured, and confident about his place in the world.

"So does that mean that Daddy is not our daddy?" Epiphany scrunched her face.

Gina knew this was her cue to step in, but she was afraid. She hesitated.

Now Trey looked unsure. He flicked the sand into the air, and it landed in Epiphany's hair. Gina felt her heart melt when his little hand reached up to brush the sand out of his sister's hair.

"I don't know." Trey wrinkled his nose in confusion. "Daddy said it on television, so it must be true."

"So is Mommy still our mommy?" That was a really insightful question for a three-year-old to ask.

Gina knew that it was time for her to intervene and inject as much clarity as she could into the situation.

"Epiphany, of course I'm your mommy," Gina said. She lowered her petite frame into the sandbox and sat with her children. Though she was dressed in jeans and a buttercup-yellow summer cardigan, she didn't care about the sand. She needed to bond with her children and help guide them through all this mess she'd created.

"And Uncle Keith is our real daddy," Trey said. He looked at his mother with such confidence and openness that Gina felt her eyes water. Children were so trusting at that age. Gina knew that she did not deserve it.

"That's good, 'cause I like Uncle Keith," Epiphany chimed in. "I want him to be my daddy. Daddy is not as nice as Uncle Keith."

Gina's mouth popped open in shock at the sharpness of a mere three-year-old. How could she have picked up on Michael's ambivalence toward her? She would choose Keith, a man she had seen only once and knew about through pictures, to be her father over Michael. That was telling. Gina had often been told how children could pick up on things, but she was floored by Epiphany's revelation. But then, Epiphany was gifted beyond her years. She'd reached a lot of milestones ahead of time from an early age.

Gina had prided herself on being able to cover up the disparity in how Michael treated Trey versus Epiphany. However, it was clear that her efforts had been futile. Epiphany knew how Michael felt about her. He had given her everything and had been polite, but Epiphany had felt the truth.

Gina sunk farther into the sand and bent her head to hide the tears. She knew now without a doubt that she had made the right decision when she signed the divorce papers. What she had done was heinous. But what Michael had done in retaliation was unforgivable.

Michael had taken his resentment out on an innocent child. He had treated Epiphany with aloof disdain. He should not have made Epiphany bear the consequences for her mother's actions.

Gina could not resist. She folded her daughter in her arms and kissed the curls on top of her head. "I know you won't be able to understand a lot of what I'm saying to you, but I'll try. A long time ago, I made a mistake. I was so afraid to get in trouble that I didn't tell anyone and I wasn't honest. But I see that I should've told the truth." She exhaled. She wasn't sure if she was making sense.

"So you didn't know Uncle Keith was our daddy?" Epiphany asked.

Gina nodded. She vowed to set a counseling appointment. She needed professional help for all three of them. She hoped she hadn't botched her attempt to explain. *Small steps,* she told herself. *Healing requires time and small steps.*

"Is Daddy coming to visit us?" Trey asked. He didn't wait for a reply but instead sighed and said, "I'm glad it's okay for me to talk about my sister. You said it's okay, right, Mommy?"

Gina rotated her body so that she could take both her children in her arms. She snuggled them close to her. She didn't know how to answer the question. Or, better put, she didn't know which father Trey was referring to. The one he had called Daddy for his entire life or the one he had discovered was his father?

"You can talk about your sis as much as you want," Gina said. She listened to herself. This was a crazy conversation. It felt surreal. Her poor kids. How had she allowed Michael to do this to her family? How had she been so foolish?

Epiphany chimed in with her thoughts. "Yeah, is Daddy Keith coming to see us?"

Gina looked as two pairs of excited eyes waited for an answer. She was relieved to know whom they were referring to, but Gina was nonplussed by their adaptability.

"Are you okay with Uncle Keith being your dad?" She asked the question with a great amount of dread.

"Yes," Trey said, speaking for both of them. "Mommy, you don't think he wants to be our dad, do you?"

A similar conversation was taking place in Keith's home in Jamaica Estates, New York. With a quick wrench, Keith's strong hands tore the fancy tie from around his neck as he stood in the living room.

He had stood beside Ned Winthrop as his best man. Ned and Penelope had been like teenagers. Their love was mutual and apparent. Keith had been moved and honored to perform the wedding ceremony.

Keith had opened his home for the special occasion. Penelope had a special surprise planned for Ned and delegated Keith as her husband's "babysitter" until she was ready. The two men watched as Penelope and her numerous cousins and sisters departed. Then they chuckled, knowing that whatever that night brought, Ned was not going to complain. It was evident to anyone who knew Ned that he was content with whatever happened as long as he had Penelope.

Wanting to share his happiness, Ned asked Keith, "How are you progressing in your search for Gina?"

Keith replied, "So far my efforts to locate her have been futile. It's like she's disappeared from the planet."

"I can see you're worried," Ned said. "And we can't have that. You're going on the air in a little over a month, and I don't need you looking haggard or stressed."

Keith nodded in amazement at the turn of events. The January 14 date had been set. *Second Chances* had been a hit in all the pilot cities. News of the show's launch had already started spreading by word of mouth in the industry. Reporters were calling Ned's office, looking for confirmation.

"I'm going to have to confirm the rumors within the next few weeks or so. But for this venture to be successful, I need you next to me on the podium with your wife, Gina. Your union is the key to the show's success."

"I know, and I want her by my side. It's what I've always wanted." Keith hung his head. "Maybe our love wasn't strong enough."

"Nonsense," Ned said. "I am now a firm believer in the power of an intense love like what you and Gina share. Love like that doesn't die easily. If ever." With a quick wave of his hand, Ned retrieved his cell phone from his pocket and punched in a number, using his speed dial. He shifted his body away from Keith.

Keith gave Ned legroom, knowing that the caller on the other end was not the type of man a minister would consort with. He heard Ned whisper orders in rapid-fire succession. Keith held up his hands to signal to Ned that his assistance was not necessary.

"You have five minutes," Ned commanded and disconnected the call.

Keith smiled as Ned shrugged. He gave Keith a thumbs-up, indicating that all would end well.

Keith prayed. His heart rate escalated. He knew he would not appreciate the unsavory character Ned was using, but Keith still prayed for results. Sometimes you had to go to Egypt when there was famine. Keith comforted himself with the old Bible story of the sons of Jacob, worshippers of the one true God, who had to venture into the land of idol worshippers to get food.

Time crept by. Keith tried to tune out the sound of the clock's ticking, but it was pointless. A couple of times he tried to start a conversation, but Ned did not take the bait. After what felt like an interminable wait, the shrill ring of Ned's phone echoed off the walls.

Keith exhaled, signifying his impatience. He tapped his feet, rubbed his head, and paced back and forth throughout the entire call.

Ned disconnected the call after what felt like forever.

"Go check your fax," he said.

"You found her?"

"I found her."

Chapter Thirty-seven

Gina pulled into the driveway of her father's home. She saw Jeff peek through the window before coming outside the house to greet her. He helped her unload her kids from the backseat.

There was a huge black truck in the next space. "You have a visitor?" Gina asked.

"Yes." Jeff wiped his hands on his pants in a nervous gesture.

Seeing Regina standing by the door, Trey and Epiphany raced inside, knowing she had special treats for them. Regina was a superb baker. She made everything from gourmet cookies to professionally decorated cakes. Gina knew she had to stay away from the mirror. She had packed on at least five pounds because of Regina's cooking.

Jeff held on to Gina's arm and led her into the house. He stopped in the entryway. Gina gave him a curious look.

"Keith's here," he told her.

Gina felt her knees buckle at her father's words. In fact, she would have fallen if Jeff hadn't maintained a firm grip on her arm. Gina did not know why, but she felt the urge to turn and run in the opposite direction.

Yet at the same time something compelled her to run straight into Keith's arms. Her traitorous body started quivering in anticipation at the thought of seeing him. Even though her exile had been self-imposed, she missed him. She had thought about him and ached to touch him.

Her father interpreted the myriad of emotions sweeping across her face. Gina had told him the entire story of her debacle with Keith and Michael. She was grateful that she had a relationship with Jeff—it had been after several intense sessions of counseling that they'd gotten here.

He took her hand and led her into the kitchen, away from Keith, who was now playing with his children in the family room. "Gina, you can't run from your destiny."

"I never saw Keith as my destiny. My temptation, my trial . . . but not once did I imagine that we could end up together."

"Why not?"

"It's too complicated. I was married to his brother. Marrying Keith now would be tacky. Too impossible."

"God specializes in impossibilities."

"But this is just—"

"It's your life, Gina. No one else can live it for you. You answer to God. Not to society and not to me. At the end of this road, you must grab and hold on to the joy in your life. And, Gina, honey, from the time I met you, you've been miserable, and it breaks my heart."

Gina stiffened at first at her father's words. But then truth seeped through her being. She had been miserable before, during, and after her marriage to Michael. There had been great moments, but she had never experienced what she had with Keith.

Could this be her chance?

Gina walked into the family room with a slight hesitation. She didn't know how she was going to react to seeing Keith.

Keith looked up as soon as she entered the room. He had been playing with Trey and Epiphany. They were sitting on each of his legs, and Epiphany was swinging her legs back and forth like she didn't have a care in the world.

Gina felt tears threaten at the sight of Keith playing with her children. No. Correction. Their children. The significance of that moment was not lost on either of the two adult occupants in the room. For in spite of all that was wrong about their union, their children were right. They were precious. Too precious to ever regret.

Keith held out his hand like he needed to feel a connection with the woman who had given him these precious blessings.

It was as if only a day had passed, instead of months. All the anger and hurt dissipated when she saw him. All the words she thought she'd say were stuck in her throat. Gina grabbed his hand and allowed Keith to pull her so that she sat in the chair next to him. Trey and Epiphany wandered off to the other side of the room.

She heard Keith inhale as the fragrance of her perfume drifted up to his nostrils. He leaned over and inhaled deeply. "I had to get another whiff of that scent. It's titillating my senses. I've missed you," he said. "And I'm understating the truth."

"I missed you too," Gina confessed in a conspiratorial whisper. Not for one second was she fooled by Trey's apparent nonchalance. Her son's ears were well tuned in to his parents' conversation.

Keith stretched his arm across her chair, and she leaned back into the comfort of his arm.

Feeling uplifted by the promising sight, Trey ambled over to where his sister was playing.

Keith leaned in to speak to her in confidence. "Marry me, Gina."

Gina was startled by Keith's sudden statement. Or, rather, his command. She expected outrage and at least a lot of questions. She didn't expect this and sought to put space between them.

Keith read her intentions and held on to her shoulders with determination. "You think after all these months I'm going to let you get away without a fight? Once I knew you were here—and don't think I didn't think to look—I was packed and on the highway to the airport in less than twenty minutes. After months of missing you and wanting to see my children, I refuse to let another day go by without you. I understand you. I know you. I love you."

Keith decided that the time for small talk was over. He and Gina had wasted an eternity on begging and pleading. He was here to claim his family. He had engaged in much fasting and prayer, and he had beaten himself up enough over the situation. Even though the nation might salivate over his blunder, Keith felt assurance in God's Word.

God did not hold the sins of the past against him. All his former deeds had been forgiven. God had forgiven him. It had taken soul-searching, prayers, and fasting, but Keith had forgiven himself. Now he needed Gina to do the same.

Reaching inside his jacket pocket, Keith extracted the small box holding the three-carat solitaire. Keith didn't view marriage as a trivial commitment. He had invested his time and energy in finding the perfect ring, one that commemorated his lifetime of love for Gina.

He placed the box on the coffee table.

Gina saw the little box and understood its implications. Taking a deep breath, she put her hands in her hair, which, as she suspected, was in disarray. In fact, in her opinion, she looked a hot mess. She had spent the past six hours with the children at the zoo. She stunk like animals.

She jumped to her feet. This would not do. "If that is what I think it is, I'm not doing it like this."

"What?" Keith also jumped to his feet.

"You waited all this time. You can wait while I shower and change."

"Gina, it doesn't matter to me."

"You can wait." Gina's stubbornness was evident. She left the room in a huff. There was no way she was going to get the proposal of a lifetime in what she was wearing and when she was looking like a hot mess.

Chapter Thirty-eight

After eight years, does she thinks I care what she looks like? Knowing that he would not win that battle against the female mind, he redirected his thoughts to his children.

Trey and Epiphany leaped over to where he remained standing. Regina came to retrieve Epiphany for her bath. He decided to take care of Trey himself. His hands shook when he helped his son undress and drew his bath. For years, Keith had longed for a family. And now it seemed as if God was about to grant it all to him.

He felt somewhat overcome with emotion and sat at the edge of the tub, thanking God. What had he done to deserve this? Keith didn't realize that tears were falling until Trey spoke up.

"Why are you crying?" Trey's hands were filled with soap, but he reached over to pat his father's hand, seeking to comfort him.

Tenderness swelled inside Keith at the gesture. "I love you and thank God for you."

"I love you too, Uncle Keith."

Keith noticed that Trey vacillated between calling him dad and uncle. Keith answered to either one, knowing that this was a normal period of adjustment. It would take a little time for Trey to get it right. He imagined that Trey understood a little of what was going on with the adults in his life, and knew that he needed to speak with his son about this.

"Trey, I know you must feel a little confused at times, and I want you to know that you can talk to me about anything you don't understand."

Trey jumped out of the bathtub. He had lost interest in the assortment of toys for bath time fun, now floating, forgotten, in the tub. "Well . . ."

"Why don't we get you dressed and then we can talk?"

For a moment, Keith thought about how Gina would react to him talking to Trey without consulting her first. Then he pushed the thought aside. Trey was his son, and the sooner he assumed the role of father with both him and Epiphany, the easier the transition would be.

Once Trey was dressed in his pajamas, he ran into his bedroom and Keith tucked him in bed. Regina and Jeff popped in to see if he needed their assistance, but he waved them off. He was pleased at how adept he was at handling a precocious seven-year-old.

As soon as he was settled in bed, Trey wasted no time in asking his question. "Is Daddy going to take me and Epiphany away from Mom?"

Keith's brows quivered. An eerie sensation struck his being, but Keith prayed that he was wrong. "No, Trey. Why would you be worried about that?"

Trey whispered. It was obvious that he was frightened. "Well, Daddy used to be nice, and then he started kind of being mean."

"To you?" Keith's breath caught in anticipation. If Michael had done something to his son, he would not be responsible for his actions. He could somewhat come to terms with his brother's pervasive cruelty to Gina, but Keith would not rationalize that behavior if the children had been on the receiving end of it. He hoped his brother was above that.

"No," Trey said. "He used to be much nicer, but then Daddy started being mean. He was always working. He wouldn't play with me if I wanted Epiphany to play too. It had to be only him and me. That's why most of the time I would just . . . I would just . . ."

Keith watched as his son struggled to find the words. It was tempting to help, but his years as an attorney had taught him to wait for Trey to find the right phrase. He wouldn't lead or prod the boy, because he did not want to get a tarnished version of the truth. The unadulterated truth had to come from Trey's own lips, with no help from him.

"I would just play with Epiphany. I think Daddy . . . I mean, Uncle Michael . . . was mad at me for doing that, so he stopped playing with me." Trey started to cry.

Keith's heart constricted. He sat down on the edge of the bed, hugged his son tight, and tried to find the right words to comfort him.

Michael's actions were unbelievable. In essence, Michael had forced Trey to choose between his father and his sister. Then, when his ploy failed, Michael had closed himself off from his son. His selfish actions proved why the Bible warned against holding on to bitterness and anger. Michael's bitterness had festered until it had hardened him and changed him. Keith did not think Michael knew how perceptive and discerning Trey was. He was sure that Michael had been crafty, but Trey had seen right through him.

"Your uncle Michael wasn't thinking," Keith explained. "I love you, and I would never make you choose. You can love me, your mom, your sister, your toys, your bed. . . ."

Trey giggled, already feeling better. Then he sobered and said, "Daddy, do you think it is my fault why Mommy had to leave Uncle Michael? She told us we're going to live in a new house and we weren't going back there."

Keith knew he would have to tread with care. Trey was already trying to adjust to his transition from uncle to dad. Keith did not want to do anything that would contribute to the emotional scars. This was a traumatic experience for anyone, much less a little boy.

"No, son. Nothing that has happened is your fault," Keith assured him. "It's us, the grown-ups, who are to blame. You have not done anything wrong. Don't think that for a moment. I promise you that all you need to know is that we all love you and your sister." Keith moved off the bed and lowered his body so that he could look Trey in the eyes. "I'm sorry, Trey." Keith uttered the sentiment in a soft voice.

"That's okay, Dad. It's not your fault." Trey grabbed on to him and started to cry. Keith saw the tears form a pool on his shirt. Trey was crying his heart out. He felt the familiar guilt rack his body. In a way, it was his fault. He had driven a wedge between Gina and Michael.

But if it weren't for him, Trey and Epiphany would not be here. He couldn't feel guilty for their existence. Children were precious gifts from God, to be treasured and cherished. Somehow, God had taken all of his faults and all of his mistakes and was now using them for good and for His purpose. His television show was evidence of that.

Keith provided soothing words of comfort for his son. He knew that the gut-wrenching pain in his own heart was something that would subside with time. But now it felt like a ton of bricks was tearing at his heartstrings as his son cried.

Keith could not stop the tears from pooling in his own eyes.

At that moment Gina entered the room to see her son wrapped in Keith's arms. Both were emotional. Gina could discern what was happening.

She gave Keith a thumbs-up sign and left the room without Trey knowing she had been there. Gina wanted to give Keith as much time as he needed with his son. They had to bond on that level.

She searched for Epiphany. She found her daughter bundled under a collection of teddy bears in her bedroom. Gina had to move a few of them on the floor before sitting on the edge of the bed.

Epiphany was not yet asleep. "Mommy," she called out.

Gina took her daughter in her arms and rocked her back and forth.

"Where's Daddy?"

"He's right here," Keith said. He had settled Trey in bed and come to check on Epiphany. He crossed the room to the opposite side of the bed and plopped down.

Without a moment's thought, Epiphany left Gina's arms and bounced into Keith's arms. Slanting Gina a teasing grin, he held his daughter.

"Traitor," Gina mouthed, but her words belied her feeling. She was thrilled at the sight of Epiphany in Keith's strong arms. Somehow, Gina felt even more assured that everything was going to be all right.

Later that evening, once the children were asleep, Gina accepted Keith's proposal. Watching the ring slide up her finger, Gina felt all the sins of the past fade away. She'd waited her whole life for this moment.

Keith held Gina's hand and stared at the ring on her finger. It looked and felt right. "Thank you, Lord," Keith whispered with reverence. "You've answered the yearning of my heart. My steps are truly ordered by you. You've worked everything out for my good."

Gina hid her momentary surprise. This was she and Keith's moment. He'd brought God into it. She hadn't expected that.

He's a man of God, so why should that surprise you? Hmm . . . good point. Gina felt a quiver of fear surround her heart. After all that Keith had been through, would God now come between them?

Chapter Thirty-nine

"Is he out of his mind? This is just plain tacky." Michael couldn't believe his brother's gall. Keith had sent him an invitation to his and Gina's upcoming nuptials in Arizona. *The ink on our divorce papers hasn't even dried yet. They should elope or something,* he scoffed silently. The invite was a lame attempt at burying the hatchet and letting bygones be bygones—an olive branch of sorts.

He resisted the childish urge to tear the paper into small pieces and burn them. Instead, he threw the invitation in the trash basket and turned on his computer. But his eyes kept straying to the five-by-seven card with the date November 17 so prominently displayed.

Throwing his hands into the air, Michael admitted that it was pointless to try to get any work done. His mind was preoccupied with thoughts of Keith and Gina. It shouldn't have surprised him that Keith and Gina would make their adulterous affair legal. This must be Keith's way of making things right with God. Well, he didn't see how God would ever be right with a man stealing another man's wife.

He reached up to touch his now bare chin. In an act of defiance, Michael had shaved his goatee. He knew how much Gina loved it, and he hadn't wanted any reminders of her. He kind of missed it, though.

There was something else that Michael missed. Or, rather, someone else.

He pulled open his desk drawer and stared at the picture he kept there. He missed his son. Michael stared at the picture of Trey and Epiphany. His chest deflated with emotion. He even missed Epiphany.

Michael had had no idea that he would feel this way. Regret tore at him. He should have thought of the agony of losing his children before choosing this path.

Correction. Keith's children.

Michael drummed his fingers, feeling misery creep up his spine and twist around his heart. There was something in the deep recesses of his mind that puzzled him. Something that he hadn't considered. He strained to bring the missing piece of the puzzle to the forefront. He closed his eyes. He could recall in stark detail holding Trey as a newborn in the hospital . . . changing his diapers . . . watching as he took his first steps.

He'd been a good father! Michael thought, consoling himself. He had signed those papers and had taken care of . . . *That's it! The papers!* Michael sat ramrod straight as everything fell into place. He whooped with delight. His laughter sounded maniacal as it echoed off the walls in the otherwise empty house.

Michael placed a call. He was going to give Keith and Gina a wedding present they would never forget.

Gina opened her father's front door. She screamed and launched herself into Colleen's arms.

"When we received your invitation, we couldn't wait to book our flights. I'm so thrilled for you," Colleen declared.

"Sorry for such short notice," Gina said.

Colleen flashed her hands. "Girl, please. After eight years, I'm surprised you waited this long."

Gina grinned, echoing her sentiment. "If it were up to Keith, we would be at the justice of the peace." She stepped aside to let Colleen and her husband inside. She noticed Terence's less than enthusiastic response. "Terence, what is it?"

Terence shrugged his shoulders. Patting Gina's shoulder, he said, "I'm happy, but I'm a little . . ." He trailed off. "I promised Colleen I would keep my mouth shut and be happy."

With that, Terence moseyed off in search of Keith. He was standing in as best man and had to perform his duties.

"What's his concern?" Gina asked, prodding Colleen with an arched eyebrow. Her eyes scanned her friend's, trying to read her mind.

"He's being cautious," Colleen said. Colleen held her hand and walked her over to the love seat in the living room.

"Let's hear it. What's on his mind? You'd better tell me, or I'll hound you until you do." Gina wasn't biting her tongue. She was getting married in two days.

"He doesn't think you and Keith should've rushed into anything. I don't agree, of course. After all you two have been through, I am rejoicing."

Gina nodded, but she needed clarification. "*Rushed?* This is eight years in the making. How can he say we are rushing?" She didn't know why Terence's opinion mattered, but it did. She wanted to know.

Colleen stammered, "He's l-looking at the fact that Keith is saved, and you're still . . ."

Gina's eyebrows shot up in warning. "Undecided?" Gina asked, supplying the word, avoiding Colleen's eyes. She would be lying if she said that she hadn't thought about that. "I think I understand his concern."

"He said that if you and Keith weren't on the same page spiritually, your marriage might be doomed before it even begins. There's a scripture in Amos that says, 'Can two walk together, except they be agreed?'"

Gina was on the defensive. "Keith's in love with me. When he looks at me, I see nothing but love in his eyes. I know I haven't said the words, but I do a lot to help others, and I respect everyone. I love Keith, and I want the best for him always. Nothing can come between our love." Terence was lucky he'd left the room, or she would be on him right now.

Colleen responded, "Gina, now that we're talking, I realize Terence has only your and Keith's best interests at heart. Keith loves you, but he will be miserable in the long term if you don't accept Jesus as your personal Savior. That goes against everything Keith stands for and upholds. I know from experience that love is not the only ingredient that holds a marriage together. God is the secret ingredient."

Gina's shoulders drooped.

"Salvation is a gift. It's one you have to choose to accept. What's so hard about it?"

"There are Christians out there who are unforgiving and hypocritical, even though they're saved. But me, I'm a good person," Gina said. The words sounded hollow to her ears, but she was stubborn.

"Being good won't save you. It's not enough," Colleen admonished. "I love you so much, Gina. Please believe how hard it is for me to say this. But why can't you admit that you need God in your life? We all do. Everything that's happening to you is because of Him. He's working everything out for good in your life. He orders our steps and knows what is best for us, even when we don't have a clue."

Colleen slid to her knees and pulled Gina down beside her and prayed. Gina didn't argue, but deep down all she could think was, *What do I really need God for?* She had Keith, and he was all she needed. She wasn't letting him go.

***

The day of the wedding was picture perfect. It was sunny, and the temperature was in the upper seventies, which made for a perfect fall wedding. Gina had even lost the ten pounds she needed to shed in order to fit into her wedding dress. She was ecstatic. Looking into the full-length mirror, Gina beheld her reflection with amazement.

She looked gorgeous, and she felt it. Gina beamed as she imagined the look on Keith's face when she entered the sanctuary. She did a girlish twirl, letting herself go as she relished the rare feeling of exultation that she had gotten her heart's desire.

She saw Colleen enter the room and stop short. "You're a vision, and your gown is off the charts. Plus, your hair is gorgeous. Shelley hooked you up."

Gina smiled. "When I saw it, I knew it was perfect." Her Vera Wang wedding gown looked deceptively simple but it accentuated every nuance of her curves and flowed with her every movement. The train would make Cinderella proud. But it was the shoes that were going to be the star of the show. They were smoking-hot glass shoes, guaranteed to make any man salivate.

Colleen's eyes ran down Gina's gown, widening when she saw her shoes. "Those shoes are so you. I'm keeping my eyes on Keith when he sees those peekaboo hooker shoes. He's going to have a conniption."

Gina shivered and clapped her hands with delight. "I couldn't resist them, and wait until he sees my matching see-through lingerie. It makes these shoes look like playthings."

"Well, they are so you."

"Thanks. You look amazing." Gina eyed her friend. Colleen was wearing the floor-length red gown that Gina had chosen for her to wear. It was one-shouldered, but it came with a small cape, which she would wear in the church. Colleen had searched for but couldn't find matching stilettos. She'd settled instead for a pair of black shoes that would be hidden under her gown.

"Might I say that you are my favorite matron of honor," Gina declared. "And you look good in red . . . again." Colleen had worn red for Gina's marriage to Michael too.

Colleen rolled her eyes. "I'm also the sole bridesmaid. Terence should be here soon."

Gina made a face.

"Please, don't be mad at him."

"I'm not—not really," Gina said. "I can't be mad at his opinion, but if he feels that way, then why is he here as Keith's best man?"

"I asked him the same thing. He said that he's not about to do God's job for Him. God's got it, so in the meantime he will be here for both of you."

Keith and Gina had wanted a simple private ceremony that they could cherish together. They declined the network's offer to air the wedding live. But after much pressure from the network, they had acquiesced and given permission for one cameraman and one commentator to tape the wedding, which would be aired at a later date. They would have the final say in the editing process.

Second Chances with Pastor Keith Ward test runs had catapulted to top-billing status. His ratings were climbing, even with the overwhelming number of reality shows. His viewing audience had written in by the droves, begging to see the wedding ceremony live.

"What a beautiful day." Gina hugged Colleen with excitement. "I can hardly wait to walk down the aisle, or to enjoy my wedding night. Keith's going to flip when he sees me, or rather, what I have on underneath." She wiggled her hips.

Colleen laughed. "I'm liking this carefree Gina, the one who is rambling on and prancing around the room. You're usually so reserved, matter-of-fact, and cynical that it's a relief to see you so giddy. I've never seen this unabashed joyfulness in you. Ever."

Gina blushed.

The door burst open, and Epiphany and Trey entered the room. Tears came to Gina's eyes at the sight of her children. She exclaimed, "You look like angels!" Trey, the official ring bearer, looked like a smaller version of Keith, and Epiphany, a mini bride. The little girl wore a white dress and red baby doll shoes.

They ran over to Colleen for a hug and would have toppled their mom over had she not reined them in.

"We're here to get you, Mommy," Epiphany said, jumping up and down. "I'm a fairy-tale princess, and Daddy fainted when he saw me. But he's okay, though."

"Yeah, Daddy said to hurry up, woman." Trey cracked up as he delivered his father's message verbatim.

Gina and Colleen laughed and scooped up the items they would need.

"Here I go again, girl," Gina said.

Colleen smiled. "Yes, but this time it's right."

Colleen retrieved her bouquet of red lilies, and Gina grabbed her bouquet, which had a mixture of red and yellow flowers. They hurried out. Gina knew Keith was not known for his patience or decorum. He would come and get her caveman style if she didn't get a move on. Gina balked at the thought of going down the aisle bottom up.

Colleen took her place with Epiphany and Trey.

Jeff came over to assume his position. He crooked his elbow and waited. Feeling shy, Gina placed her hand through her father's arm. When she asked him to walk her down the aisle, he cried, confessing that he had been afraid that Gina wouldn't want him to. She'd been surprised by his response. "You're my father. I wouldn't want anyone else to take your place," she told him. He had been overcome with emotion then at her heartfelt words.

As they were about to enter the sanctuary, Keith's mom came over to Gina. Gerry looked her in the eye for several seconds. Then she enfolded Gina in a hug and whispered, "Welcome to the family again, Gina."

Gina relaxed. That was the best she could ask for, considering. Gerry remained gracious to her, even though for all intents and purposes, she should hate her. Her love and admiration for Keith's mother intensified at that moment.

With Gerry's blessing, and her father at her side, Gina walked down the aisle to marry the man of her dreams.

As she walked by, Gina nodded at Natalie and smiled at Kelly and Kendall, who looked so handsome in his little suit. When he saw Gina, he stretched his pudgy arms toward her. Gina blew him a kiss.

Regina sat in the front row. Gina gave her stepmother a tender smile. She wished her mother were here, but she couldn't complain. All was well in her world.

There wasn't a dry eye in the place when Keith and Gina said their vows. Their love and devotion for each other was evident. Everyone present was awed by the sincerity displayed, knowing that they were getting a glimpse of a mutual, transcendent love that was ordained by God.

Gina was so ready for her "happily ever after" ending, but for the moment, God had other plans.

Chapter Forty

"You are a conniving, sadistic liar!" Michael screamed. He doubted he had ever been so furious in his life. "How dare you spin such a wicked, spiteful lie! Especially after what we just shared." He'd made her body sing a mere hour ago and had come into his study to work.

Wide-eyed, Lauren backed away from him in stunned disbelief. Her heels knocked against the leg of the table. She reached to grip the back of a chair to keep from falling. But Michael didn't care if she was hurt.

He was not having it. She was not getting away from him that easily. Not after she uttered words that twisted and turned his heart, bringing all his pain and shortcomings back to the surface. Grabbing her arm, not caring that she would have telltale red welts, Michael struggled to bring his temper under control. His chest heaved with effort as he tried not to entertain the overwhelming impulse that was urging him to wring Lauren's neck.

Tears flowed from her eyes. "I . . . am . . . not . . . lying. . . ." Lauren repeated with a calm voice. However, her eyes showed she was terrified and Michael knew she was trying to present a brave front. "I thought you would be happy." Spotting the condom on the heel of her shoe, Lauren reached down to grab it, a rosy hue filling her cheeks. Michael watched her search for a trashcan but he had her cornered, so she tucked it into her pants.

Michael reached up and twisted her ear. "Are you listening to me, woman? Do you think I don't know that you are feeding me garbage so rancid, I can smell it up to here?" He shoved his fist in her face. "And how do I even know that it's mine?"

Lauren's body contorted with pain. "I won't dignify that with an answer. I'm not taking this abuse from you or any man." She sank her nails into his arm. She held on like a leech until he shrieked and let her ear go.

Michael turned his back and stomped back over to his desk. He saw when she smiled with satisfaction, knowing that she had drawn blood. The evidence was seeping through his otherwise immaculate white shirt. Emboldened after her stunt, she walked over to his liquor shelf to get an ice cube for her ear, which was splotchy red.

Michael plopped into the chair behind his desk and hunched over, with his head in his hands, and calmed himself. *What was he becoming?* he said to himself. He eyed his bloody shirt and acknowledged that he deserved that. Lauren was like a tigress when riled. In spite of himself, Michael smiled at her spunk.

She sensed the worst was over and stomped over to sit across from him. She was now simmering with righteous indignation at his mauling. With an upturned nose, she growled, "Don't you ever put your hands on me again, or you'll live to regret it. I promise you that."

"I'm sorry. I shouldn't have manhandled you," Michael responded, contrite. His anger evaporated. He had a good idea why Lauren had resorted to pulling such a low stunt. "Lauren, I know you don't think I should, but I'm still going through with my plans. Nothing that you say or do is going to change my mind. Not even your current wild, harebrained scheme, which is an ill attempt to get me to deviate from my decided course of action."

Lauren blinked. It was obvious that she was at a loss for words, which was rare. She continued to eye him for several minutes before she declared, "I can't imagine you'd believe I would lie to you about something like this, Michael, after all that we have been through. I put my career on the line for you."

Michael should have listened to her tone, but he refused to listen. "Yes, but you reaped the benefits. There was something in it for you. So tell me. What's in it for you this time? You think I would buy this stunt? What are you looking for? Another TV interview?"

"Michael, I know this thing between us is an arrangement for you, but my heart is involved," Lauren admitted. Michael cringed at her confession. "Yes, Michael, I broke our unspoken arrangement. I fell in love. If you cannot accept that, and this gift, then you are not the man I thought still existed underneath all that bitterness."

Lauren jumped to her feet and retreated to the doorway. She turned and said with disgust, "I'm going to give you one more chance to come to your senses and take what I'm offering you. I'll give you a second chance, even after your awful behavior toward me."

Michael's heart hardened. He would not budge on this. With a determined gaze, he told her, "Lauren, it's done. Gina and Keith already received the papers." To further prove his point, Michael opened his drawer and retrieved his copy of the documents.

"Michael, I'm asking you, for my sake, let this go. No, I am begging you not to do this. Think about the children."

"I am."

"No, you are thinking of yourself." Lauren's voice broke. "This is a reality check. I can't believe I fancied myself falling in love with such an uncaring, selfish man. I can't believe you would disrupt the children's lives again, after all you've put them through already. Children whom you say you love. It's cruel and beneath you."

"I do love them," Michael stated. "That's why I am doing this."

"I see there is nothing I can do to change your mind." Her shoulders sagged. In a defeated tone, she said, "It's like you're on this road to destruction and you don't care who you hurt along the way."

Michael basked in his own cleverness. "Admit that you lied earlier."

Lauren opened her mouth and said, "I can't utter the words. From today onward I'm done with you. If you think I'm lying, then I am."

"Spoken like a true reporter," Michael replied. His arrogance had surfaced. He was more than ready to call her bluff.

"I was never a reporter with you, Michael," Lauren informed him. "I was always a woman. A woman whom you rejected, I might add. For your sake, I hope your revenge merits all that you're losing."

With that Lauren strode out of his life. Michael had already dismissed her and her drama, too caught up in his malicious scheme to give her a second thought.

Chapter Forty-one

Alone in the master bedroom she now shared with Keith, Gina was inconsolable. Keith had been able to rent the same house in Atlanta as before. She'd been tossing and turning the past two weeks, feeling the torture of Michael's latest ploy. Keith was locked in his study with Nigel Lattimore, a top attorney at his old law firm, Bohlander & Associates.

When Keith had called him, Nigel had agreed to oversee the case himself, flying to Atlanta from New York. He was a slender man, a little taller than Keith, and looked like he should be on the basketball court instead of in the courtroom. He had boyish good looks and a charm that Gina would have found appealing had she not been so worried about losing her children.

Keith had crooked his arm about her shoulders when he made the introductions. He was possessive and was staking his claim. Gina resisted rolling her eyes. He needed not have worried. She had eyes only for him. It was because of her inability to stay away from him that they were now in the hot seat.

Since then, Keith had been working nonstop. It was now past midnight, and the two were still pouring over legal statutes and cases, preparing a defense for a case for which Gina would never, ever be prepared.

"Michael doesn't really have rights, does he?" she asked Keith the other day. "I mean, he went on national television and acknowledged that Trey and Epiphany were yours."

Keith touched her cheek. "The law doesn't see it that way, Gina. His name is on their birth papers, so he's their legal father, and he has rights."

Gina had been too distraught for words. How did she prepare for the possibility of losing her own flesh and blood?

Her children were her life. They were her heartbeats. She couldn't lose them.

"Gina, no judge in their right mind would take children from their mother. You've got to believe me. Michael is wasting everybody's time with this nonsense. I don't even know how he got a judge to entertain this case," Keith had assured her.

Though she heard Keith's words, Gina hadn't been mollified.

Giving up on sleep and tossing the covers back, she tiptoed out of the room to stand outside Keith's locked study door. Gina pressed her ear against the doorjamb, hoping to hear something that would ease her mind.

She'd been involved in the process, but her lack of sleep and nutrition had taken a toll after a week and a half of nonstop research. Seeing her lackluster, tired expression, Keith had banned her from his study and ordered her to bed.

Feeling useless, Gina moved her ear from the door. She heard nothing. It had been a pointless attempt, anyway, since the room was soundproof. Next, she went to look in on Trey and Epiphany, who were sound asleep.

Heading to the refrigerator, Gina snatched the pint of pistachio ice cream from the freezer compartment. She'd given up ice cream for the past three months, but now Gina refused to resist the temptation. She moseyed over to the large living room and plunked herself down on the soft red leather couch. It contorted to fit her curves. To kill time, she turned the television on and ate ice cream while she channel surfed.

Gina intended to waylay Keith and Nigel when they came out of the study. She wanted answers They were not getting rid of her so easily.

Keith found Gina asleep on the couch after Nigel had left for his hotel. Keith looked at the cable box and was surprised to see that it was almost one thirty in the morning. He even looked at his watch for confirmation.

Michael's case was reminiscent of those days when he used to burn the midnight oil. He felt confident with what he and Nigel had prepared, but it was Gina, their star witness, who would take the most prepping. Gina had never been in court before, so of course, she would be nervous. Keith's heart twisted, because he knew that Michael's defense attorney was going to paint Gina in the worst possible light.

Putting one hand on his head, Keith took the remote control, which Gina still clutched in her hand, and turned the television off. He picked up his wife, who did not stir. That spoke volumes about how tired she was. He carried her into their bedroom.

As he positioned her on their king-size bed, Keith laughed to himself. He had not yet made love to her since she officially became his wife. He undressed and settled in to cuddle with Gina spoon-style.

Looking up at the ceiling, Keith closed his eyes and whispered a quick prayer to God. Closing his eyes, Keith pictured Gina as she had looked on their wedding day, until Michael had ruined it with his special "surprise."

Gina had been radiant and glowing, as any bride in love should be. When Keith saw her coming down the aisle, he had done all he could to keep from running and grabbing hold of her. She was absolutely breathtaking. Keith remembered how he grabbed her hand as soon as she was close enough. He had wanted—no, had needed—to touch her. Terence had held his arm, or he would have planted a solid kiss on those lips before the right time for that.

The rest of the ceremony had flown by, and Terence had to tap him to end the searing kiss. Keith had almost lost his composure then. He groaned with horror, as he had seen that kiss repeated on screen so many times that he had count. Their lip locking had made the devastating news even more sensational.

Keith and Gina had decided to have the reception at the same venue, because they intended to make a speedy retreat afterward to start their honeymoon. But in the middle of the celebration, a flashily dressed messenger arrived. He was a young man in his early twenties. His getup and mannerisms screamed that theatrics were afoot. The young man got everyone's attention and told them to gather round. Then he presented Keith and Gina with an embroidered envelope. Of course, caught up in the festivities, the crowd and the camera crew had eaten it all up.

Enthralled, everyone watched as Gina opened the envelope to read the contents of the enclosed letter. In a matter of seconds her face had frozen with shock. This must have been his cue, because the young man then executed a theatrical bow and proclaimed at the top of his lungs, "Congratulations, Keith and Gina! You've been served! Michael is suing you for full custody of his children!"

The loud gasp from the crowd was quiet in comparison to Gina's reaction. She let out a bloodcurdling scream and pounced on the messenger, who had been making his way down the driveway toward a waiting car with rapid speed. Keith let the young man go, because he knew that the messenger was just another pawn in Michael's plot for revenge.

To their chagrin, Keith and Gina's humiliation was now a YouTube sensation. Even Keith's broadcast station had replayed the day's events with alarming speed over and over again. Once again his life had become more outrageous than a soap opera.

From that moment onward, Keith had been hitting the law books. Nigel was the crème de la crème at the law firm, and Keith trusted his judgment. Terence and Colleen had also come to his support. They had been praying and fasting with him in earnest two days a week. In fact, he needed to turn his brain off, because they would be at his door at 8:00 a.m. The only one missing from the group was Gina. Keith excused her, however, knowing how distraught she was.

But another part of him felt a small niggling doubt. Keith pondered Gina's spiritual beliefs. He knew it was a little too late to wonder now, but Keith had never questioned Gina's convictions before. He had been too in love to let her go. However, he acknowledged that he wanted and needed a firm woman of faith.

Keith knew Gina was not an atheist. She believed in God. She accepted God. But he realized that Gina had not yet discovered her own personal relationship with God. She did not know how much she needed Him.

Caught up in his thoughts, Keith played with Gina's hair. She looked so tiny in her sleep, but that was deceiving. Gina was a powerhouse, a force to be reckoned with, and he would not have her any other way.

Lord, thank you for giving me the woman of my heart. I will wait for you to complete the work.

Chapter Forty-two

"Why is this day so warm and sunny when I'm in turmoil?" Gina said as she sulked, sinking deeper in the seat. She crossed her arms and covered her eyes to keep the sun from hitting them.

Keith, however, was uplifted. He took the unseasonably warm weather in December as a sign that God was still in control and that there were brighter days ahead.

They had dropped Trey and Epiphany off at his mother's house. They would stay with her for the day. In lieu of driving, Keith arranged for a car service to transport Gina, Nigel, and himself to the courthouse.

After hugs, kisses, and tears at Gerry's house, Keith and Gina were on their way to meet with a mediator to resolve the issue. If the mediation proceedings were unsuccessful, they would be facing a lengthy trial. Keith hoped and prayed that it would not go that far. He hoped that Michael's foolish lawsuit was dropped and that his name replaced his brother's on the children's official birth papers since he was their biological father.

Against his wishes, Gina wanted to speak during the mediation proceedings. She felt that as their mother, she needed to at least defend herself and her children. Keith tried to talk her out of it, but Gina would not budge. She was going to plead with the judge on her children's behalf. The only saving grace was that the mediation proceedings were closed, so the media fanfare would be absent, at least inside the courtroom. Naturally, a huge number of news stations and reporters were hanging around outside the courtroom.

When Gina, Keith, and Nigel stepped out of the car at the courthouse, Gina slouched farther into her oversize cashmere coat, and Keith gave her a thumbs-up for encouragement. Nigel, Keith, and Gina had to tackle their way through the reporters to get inside the courthouse. Keith shielded her against his large frame. Her petite body was undetectable, as both Keith and Nigel hid her from the onslaught of curious onlookers and the media frenzy.

Michael was already seated in the courtroom with his attorney when they arrived. Seeing the woman with him gave Keith momentary pause. Verona "Tiger" Stachs was, to put it mildly, a piranha. She too had come to Atlanta from a competitive law firm in New York. Verona was tall, willowy, and was dressed in a no-nonsense black suit and a sensible white shirt. Her hair was dyed cinnamon brown, which accentuated her honey-colored eyes. Those eyes had earned her the moniker "Tiger."

As far as attorneys went, Michael had chosen well. Verona was all about winning, and she didn't care who she devoured or hurt in the process. She had graduated at the top of her class from Stanford. When he was still at Bohlander & Associates, Keith had even deliberated inviting her to join the practice, but at the last moment, he had a change of heart. Instead, he pursued Nigel, who was second in the same class at Stanford.

Keith whispered a silent prayer for strength.

Nigel grunted at Verona. It was common knowledge that there was a long-standing rivalry between the two. Rumor had it that they had once been in love. But something had happened, which neither of them would divulge, and the two were now mortal enemies.

The temperature in the room fell several degrees. This wasn't going to be a pleasant encounter.

Keith saw Michael's calculated smirk and resisted the urge to confront him. He knew then that Michael had selected Verona by design. His brother somehow had known about the lawyers' rivalry and was counting on that to propel Verona into getting him custody of his children.

Gina tapped him on the shoulder. "I've got to run to the restroom."

He nodded. Her trip to the bathroom was a true indicator of her nervousness. She looked so adorable in her blue striped suit. She was wearing a baby blue shirt and a multicolored scarf that was both professional and sexy. He eyed her black shoes, which added about three inches to her stature. Keith thought of another pair of shoes. The glass shoes Gina had donned for the wedding. The ones that he didn't get a chance to appreciate, because of Michael's evil doings. That was definitely on his to-do list.

Judge Marisa Wattinger entered the room about a minute after Gina returned. Gina had hopes that a female judge would work in her favor. Keith knew better. He grimaced and could not resist looking over at his brother. Michael looked like the cat that had spotted a delicious bowl of milk.

Marisa Wattinger had never had children of her own. This Keith knew because Nigel had filled him in on the common courtroom gossip. She had had about four miscarriages and yearned for children. Instead of making her sympathetic toward mothers, her experience had served to make her react harshly when she perceived any sign of unfit motherhood. But Keith was counting on a higher power to change the outcome. Michael didn't know who he knew.

Keith concluded that Gina was going to have to speak whether he wanted her to or not. Judge Wattinger would want to hear from her. She had been known to pose questions herself as well. Keith reached over and squeezed Gina's hands to provide reassurance. *Our God shall fight for us*. He silently recited the verse from Nehemiah to remind himself that God was in control.

When Keith and Gina left the courthouse that day for lunch, they felt as if they had been run over by a freight train. Gina ran into the waiting car in tears. Keith could not comfort her.

Judge Wattinger had put her through the wringer. Verona had painted her in a vicious light with her pointed questions. Gina felt frayed, believing that both women had it in for her. The worst part was that Michael had witnessed her demise. He had seen her reach the breaking point, and he had sat there, wearing a smug look of satisfaction. Nigel had tried to speak up on several occasions, but the judge silenced him. This left Gina swimming on her own in deep, shark-infested waters.

"I'm going to lose my children. The judge hates me," she cried.

Keith gripped her shoulders and pulled her close. "Gina, listen to me. It's almost impossible to prove a mother unfit. You're not a drug addict, and you're not abusing your children. You would have to have an extensive record of serious abuse or neglect for them to take our children."

"I'm going to lose my children," she repeated with a wail. "You saw how she treated me."

She was inconsolable and could not hear him, so Keith tried to calm her. "Don't let this process get to you. Try not to take it personally."

Gina shoved out of his arms. "How can I not take it personal, Keith? Those women are maligning my character. Judge Wattinger is anything but impartial. It is evident that she is not remaining neutral."

Keith knew that she spoke the truth. "I know it seems as if we are in a losing battle, but the battle is the Lord's. He will fight for us."

Gina's lips trembled. She couldn't hold her tongue. She lashed out at Keith. "At this moment, I don't feel like hearing your paltry words of appeasement. Right now they mean nothing to me. This is my reality. I'm about to lose my children. Could God relate to that?"

"God lost His only child for us," Keith said.

"Yes, God gave His Son up, but it was by choice," Gina argued. "I'm not trying to give mine up at all."

"What I am trying to tell you, honey, is that God understands what you are feeling right now. He could be allowing us to go through this for a reason."

"Don't you dare come to me with that argument. Your reasoning is weak, Keith."

"I know that God can work everything out according to His purpose. And that faulty reasoning is better known as faith, Gina. Faith."

"I can see that your faith in God is not shaken by this whole debacle, but I'm shaken. I'm shaken."

The driver dropped them off at a nearby restaurant. Gina remained silent during lunch. Sensing her inward rebellion, Keith left her alone. He knew his charms were wasted on his wife at the moment.

Nigel met with Gina in a small room to prep her for her closing statement. Michael gave his first. When he was finished, even Gina felt sorry for him.

"He sounds like he should be knighted or given saint-hood," she muttered to Keith. But all her husband did was squeeze her hands.

Gina was poised and ready to give her statement. She didn't even get two words out before the judge interrupted. "Mrs. Ward, I am going to stop your attempt at a defense. What I want to know is why you should be awarded sole custody. Michael Ward, your ex-husband, is well capable of taking care of the children. So why not shared custody?"

"Because he's not their biological father, Your Honor."

"However, his name is on the birth certificates, and he's been providing for the children, has he not?" the judge asked.

Gina nodded and bit her lip.

"Your Honor, I am the biological father, and I'm more than willing to take over their care and provide for them," Keith interjected. He saw that Gina's misery mirrored his own.

"Hmm," was the judge's ambiguous response.

"Your Honor, if I may continue," Gina began again. She had to fight for her children. "I know that my actions were immoral, but Michael doesn't love my children, as he should. He treats my daughter, Epiphany, with total disregard. I—I think he hates her. He can't be allowed to have them. It would damage them." Her lips quivered, and the tears fell. "I'm a good mother to both my children. I love them with all my heart and will be a good example to them."

"You call your moral turpitude a good example?" Judge Wattinger bellowed.

Nigel opened his mouth to object but remained silent. He could not object to a judge.

"Judge Wattinger, if I may," Keith interjected, infusing his voice with every ounce of deference and respect he could muster. "I know that our previous actions were questionable, but we were remorseful and have changed. We have changed our lives and have found spiritual guidance to keep us on the right path."

His words and mannerisms seemed to appease the temperamental judge for the moment. The "torture," as Gina called it, continued. She was so glad when five o'clock loomed. The judge promised to give both parties' arguments great consideration.

Keith and Gina left the courtroom in a somber mood. Gina could no longer stop the tears she'd been holding in. She cried during the car ride to Gerry's house. She cried when she saw the children running to greet her. She cried during the drive home. Once they got back to the house, Keith allowed her to flee while he tended to the children. Gina cried for a good hour until she fell asleep.

After he put the children to bed, Keith also cried. His pain and guilt over the past overwhelmed him. It was because of her love for him that Gina was now facing this agony. But, somehow, through his tears God provided solace. Keith remembered that his weeping would last only so long. He would feel joy soon. His joy was going to come.

Later that night, Gina woke up.

She looked around the dark room in alarm. She could have sworn she'd felt someone tap her shoulder. She should have been alarmed, but instead, Gina felt an odd sense of comfort. Then she remembered the havoc in her life, which she had created.

Feeling suffocated, Gina eased out of bed, not wanting Keith to awaken. She knew how worried he was about her and the possibility of losing their children. However, unlike her, he seemed calm and at peace almost. That was because he wasn't trying to carry the burden himself. Or so he'd said.

Keith's words about God giving up His only Son came back to her like a whisper. The words washed over her. God did know what she was feeling.

Gina walked out to her living room, but this time she fell to her knees. Again, she cried, but this time she poured her heart out to God. "Lord, I really never needed You before," she sobbed. "I know I don't deserve it, but I beg You not to let that judge take my children from me. They're my most precious commodities. I'm not me without them."

In her heart, she vowed that if God performed this miracle in her life, she would serve Him with all her being. She continued to pour out her deepest feelings. "I realize that everything I've gone through in my entire life has led me on this path to You. I'm here, ready to open my heart to you. I do need you, Lord. Thank You for loving me enough to provide for me even when I didn't see it. You've been there all along. Please don't leave me now." Though Gina still cried, this time a sense of comfort followed her tears. She felt a warmth envelop her being and wash over her soul.

Spent, Gina went back into the bedroom, dove back into her bed, and curled up next to Keith. For the first time in weeks, she slept like a baby.

Chapter Forty-three

The next morning, Michael entered the courthouse, positive that he would be retrieving his children that very evening. He was hoping to hear that he'd been awarded shared custody. Verona was already there when he arrived.

Figures, Michael thought. He did not want to enter the courtroom and be forced to engage in meaningless conversation with his attorney. So Michael left the courtroom and took the elevator to the lobby. He decided to grab a cup of coffee from the coffee shop across the street. He was about to pay for his order when a pair of beefy hands tapped his shoulder and someone said, "Hey!"

It took a moment for Michael to place the face, but then he recalled Lauren's cameraman, "Tiny." The man's nickname was an oxymoron. At over six feet and almost three hundred pounds, he was anything but miniscule. Michael greeted Tiny with a warm smile.

He felt a funny surge in his heart. Tiny's presence meant that Lauren was somewhere in sight. He was a bit surprised at the emotion. He didn't expect to feel anticipation at the thought of seeing Lauren again.

Michael had kind of given up after calling her for over two weeks and getting no response. He chalked up their time together as a brief encounter and was determined to keep moving. However, Michael could not admit that he had not started moving yet.

"So where's our lady?" Michael asked with a slight grin.

"You didn't hear? She quit the station and disappeared," Tiny bellowed with a loud guffaw.

Seeing the scrutiny of the other customers, Michael decided to steer Tiny outside to continue their conversation. His interest was piqued. Glancing at his watch, Michael realized that he had about a half hour before Judge Wattinger was due in court.

His heart did a telltale drop as Lauren's last "revelation" sank into his system. He needed to find out what was going on, because if Lauren was not lying, then . . .

Keith and Gina made it to court with five minutes to spare. Both Nigel and Verona were already present. The tension between the attorneys was even more palpable.

Keith lost his patience and grunted, "Listen, whatever is going on with both of you needs to stop this minute. Gina and I are here fighting for our family—our lives. Whatever squabble you two have can wait."

"It's not us," Nigel replied, mortified. Keith knew that his attorney was not aware that his and Verona's rift was so evident or well known.

"Then what is it?"

"Michael has decided to . . ." Verona trailed off as Judge Wattinger entered the courtroom.

Keith's brother was nowhere to be found.

"Where is your client, Ms. Stachs?" Judge Wattinger asked without preamble.

"Ahh . . . ah . . . " Verona sputtered and fiddled with her blouse. She was clearly out of her element. Her demeanor made Gina nervous.

"Spit it out," Nigel commanded, not withholding his delight at her uncharacteristic discomfort.

"Judge, Michael Ward has dropped the case. He is no longer seeking custody of Trey and Epiphany Ward,"

Verona begrudgingly admitted. She shifted the papers around on the table, trying in vain to keep the blush from spreading across her cheeks.

Judge Wattinger couldn't disguise her surprise but pasted on a plastic smile. She addressed Gina. "Well, Mrs. Ward, I guess this hearing is over. I hereby grant you full custody of both Trey and Epiphany Ward, and I further move to remove Michael Ward's name from the birth certificates. Keith Ward's name will now be placed on their birth certificates as their biological father." At the end of that comment, the judge banged her gavel and departed the courtroom in a huff.

Keith pulled Gina into a tight embrace. "God is the ultimate, victorious judge. No one can fight a battle like Him."

While her husband praised God with fervency, Gina looked up and whispered, "Thank you, God. You answered my prayer, and you came through. I will keep my promise. I give you my heart and all of me. My life is in your hands."

Keith and Gina jumped with triumph. It was over.

Keith heard Nigel needle Verona so that she would spill the beans about Michael's sudden retraction, but she wouldn't budge.

Keith and Gina questioned what happened for a brief moment, but they were too exhilarated to debate the topic for long. They both knew to whom the credit really went. They knew that God had fought the battle for them and won. They headed home.

As soon as they entered their home, Keith swept Gina into his arms. He was free. Free to love Gina. Free to father his children. Free.

Keith would not delay another moment. He called his mother, whooping for joy, and made sure she was up to keeping the children for a couple of nights. Of course, she was thrilled and more than happy to give him time with Gina. Gina was too overcome with emotion to speak. She was still busy crying from relief.

Next, he called Colleen and Terence and told them the good news. He also warned them not to call for at least two nights. He had pressing business with his wife that he needed to settle—yesterday.

Then he made Gina don her wedding gown and those remarkable glass shoes. He grinned in delight when he saw what she was wearing underneath. They stepped outside the front door Keith lifted her over the threshold, signifying that they were about to embark on a fresh start to the rest of their lives. Then they made a beeline for the bedroom.

Keith was going to make love to his wife. No holds barred.

And he did.

All night long.

All through the morning.

Through lunch.

Through dinner.

And . . . God give him strength . . .

Till daybreak.

Epilogue

Lauren sat in her newly rented house with her feet propped up on the coffee table. She looked around the sparse room. Like the rest of the house, it was almost bare. All she had so far was a sleeper couch, the coffee table, and a TV. Reporting and news were in her blood. She had to know what was going on in the world.

Lauren knew that she would have to get the place ready soon.

She hugged her tummy, which was expanding and showing the life growing inside. Or, she should say, lives. Dr. Kline had told her he heard two heartbeats, instead of one. She would be going for an ultrasound in a couple of weeks to confirm that she was carrying twins.

She felt her eyes brimming with pity tears again. With a brisk wave, Lauren wiped them away. Her emotions were so topsy-turvy. She cried about the oddest things and at the most inopportune times. It was downright annoying.

She put the television on and angled her body so that she could watch it, as it was sitting on the coffee table. She flipped through the channels until she came to a rerun of, of all things, her interview with Keith and Michael. She quickly hit the record button.

Lauren cried when Tiny zoomed in on Michael's handsome face. To her, he was the more gorgeous of the two brothers. She did not understand what Gina saw in Keith, why she'd chosen him over Michael.

The last segment was playing now, when Keith looked directly into the camera to address the audience. She perked up. His speech was one that she would never forget. Lauren supposed that it was not by chance that she was now about to hear it again.

Once again, Lauren was enraptured as Keith spoke from his heart. "I must admit that if I were in your shoes now, I would be enthralled by this scintillating piece of gossip. But this is my life. Yes, a few years ago, I fell in love with Gina, who is now my brother's wife. I can say that I'm sorry, but I would be lying if I said I had regrets. How can I regret the woman who, besides God, has been my passion and my . . . everything? I know that there are other women out there, but they are not Gina."

Gina had left by then, but Keith had still paused a moment to address her. Lauren wondered if Gina had ever heard Keith's statement. "Gina, darling, I love you. I always will. My life is meaningful because you're alive. I know we may never be together, but you've always been in my heart and you always will be."

Lauren saw herself squirm in the face of Keith's intense declaration. She remembered trying to remain professional, but she had been moved. Lucky for her, Tiny had chosen that moment to take a close-up of Keith's face.

Keith had turned toward the camera and allowed the world to see his agony and torment and lack of caring. His final words had made the world forgive him and the women's hearts melt. "I know I could sit here and deny what's in my heart to make myself look good to you. But I'll never do that. I could never deny my love for Gina Ward, and now for my children. I profess it willingly. I love Gina. My heart beats for her alone. No other woman can take her place. No other woman will do."

As she hit the REWIND button, all Lauren could think was, *Will Michael ever feel that way about me? Is he even capable of such a love?*

Coming May 2015

Book Three of the "On the Right Path" Series

The Fall of the Prodigal

A Condemned Man. His Two Brides. One Untimely Death.

He had it all. Will he have to lose everything in order to save his soul?

Michael Ward is at the top of his game. He didn't need anyone or anything and he liked it that way. Money is his new best friend. Until he's arrested for a heinous crime he didn't commit. As much as he hates to admit it, Michael needs his brother, Keith Ward, the man who stole his wife and children. Will Michael open his heart to forgive his brother?

Verona "Tiger" Stachs has been Michaels' attorney for years. She's in love with him but is tired of being treated as his guinea pig. A backslidden Christian, Verona finds herself being drawn closer to God. She thought she was through with God, but He's nowhere through with her. Which relationship will she choose?

Keith Ward's a prominent minister and family man, yet he yearns to rekindle his relationship with his brother. When Michael calls him citing that he desperately needs his help, Keith jumps at the chance to set things right with Michael. Will Keith be able to lead Michael into the light?

Readers' Guide Questions

1. Gina, Michael, and Keith were parents who had to take care of a sick child. Though Trey recovered, what are some thoughts we can offer families who lose their children and question or blame God? Why do you think God allows children to be sick?
2. Gina wanted to have another child, but she didn't like the idea of having one for the sole purpose of saving another. Share your thoughts on whether or not you think it's okay to have children for this purpose.
3. Gina was married to one man while being in love with another. Keith constantly filled her thoughts. As Christians, how can we counsel someone who is facing this struggle?
4. The story is based on the scripture Psalm 37:23, and the events show that Keith's steps were truly ordered. What are some incidents or experiences that you've had that prove that God is with you every step of the way?
5. Gina felt that she was a good person and that she didn't need God. Are there friends or family members in your life who you know behave better than those who profess to be saved? How can we minister to these individuals who have high morals and values but haven't accepted Christ? Are there any Bible scriptures or histories that back this up?

6. Throughout the novel, Gina relied on God only when she needed something. How do we engage in this same behavior at times? What are the dangers of knowing God only when we need Him?

7. Keith was unwilling to face his past, though he had converted. Although the sins of the past are forgiven, there are still consequences. How do we explain, then, that God has thrown these sins into the sea of forgetfulness? Why do we still have to face our past if it has been forgiven?

8. Keith's love for Gina made him betray his brother. Do you think there is ever a time when love justifies hurting someone you love or going against family?

9. Sometimes when we minister to people, they feel as if they're too sinful for God to really want them. Share your experiences. What scriptures or words of comfort can we offer someone who feels this way?

10. Gina and Keith had different reactions when faced with the possibility of losing their children. Discuss their different reactions, particularly from a saved versus unsaved point of view.

11. Do you think it's possible in this day/time, given Facebook and other forms of social media, to hide the fact that you have a child?

12. Though Gina was a strong woman and was unsaved, she allowed Michael to manipulate her because she believed in marriage and she didn't want Trey to grow up in a single- parent home. Should we remain in a marriage if we're unhappy, even if we're saved? Should a child influence our decision to stay in an unhealthy marriage?

13. Do you share Colleen's belief that there are some marriages that God didn't put together?

14. What advice can we give to couples that face infertility? Share some of the reasons for infertility. Do

you think it is a punishment from God to be unable to bear children?

15. Keith ignored God's voice when he was urged to confess the truth. Have you ever ignored God's spirit and done your own thing? Share your experiences and any life lessons learned.

16. Keith faced instances where his flesh and spirit struggled. He knew what was right, but his heart wanted what it wanted. What are some practical tips we can give believers when they are faced with temptation? How did Christ address this in scripture?

17. God gave Keith a second chance. Do you think he deserved it? Are there certain individuals who you feel don't deserve a second chance?

18. Michael's actions grew out of anger and malice because he had been wronged. Were his actions, though extreme, somewhat justified? Why or why not?

19. Michael used his children as pawns to get back at Gina. He didn't consider the innocent children. What lesson can we take from this? Why isn't it a good or godly idea to use children for revenge?

20. Keith and Gina's relationship was messy. She committed adultery, and he betrayed his brother. Should he still be allowed to be in ministry? Why or why not?

About the Author

Michelle Lindo-Rice enjoys crafting women's fiction with themes centered around the four "F" words: Faith, Friendship, Family and Forgiveness. Originally from Jamaica West Indies, Michelle Lindo-Rice calls herself a lifelong learner.

She has earned degrees from New York University, SUNY at Stony Brook, and Teachers College, Columbia University. When she moved to Florida, she enrolled in Argosy University where she completed her Education Specialist degree in Education Leadership. A pastor's kid, Michelle upholds the faith, preaching, teaching and ministering through praise and worship.

Her first Christian Fiction novel, *Sing a New Song*, was released in January 2013 and was an Editor's Choice feature in Black Expressions Book Club. *Walk a Straight Line* is her second work of fiction and first in the "On the Right Path Series." For more information, or to leave an encouraging word; you can reach Michelle online at Facebook, Tumblr, LinkedIn, Pinterest, Google+, Twitter @mlindorice, or join her mailing list at:
www.michellelindorice.com

UC HIS GLORY BOOK CLUB!

www.uchisglorybookclub.net

UC His Glory Book Club is the spirit-inspired brain-child of Joylynn Ross, an author and the acquisitions editor at Urban Christian, and Kendra Norman-Bellamy, an author for Urban Christian. It is an online book club that hosts authors of Urban Christian. We welcome as members all men and women who have a passion for reading Christian-based fiction.

UC His Glory Book Club pledges its commitment to providing support, positive feedback, encouragement, and a forum whereby members can openly discuss and review the literary works of Urban Christian authors.

There is no membership fee associated with UC His Glory Book Club; however, we do ask that you support the authors by purchasing their works, encouraging them, providing book reviews, and, of course, offering your prayers. We also ask that you respect our beliefs and follow the guidelines of the book club. We hope to receive your valuable input, opinions, and reviews that build up, rather than tear down, our authors.

What We Believe:

—We believe that Jesus is the Christ, Son of the Living God.

—We believe that the Bible is the true, living Word of God.

—We believe that all Urban Christian authors should use their God-given writing abilities to honor God and to share the message of the written word that God has given to each of them uniquely.

—We believe in supporting Urban Christian authors in their literary endeavors by reading their titles, purchasing them, and sharing them with our online community.

—We believe that everything we do in our literary arena should be done in a manner that will lead to God being glorified and honored.

We look forward to online fellowship with you. Please visit us often at www.uchisglorybookclub.net.

Many Blessing to You!

Shelia E. Lipsey,
President, UC His Glory Book Club